Sweetened

With A Kiss

LEXXI CALLAHAN

CHAPTER ONE

The only thing Stefan hated worse than riding in a limousine was wearing a suit. Martin, his father's executive assistant, had shown up with both. On a Saturday morning. A Saturday morning that Martin knew Stefan was training for the New Orleans 70.3. Everyone knew that Saturday mornings were off limits. Saturday mornings before the New Orleans 70.3 were sacrosanct. Real threat of death type stuff.

So, something wasn't just wrong. It was bad wrong.

Stefan sat up on his bike. It wasn't like his head was in the game anyway. Not with Jen's plane already halfway across the Atlantic. He glanced at his watch, telling himself he still had time. Dinner was handled. His sister Lizzie had the party under control for tomorrow night. Everything was ready.

He waved at the friends he trained with to keep going and was off his bike before the wheels stopped spinning. Martin straightened up from leaning against the STI limo and held out a cell phone. Not Stefan's phone. His iPhone was still strapped to his bicep but turned off because no one would call him while he was training for the triathlon that would qualify him for this year's Ironman Hawaii. Everyone knew better.

"Who is it?" He stripped off his fingerless gloves, not looking up at Martin, before he took the phone.

"Nic Maretti."

Of course. Everyone knew better but Nic. Nic just didn't care. But if Nic called, it was worse than threat of death type stuff because Nic took his silent partnership in Stefan's investment group to the extreme. As in invisible. So this wasn't good. "Maretti? You couldn't wait an hour?"

"I can wait all day," the deceptively calm voice with the light Texas drawl matched Stefan's New Orleans city sarcasm perfectly. "But you have about forty-five minutes before Volikov lands in Houston to meet with my father and his cronies."

Stefan stopped, cold suddenly despite the unseasonably warm January day. He stared at his hands, not seeing them as his brain rebooted out of training mode and into business mode, lists of things he would have to do forming and prioritizing without much effort. A heavy weight settling on his shoulders that he'd almost started to believe would be gone by now. Not anymore. Before he could say anything, Nic continued.

"Andreas is showing off and flying him over on the company jet. But the pilot works for me so I can give you another half hour delay if you think it will help."

"It won't hurt."

"This conversation never happened."

Stefan and Nic had lots of conversations that never happened, so his response was automatic. "Is this phone going to self destruct?"

"No, I would have sent that phone to my father."

"I owe you," Stefan said.

"Yes," Nic said completely unconcerned. Stefan knew better. Nic would collect. He knew it. Stefan knew it. That went to the bottom of his priority list. That could wait.

Instead, he gave himself a moment to feel the anger trying to incinerate him. This Saturday? Of course it would have to be this Saturday. Then he shut it down. No time for that right now either. He should have run this morning instead of cycling, but he'd needed to improve his bike time. He wouldn't think about that either. Not yet. "The limo's a bit much," he said to Martin, his voice flat.

"Your father's at the Tower. I thought you'd want to change."

"Does he know?" Stefan asked.

"I'll let you make that call."

"Fine."

"Do you want me to send a driver for Miss Taylor?"

"No, I'm going. Keep the limo on standby." He tossed Martin the key to his SUV, not quite believing he had committed himself to not one but possibly two limo rides. "Follow us."

He changed while the limo pulled back onto the road. He finished buttoning the pinstriped shirt then began to wrestle with the tie. Funny. His hands were shaking. Jen's plane landed at eight. He had roughly six and half hours to sort out this mess because he was not missing her flight. They needed to talk and if she set foot back in New Orleans before he saw her, he'd lose the upper hand. He wasn't going there again.

When Stefan finally managed to get the half-Windsor finished on the tie, he called his father.

"Why aren't you on your bike?" Mac barked, instead of the usual hello.

"Alex Volikov is on his way to Houston."

Mac Sellers got real quiet on the other end of the line. Real quiet was not a good thing for Mac Sellers to be. It made the hairs on the back of Stefan's neck stand up. "I'm calling that Russian prick," Mac said, sounding calm but Stefan knew he was anything but. His father did not play games.

"This is just a courtesy call, old man. I'll handle it."

"I thought this was all settled."

"It is. Alex is a pain in the ass. He's playing with us."

"On a Saturday morning?" Mac chuckled. "That crazy Russian likes to play with fire, doesn't he?"

"I've got this."

He was rewarded with a low laugh that would have scared the hell out of most people. Mac Sellers was a scary bastard, but he loved his son. He hadn't wanted to go near this Russian deal but he'd believed in Stefan enough to let him do it. And Stefan thought it was the future. If Alex Volikov actually succeeded where others had failed off the coast of Cuba, it would mean more jobs in a depressed area and another expansion of their plant in North Mississippi, which was already operating at capacity. There was no way Stefan would let Andreas Maretti undercut STI's deal with Volikov.

"OK, you handle the Russian, son, but if this blows up, Maretti is going to get the war he's been trying to start for the last ten years."

"You'll get no argument from me on that."

"Good. Now, tell Trent to stop driving like an old lady, I'll see you in fifteen."

Stefan sat back in his seat and pushed his fingers through his hair, vaguely registering that he should get a haircut. He closed his eyes. He still couldn't quite believe it had been six months since he'd seen Jen. It seemed like so much longer. He scrolled through his phone looking for Volikov's number. He wanted this settled before Jen's plane reached Atlanta.

Any minute now, Jen was sure her brain would start leaking out of her ears. She turned her iPad screen off and leaned back against the head rest, thankful once again she hadn't been able to talk Martin out of the first class tickets. She glanced out the window, the cloud cover so much more interesting than the numbers and projections, and estimates and blah blah blah that filled pages of the business plan Jared had finished just that morning. Thank goodness he had a head for business, because Jen sure didn't. The only numbers she really cared about were ounces and cups.

She yawned and stretched her legs out again. Yeah, first class wasn't so bad. She glanced at her watch and groaned before switching the iPad back on. She had to be ready. So as much as she hated it, she forced herself to keep reading the business plan. She knew Mac would ask her a million questions when she told him she wanted to open a bakery. There was no way she was going to tell Stefan about it because he would just laugh, pat her on the head, and tell her to start picking out flowers for their wedding.

She was pretty sure that Mac would be supportive as long as he thought she had all her financial ducks in a row. If she could get Mac on her side, then she was hopeful Stefan would back down.

She glanced outside to see if there were any pigs flapping around the plane.

No such luck.

Stefan was going to flip out when he found out about her plans for a bakery. But that would be nothing compared to what he was going to do when she told him she didn't want to marry him. Honestly, Jen wasn't exactly sure how she was going to tell him.

"Tell him we're getting married," Jared had teased her earlier while they waited for her flight to start boarding.

"Have you lost your mind?"

Jared grinned, that black goatee making him look just like the devil he was. "Fine. Wait 'til I get back and we'll tell him together."

"You have lost your mind."

"No, I'm perfectly serious. I can get my half of the money from my father. I passed the damned bar, he needs to make good on his part of the deal. Your trust says you have to wait until you're thirty or get married, right? We'll fly to Vegas, do the deed, pass go, collect your two hundred dollars, then cruise down to the Dominican Republic and get a quickie divorce and a tan."

"You're serious?"

"What?" he shrugged, stretching out long denim-clad legs and folding tattoo-covered arms behind his head. He was checking out a tall blonde and her red-haired friend who were walking down the concourse but he kept talking. "Does the trust say you have to consummate the marriage? I can close my eyes and think of England if I have to. It's so simple, I'm sorry I didn't think of it sooner."

"Simple?" she echoed, still not sure whether he was serious or not. Not that it mattered. She loved Jared to distraction, but like a brother. Life really would've been so much simpler if there'd been any sort of spark between them when they met at a cooking class four years ago. She'd agreed to go out with him, hoping something would happen between them. But Jen's heart had been locked up a long time ago and mid-way through dinner both of them admitted they liked each other far too much to blow it with sex.

"I guess it would be simple," she nodded, watching the two women slow down as they walked past and checked Jared out. "I wouldn't really need the divorce considering I would be a widow the minute we touched down in Kenner."

Jared shrugged. "He could try." Then he sat up, suddenly serious for a change. "Look, just tell him you want your money, Jen. It's your money."

"I said I would talk to Mac. Stefan will just say no."

"Try wearing that black dress we found you for your birthday. See what he says then. If you could get a picture of his face when he sees you in it, that would be sweet."

Jen scoffed. "He wouldn't notice."

There was no way she was wearing that dress again. The only reason she'd had the nerve to wear it on her twenty-second birthday was the giant bottle of champagne she and Jared had consumed before they went out to dinner then a nightclub to celebrate.

"Did he suddenly go blind?" Jared asked. "Look, if he still says no, then tell him we're getting married. Just make sure you're wearing the dress when you do. And press record."

"Do you have any idea what he would do if I told him you and I were getting married?"

"Wake up, hopefully," Jared laughed, then stopped when she didn't join him.

"He still thinks we're engaged."

"Uh, newsflash, Jen, you are still engaged."

"I'm not going to marry him," Jen said. "I'm not that pathetic. But I'm not going to marry you, either."

Jared pressed his hands to his chest. "You wound me."

"Oh, please. You'd have to care first."

"Hey, I do care. I just don't understand what the problem is. You've been in love with him since you were what? Twelve?"

She shrugged. She didn't know exactly when. She'd just never not been in love with Stefan. She took a deep breath and said the words out loud, more to remind herself than anything else. "He's not in love with me, Jared."

Jared laughed then. "You wear that black dress for him, then get back to me on that."

"I wish you were right. I really do. But I gave up on that a long time ago. He thinks I'm still a kid he needs to protect."

"Screw Madlyn Robicheaux," Jared exploded suddenly. "You can't believe a word that bitch says."

"You don't even know her."

"I know who she is. My brother clerked for her grandfather and that old man is a real piece of work. I know you think she was trying to help you that night, Jen. But she has never helped anyone but herself."

"That's not true," Jen said, wondering why she was defending Stefan's ex. But then, all Madlyn had done six months ago with her careful and oh so gentle remarks was confirm what Jen already knew. But hearing the words out loud was a lot more humiliating than just thinking them. If she had not had pastry school as an excuse to leave, she would have just found something else. Maybe it still wasn't too late to go backpacking in Tibet.

"Three words," Jared had said, interrupting her crazy thoughts. "Wear the dress. I promise you, he'll notice that you're all grown up."

"Right," Jen had said, shaking her head in disgust. She could see Stefan's face as he tried to choke back laughter if she showed up in that skimpy black dress and too high heels. There was no way she was setting herself up for that kind of humiliation. Been there, done that, screw the T-shirt.

"It's that or Vegas with me, babe. Take your pick."

Jen turned the screen off again, unable to concentrate on the business plan any longer. She catnapped until the captain announced their flight was going to be late. Jen groaned. If this flight was late, she would miss the connection in Atlanta. She really didn't want to have to stay in Atlanta any longer than necessary. She really dreaded seeing Stefan again, but she also really wanted to get home.

Not only was the flight late, customs was jammed. She thought she would never get out of the crush of people. By the time she made it to a ticket counter, her head was killing her and she wanted a shower. She got lucky and there was a later flight to New Orleans, which gave her time to text Martin all her new flight information, and then find pain killers and a double-shot caramel latte.

Her new seat was not in first class. Even worse, it was next to a young couple with three small children. None of the kids were impressed with their car seats and by their red faces and snotty noses, Jen could tell they had been crying for a while. She slid into her seat which gave her a perfect view of the exhausted couple as they tried to calm the furious toddlers. The mother caught Jen's eye and gave her an apologetic smile.

Jen smiled back. "I don't blame them. I feel the same way."

The mom laughed gratefully and Jen spent the rest of the flight trying to ignore the ache building inside her. Such a sweet family. She watched the young mother drop her forehead to her husband's shoulder and he kissed the top of her head. The ache turned into something hot and jagged deep in Jen's chest. She wanted that, complete with screaming kids. Until six months ago, she'd believed it was all about to start for her. A family. A family with the man she'd loved all her life. She'd been a silly little fool. She wouldn't be again.

Stefan's second limo ride of the day was almost as bad as the first. The only answer he could get out of Alex Volikov was that his legal team was reviewing the contracts. Stefan was searching his contacts for Senator Warren's number when Trent let down the privacy screen between the front and back seat.

"She missed her flight," Trent said.

"You have got to be kidding me."

"Martin says she caught a later flight but it will be another two hours before she lands."

Stefan just shook his head. Just when he thought the day couldn't get any worse.

"We can wait for her in short-term parking."

"Fine," he snapped, then sighed. Trent had worked for his family for nearly twenty-five years. There was no need to take it out on him. "Sorry, Trent. Stop somewhere and get yourself some coffee first."

"You want anything?"

Oh, yeah, he wanted something. He had a list of things he wanted. One of them was the last six months back. He hadn't been thinking straight since Jen left. He'd had no idea not having her around would affect him so much. Completely unprepared to actually miss her, he'd found himself thinking about her in the middle of the day, wondering what she was doing in the most romantic city in the world with the tattooed freak. He still couldn't quite believe he'd let her go with Jared Marshall to Paris.

Not that he'd had a lot of choice. They'd been sitting in the middle of the Lizard Room in Bayona, one of the most romantic restaurants in New Orleans when she'd dropped her little bomb shell on him.

"Pastry school?" he'd repeated, sure he hadn't heard her correctly.

She'd nodded, her smile bright but not quite meeting her eyes - warm caramel eyes that looked everywhere but at him. She'd been so lovely that night. She'd had on a wispy little sundress that clasped at her neck leaving her long, slim arms bare. Her skin had glowed in the candlelight. She'd pulled her hair up and twisted it in an elaborate knot, but tendrils had escaped and brushed against all that tan skin, and he'd been so focused on keeping his hands from brushing one stray hair behind her ear that he'd almost missed what she said.

"Paris?"

"Yes, it's in Paris. But it's only for six months and Elliot says..."

"Six months?" He'd started to feel like a parrot. "You're going to Paris for six months?"

She'd brushed the hair behind her ear and reached for her water glass. "We've already found an apartment and everything."

"We?" he'd asked, sitting back in his seat, his gut clenching because he already knew who the 'we' was.

"Jared's been accepted too. We applied last year, Stefan. And I really want to go."

And she did. He could see this was important to her. More important than marrying him apparently. He'd brought her here tonight so they could set a date for the wedding. He'd thought Christmas would be perfect, but now she wouldn't be home for Christmas. Jen loved Christmas. He couldn't believe she wanted to spend it on the other side of the world.

Then she'd completely blindsided him when she'd carefully held out her engagement ring.

"I need time to think," she'd said, setting the ring on the table in front of him when he wouldn't take it from her.

"Put your ring back on," he'd said quietly, or at least he thought that was what he'd said. He wasn't honestly sure since the rational part of his brain had shut down.

"Six months will fly by. You'll see. And we can email and, well, I don't want anything to happen to the ring. Please, Stefan, I'm afraid I'll lose it."

He'd reached out, taken the ring, and dropped it in his pocket, his eyes never leaving her face. She was looking down on her plate, pushing the fish around. She hadn't eaten any of it.

"Six months," he'd said.

She'd nodded and, before he knew it, she was on a plane to Paris with that tattooed freak. She'd sent emails, of course, telling him all about the school, the classes, and how amazing Paris was. Nothing personal. Nothing about wedding plans. Nothing that gave any indication what she was really thinking. Nothing to indicate that her world was as upside as his. He'd known Jen her whole life and for the first time, he had no idea what she was thinking. He hadn't liked that at all. So his responses to the emails were probably not as nice as they should have been and eventually, she'd stopped sending them. He hadn't heard from her in nearly four weeks.

Not even at Christmas. It was the first Christmas she hadn't spent with his family in over ten years. Lizzie had gotten home from school and spent her whole vacation sulking.

"How can it be Christmas without Christmas cookies?"

He'd just shrugged. He didn't like cookies. So what did he know.

"This is all your fault, and you can forget about a tree."

For years he'd ragged his little sister and Jen when they made ornaments every year. With Lizzie boycotting Christmas, his mother had hired a professional to decorate the lake house. Stefan had taken one look at that elegant, glittering tree and known deep down in his gut that in a shabby little apartment in Paris there was a shabby little tree covered in popcorn, gingerbread, and construction paper. It had gutted him.

His cell phone rang as Trent pulled into short-term parking. Six phone calls later and Volikov's legal team was still reviewing the paperwork. Frustrated, he canceled the dinner reservations on his way into the airport, because there was no way they would make it in time.

"I can hold your table," Elliot assured him.

"No, we'll see you tomorrow night," Stefan said, side-stepping a woman pushing a buggy loaded with suitcases.

He sent Lizzie a text and told her to hold off on the party. He got a text right back telling him he was no fun. He checked his watch then sent Jen a text to tell her where he was. His phone rang and he tried to put out another fire.

CHAPTER TWO

I'll meet you in baggage claim.

Jen sagged back in her seat, watching the exhausted family leave before standing up to grab her bag out of the overhead. Why couldn't Martin have sent Trent to pick her up?

There was no way she could meet Stefan looking like a hot, sweaty mess, so she ducked into the first ladies room she saw. She splashed water on her face and refused to admit her pulse rate had increased. She dug through her purse until she found her make-up bag. After a little lipstick, eyeliner, and mascara, she was satisfied that she didn't look like a love sick zombie. She brushed out her hair until it fell in its usual straight curtain of nondescript brown, then pulled it high on the back of her head, clipping it with a barrette. She smoothed down the black knit dress she wore with black leggings and a battered pair of black Converse. She frowned at her favorite shoes. They'd been great for the last six months but now they were kind of disgusting.

She unzipped the overnight bag she'd packed and shifted the contents around until she found the only shoes in her bag. She groaned. She had not packed her four inch black Manolos, but here they were. Thanks, Jared! He'd apparently wanted to make sure she had them for the dress and black stockings she also found carefully wadded up in her bag. He was going to die for this. Slowly.

"I'd switch them," a lady said, stepping up beside her to check her hair and fix her lipstick. "The shoes. I'd definitely wear the heels."

Jen smiled. Whatever. She quickly leaned against the sink and switched shoes, telling herself it had nothing to do with Stefan. She didn't care what Stefan thought, she reminded herself. Not anymore. He wouldn't notice the shoes.

She took a very deep breath, closed her eyes and held it. She exhaled, then faced herself in the mirror. The extra height the shoes gave her shored up her confidence. She'd almost be able to meet him eye to eye. Almost. If she didn't pass out and fall at his feet because her heart exploded out of her chest.

Okay, she was ready.

Absolutely ready.

She forced herself out of the ladies room and into the concourse. The shoes weren't too bad. The last time she'd worn them, she'd been more than a little tipsy on champagne. Now sober, she found she could walk in them just fine. No big deal.

Just like seeing Stefan after six months. Because she was over him. She'd decided. O.V.E.R.

She was not marrying him. The engagement was over. She had her own life and things she wanted to do that did not include being Mrs. Stefan Sellers.

She faltered a little. Mrs. Stefan Sellers. She'd written that on so many notebooks over the years that it was second nature. Everyone had always just assumed it was a foregone conclusion and, well, up until six months ago, she'd just never ever considered being anything else.

But she was not that girl anymore, thanks to Madlyn Robicheaux. She was Jen Taylor, high voodoo priestess of sugar and all things sweet. And she was not marrying Stefan.

When she made it to baggage claim, she stopped short and ducked behind one of the ugly orange columns. That couldn't have been Stefan. No way. She was crazy. She peered around the column again to get a look at the tall businessman in a gunmetal gray suit talking on his cell phone with his back to her. His fingers were pushing through his too short hair. No way that was Stefan.

Her Stefan's hair was not cut short. It was longish and rumpled and caught back with whatever rubber band he could find. And her Stefan wore jeans so faded they were indecent in places and T-shirts he should have thrown away years ago.

Then the man turned and she caught his profile and she was back around the column before her brain admitted it was Stefan. And he was not happy about something.

Stefan was watching the thinning crowd with a growing sense of concern as he ended another call. He saw her luggage come around the conveyor belt but there was no trace of Jen. She should have come through the crowd by now. He grabbed the single bag off the carousel and while he was pulling it off, he caught a glimpse of a tall woman dressed all in black. His breath actually caught in his throat and a raw stab of lust stroked through him as he realized her legs didn't seem to stop. He took in a ragged breath, glancing away before he saw her face, then shifted his weight as he set the bag down and pulled up the handle. He couldn't remember the last time he'd felt anything so intense. He'd been training pretty hard since Jen left and that usually distracted him, but those legs reminded him instantly that it had been a very long time.

He glanced at his watch. Where the hell was she? His eyes slid to the brunette's legs again, then the high ponytail she wore. That rich brown swath of hair would wrap around his fist at least twice. Before he could kick himself for having that reaction to a complete stranger, he saw her face and lightning zapped the back of his head and sizzled down his central nervous system, freezing him in place.

Jen.

He wasn't sure how it was Jen, but it was definitely her. He just managed to stop his jaw from dropping as she spotted him and started straight for him. He almost backed up a few steps, he was so stunned. How in the hell could that be Jen? But it was her. She'd lost weight. She hadn't needed to lose it, but he had to admit it suited her. She was sleeker, her face more defined. She looked older, more mature. But there was no mistaking those caramel eyes, and that mouth just slightly too wide for her face—the one he suddenly couldn't take his eyes off…unless he let himself admire her legs again and that was not going to happen. Then her mouth was curving into a soft smile so familiar it hit him square in the chest and his lungs really tried hard to turn inside out.

He should have smiled back, but his face was frozen. For a panicked second, Stefan Sellers wasn't quite sure what to do. He always knew exactly what to do. Always. Instead, he shut down, looking for the place in his head that kept him centered and calm. He couldn't find it. There was nothing in his head because all the blood had deserted his brain and headed south.

Then suddenly she was right in front of him. She smelled like sugar and sunshine, and she was saying something, but his brain didn't translate the sound into anything he could understand. Instead he just leaned forward, grabbed her overnight bag from her. "Car's outside," he managed to rumble out, and turned towards the exits before he gave in to the urge to throw her over his shoulder and haul her out to the limo.

"But Martin was sending a driver," she said, trying to keep up with him as he headed towards the exits. He knew it couldn't be easy in those shoes. Too bad for her. Where the hell did she get shoes like that anyway?

"He did," Stefan said, "Trent's in short-term parking."

Jen stopped short. "You're joking. You came in a limo?"

She almost stepped back as he turned on her suddenly. She still couldn't believe she was seeing him in a suit, even if the cut made him more deadly attractive than he was in cutoff blue jeans and faded T-shirts. And really, Jen hadn't believed that was possible. He looked so much older, less approachable. She hardly recognized the cold, hard man staring back at her impatiently. He was still beautiful, but he wasn't happy to see her. He looked annoyed and distracted now, but earlier, when he'd first seen her, he'd looked just like he had the night of her junior prom. Jen had hoped never to see that expression again.

"I thought you liked the limo. You and Lizzie used it often enough." His words sounded like ice chips.

She smiled despite herself. Guilty as charged. She and Lizzie were intimately familiar with the limo. Mac didn't normally use it on the weekends and had encouraged them to use it because he didn't like Lizzie driving in the city. They'd been happy to oblige and there had been many girls' night out both in high school and college. They both owed Trent a piece of their souls for not telling Mac what had actually gone on in the limo.

At least Trent was happy to see her. She gave him a quick hug and asked about his oldest daughter. "She's starting her residency this fall," Trent said proudly.

"Well tell Bonnie I asked about her. We all need to get together," Jen said as she slid into the limo.

She grabbed two water bottles out of the mini fridge before leaning back. Stefan was on his cell phone so she barely got a chin nod when she handed him one. She took a sip and registered that Stefan was speaking in Russian. When had he learned Russian?

She shook her head in disbelief and tried to relax as they pulled out of the airport. She'd missed New Orleans. Her first impression of Paris had been almost a little disappointing. "It's just a larger version of the French Quarter," Jared had said.

"Well, yeah!" Jen had teased, then they'd laughed that whole first day playing goofy tourist and staring wide-eyed at the Eiffel Tower and trying really hard to be too cool to be impressed.

She dragged herself to the present when they didn't take the exit to cross the Pontchartrain. "Where are we going?"

"Home."

"We're going the wrong way."

He gave her a grim look and his phone rang before he could answer her. She fished her own phone out of her bag and sent Jared a text telling him she'd arrived safely. She smiled at the ten text messages from Lizzie, all demanding *Are you here yet?*

She sent back, *Yep*

Her phone rang less than thirty seconds later. "I'm so glad you're home," Lizzie rushed. It wasn't like they hadn't talked on the phone almost every day.

"Glad you're still here," Jen said, wishing Lizzie wasn't heading back to school in a week. They'd been best friends for as long as Jen could remember. Lizzie had always been more like a little sister than just a friend. And when Jen'd gone to live with the Sellers after her parents were killed, she and Lizzie had gotten even closer. They had never really been apart until Lizzie went off to graduate school.

"I'm not going back to the frozen North until you've made pancakes."

"Tomorrow morning. Promise." Jen said, then lowered her voice and turned towards the window. "What is going on with Stefan? He's really intense and he's been on his phone the whole time."

"Stefan picked you up?"

"I know, I was surprised too."

"Something's happened at STI. I'm not sure what exactly. Martin pulled Stefan off his bike this morning and Dad's still at the Tower but Mom keeps saying 'everything's fine, dear'."

"That's bad," Jen said, darting a glance at Stefan who was hanging up. "Gotta go."

She ended her call and sipped her water and pretended not to notice he was no longer ignoring her.

"Lizzie?" he asked.

She nodded.

"What did she say?"

Something in the tone of his voice raised the hairs on the back of her neck and she turned slowly. Glacial blue eyes were watching her closely, and the hairs on her arms joined the hairs of her neck in a nervous dance. "She wants pancakes. Why?" she asked slowly, wondering what he thought Lizzie had told her.

He pushed his fingers through his hair, then just shook his head.

"No reason."

Right.

"Is everything okay?" she asked carefully.

He watched her a moment, then reached into his jacket pockets. "It will be," he said and tossed a small black box at her. "As soon as you put this back on."

She jumped, startled as if he'd dropped a spider on her lap. She would've actually preferred the spider. She stared at the box, unable to even bring herself to touch it. She turned away and stared out the window. A spider would have been a whole lot better.

"We need to talk," she said, the words barely audible as her nerve started to desert her.

"Your six months are up. Put it back on."

The tone of his voice actually startled her worse than dropping the box in her lap. There was an edge to it she'd never heard before, and he was so cold the temperature in the limo was actually dropping.

She reached for the box, but her fingers were trembling. She couldn't keep a hold on it. It tumbled back to her lap and bounced onto the floor board. She leaned forward but an arm slid across her waist and pushed her back against the cool leather seats. He leaned forward and scooped the ring box off the floorboard.

He snapped the box open and the solitaire that had once taken her breath away, now made her insides as cold as the atmosphere in the car. Warm fingers curled around her hand and he slid the ring onto her shaking finger. His touch was gentle, as usual, but it nearly burned her. She turned her face towards the window, unable to face the fire in the perfect stone. It just hurt too much. Nothing that beautiful should be based on a lie.

Then she realized he was still holding her hand, his thumb stroking gently across her knuckles. The gentle caress hurt deep in her chest. She wasn't even sure if he realized he was doing it. He normally didn't touch her, other than a light hug or a quick kiss on the forehead. But caressing her fingers like that? She needed it to stop and tried to pull her hand away. He didn't let go.

"We really need to talk about this," she said.

"No, we don't." He released her hand and reached over to pull the barrette out of her hair. Her hair came down in a straight brown wave. He pushed it around with his fingers then threaded them through her hair until it fell the way he liked it. "That's better," he said. "You've lost weight. How can you lose weight at pastry school?"

Almost paralyzed by the light touch of his fingers around her neck, she had to swallow hard before she could ask again, "Where are we going?"

He didn't answer her. She wasn't surprised. If he didn't want to answer a question, he usually ignored it. If he didn't like her answer to one of his questions, he ignored that too. Instead he just watched her. She could feel his eyes skimming all over her.

"I don't want to get married," she finally said out loud, no longer able to contain the words.

"I agreed to give you six months. Time's up. Come here." His hand tightened on the back of her neck as he eased her closer to him.

Six months ago, she would have plastered herself to him at the first opportunity. She had tried a few times only to have him pull back and keep things light. Now, he was actually pulling her into his lap. An unwelcome but familiar ache came roaring back through her without any warning as she balanced herself against rock hard shoulders and legs.

"Be still," he snapped, but she couldn't. She just couldn't handle being this close to him. Panic swirled up in her, and she struggled against him until he clamped his arm around her waist and his other hand laced painfully into her hair. "I haven't seen you in months and all I get is an angry kitten."

"Let me go," she whispered, wishing desperately his phone would ring so he would have to let her go.

"Can't do that," he said, his voice sounding like gravel. The fingers still threaded through her hair, tightened suddenly and he pulled her head down closing the short distance between them. She closed her eyes and tried to turn her head but his mouth crashed into hers, his tongue sliding in between startled lips, laying ruin to every single shred of defense she had gathered up in the last few months.

She couldn't actually seem to stop her arms from going around him and her body from melting into his. She'd forgotten how big he was. He was easily over six three and years of training had carved him down to lean, hard muscle. It had never intimidated her before, but now, like this, she felt small, delicate, almost fragile.

Jen hated to feel fragile. Jen refused to feel fragile. She tried to pull back but his arm tightened and he tilted her head, taking the kiss deeper, teasing the hunger that always simmered below her surface until she was lost. She kissed him back, meeting the hot glide of his tongue, letting herself taste him, opening up even more to him, letting him in, dropping her guard, exposing her heart.

And the second she did, he eased back and broke the contact of their mouths. Her eyes flickered open to find his expression far from glacial anymore. The lust raging just below his surface singed her skin. Her lips parted and ached for him, but before she could kiss him again he set her away from him so quickly she nearly fell across the seat of the limo. It took her a second to register that all the delicious heat was no longer there. For one wild, hysterical second, she almost flung herself back at him.

He had shut them down the moment she had let go.

Lust boiled and transformed into an unfamiliar anger for Jen. Probably for the first time in her life, Jen actually got mad at Stefan. It was impossible to tell which one of them was more shocked when she said, "It must be nice having an on/off switch like that. But don't bother flipping mine on again if you can't handle the results." She dragged air into her lungs, feeling like she'd just woken from a disorienting dream. She almost laughed at the way he was watching her as if seeing her for the first time. The smile that curved his perfectly sculpted mouth made her fingers curl and her nails itch to scratch his eyes out.

"Well, Paris was good for something." His eyes glittered with amusement, but his breathing still wasn't steady. "Our kitten grew claws."

"Go to hell." She crossed her arms against her chest so she wouldn't lash out at him again. She sat up in her seat and threw her one leg across the other. Kitten? Kitten! She flexed her fingers wishing for a second that she did have claws. She was not fragile and she was certainly not a kitten.

"I'll let you in on a secret, Jen."

He was leaning close to her again but she refused to meet his eyes. The anger felt so good, and she positively clung to it. Her blood was finally moving through her veins again. She felt...alive. It felt great.

"I like claws," he whispered, the husky voice sending wildfire rushing under her skin again.

She turned her head and found he was much closer than she expected. She had no way to describe the expression on his face, but it quickly melted into shock when she closed the distance between them and ran her tongue across his bottom lip.

"Meow," she purred, and swallowed down bubbles of laughter as she watched at least fifteen different emotions clobber him at once. "I don't need claws," she informed him.

Thankfully his cell phone rang because her heart really was about to blow right out of her chest. She smiled to herself as she heard how rough his voice was when he answered the call. She bit the inside of her mouth to keep from laughing. She had no idea what had just happened to her. Never in a million years would she ever have thought she'd do something like that. She felt his eyes on her and slowly licked her lips.

He made a slightly strangled noise and he was having trouble sitting still. Maybe he wasn't quite as immune to her as she'd thought.

She'd gotten to him. She'd actually scored a few points. Maybe she had grown claws. She watched her fingers as she flexed them. Her fragile kitten days were well behind her. And they were still going the wrong way.

"Where are we going?" she asked again, when the limo turned onto St. Charles.

Still on his phone, he just shook his head at her before turning away. She didn't have to understand Russian to know he was aggravated. Whoever he was talking to obviously didn't know him very well. Stefan Sellers didn't respond well to anything that wasn't exactly the way he wanted it. She almost felt sorry for whoever was on the other line. Stefan was wearing them down, that was obvious even to her.

Trent stopped at a red light and a street car packed with tourists passed by. St. Charles was still full of activity at night. Jen loved the Garden District. She had lived here when she was a child with her parents before they were killed, so it felt like home even if her memories from before the accident were fuzzy.

She and Lizzie had gone to school on St. Charles until Katrina had forced them to evacuate. They had explored the neighborhood more than they should have as teenagers. When the limo stopped in front of the huge Victorian house on the corner of Nashville and St. Charles, she had to smile. She always loved that old house with its wrap-around porch, formal landscaping and elaborate wrought iron fence. It was not one of the fussier houses on the street. Unlike most Victorians it was very understated. Someone had painted it recently, but Jen was glad they had stayed with the original ivory color and not tarted it up. She noticed a carriage house had been added when the limo turned onto Nashville and pulled into the driveway.

The driveway? She turned on Stefan. His expression was completely blank.

"What is this?"

"Our house," he said, his words crystallizing into ice as they hit the air. He didn't wait for her response, just got out of the car and slammed the door.

When her heart started beating again, she took a deep breath. He really had just said "our house". She knew her memory wasn't the best in the world but she had not imagined that. "We don't have a house," she said, getting out on her side when Trent opened her door.

"I bought it last year. Rogan finished the renovations about three months ago. It was meant to be a surprise but you surprised me instead by running away to Paris."

"I didn't run away."

"No?" he asked, heading around to the front door after getting her suitcase from the trunk.

"I didn't!"

"What do you call it then?"

"I applied to pastry school a year before you decided we should get married. I'm sorry if my life interfered with your plans," she yelled after him, not knowing who the hell she was for a moment, but not really having a problem with this sudden change in her attitude.

Trent cleared his throat politely and Jen flushed bright red.

"Sorry. Thanks for coming to get me, Trent."

"Go easy on him, Jen. He's been under a lot of pressure today," Trent lowered his voice, glancing up at Stefan, who was still glaring at her from the wrap-around porch.

"I'm not making any promises," Jen said, but she smiled and Trent seemed satisfied and got back into the limo.

She stepped up on the porch, easing around the old swing creaking on its chains. Stefan was still watching her with that pissed off glare and she started to tell him what he could do with it when something blue caught the corner of her eye.

Jen looked up, and her heart just stopped. The porch ceiling had been painted haint blue.

She closed her eyes against flashes of hot Georgia summer, lemonade, and Granny's gnarled fingers spinning yarn into gorgeous afghans without patterns or sense. "The slaves claimed ghosts thought the blue paint was water. They won't cross it so they won't haunt your house." Granny had explained when Jen asked why the neighbor boy was painting her porch blue.

That had been the summer before her parents were killed. Granny had been her only living relative and far too old to take her on after the accident. Granny had died six months later, leaving Jen completely alone in the world. Having no living family was a strange kind of emptiness. A hole that never quite closed. Jen had stopped expecting it to a long time ago.

Now, staring at the blue ceiling of the porch of her favorite house in the city of New Orleans, she discovered an entirely new level of pain and loss. Like the ring, this house was perfect. More of her dreams coming true for all the wrong reasons. And the worst part was he'd thought she would love it. He had no idea he was breaking her heart into smaller and smaller pieces.

He was still watching her, his expression completely unreadable except for the tightness around his jaw. He opened the front door and stood back waiting for her to go inside. She wanted to run the other way as fast as she could. Every single instinct screamed at her to flee. But running from Stefan would be about as effective as running from a lion. In fact, she'd have better luck escaping from a lion. Stefan could run a hundred meters in under twelve seconds if he tried. She wouldn't get a step.

Stefan watched as Jen started to take a step back. Icy disappointment overwhelmed him and he realized he'd been holding his breath, waiting. Waiting for what? Not this step back. She was supposed to at least smile. She was supposed to burst into tears of absolute shock and joy. Launching herself into his arms would not have been out of place either. She wasn't supposed to run away from him.

"Jen." Her name escaped him before he could stop it. His voice sounded like gravel but it froze her in place. Then he heard himself say, "Don't run." The warning in his tone made his own blood run cold. He watched her go pale and her whole body flinch away from him. For at least the five millionth time today, Stefan wanted to break something.

This was not supposed to be happening like this. She loved this house. He'd listened to her and Lizzie dream out loud about the house on the corner of St. Charles and Nashville for years. They had made up the most ridiculous stories about the magical people who lived there and the huge parties and the dresses and everything little girls loved. Now she was staring at it as if it were a cell at Angola.

Irritated, he suddenly didn't really care anymore. He'd bought her this house and spent a fortune remodeling it. She was damned well at least going to look at it. He held out a hand for her, giving her a chance to take it before he gave in to that lingering instinct to sling her over his shoulder.

She surprised him by taking it. She was trembling and that had him swallowing back the anger he never let himself feel. He pulled her inside a little harder than he'd meant to and flipped on the lights. Her sharp intake of breath gave him a little satisfaction as she pulled away from him to step further into the huge foyer. She turned in a circle to look at the monstrous chandelier and at the wooden staircase that wrapped around the two-story entrance so large a helicopter could have easily set down in it. Then she looked down, her lips parting in surprise and her eyes widening at the intricate black and white marble floors. Rogan had insisted they try to save the floors and Stefan had warned him not to even tell him what it cost.

In fact, Rogan had never actually given him a final figure on the renovations because Stefan really didn't want to know. It hadn't mattered. Jen had been through so much in her life. He'd wanted her to have the home of her dreams and he wanted it to be perfect. Better than perfect.

"Rogan saved a lot of the original fixtures," Stefan told her now. "And the doors. We only had to replace about half the windows but they matched them pretty closely. And the mantles weren't in bad shape. There are fireplaces everywhere. Some still work."

Jen didn't know where to look first. "Rogan's a genius," she breathed.

"Dining room's this way," he said. "Lizzie has furniture on hold at some of the antique shops in the city."

Jen nodded, but she still wouldn't look at him. So he watched her move through the huge dining room to the butler's pantry that he'd been so sure she would love. Instead, she stopped dead, turned quickly on her heels and headed for the front door. It might honestly have been kinder of her just to gouge his eyes out. Stefan had only experienced the angry pain that blinded him as she swept past him once before in his life. He certainly hadn't expected to feel it again and not under these circumstances.

Run. Run faster, was all she could think. Her heart was beating like crazy. If she went in that kitchen she'd never want to leave. She would be well and truly trapped. And he knew it. He'd done it on purpose.

He caught her by the arm when she reached the foyer. "Oh no, you don't," he snapped, pulling her back before she could reach the door.

"Don't," she whispered. "I've seen enough."

"You haven't started." He dragged her back through the dining room into the most amazing kitchen she had ever seen. The island alone could seat twelve people. The marble counter top offered an incredible workspace and the stainless appliances included a commercial-grade range. Then another set of full-sized single ovens, double-stacked in the cabinets. And it all still managed to look like a farmhouse kitchen.

"Tell Rogan the kitchen is perfect," she said, the painful lump in her throat making her voice lower than usual.

"You can tell him yourself. He's staying in the Carriage house."

"Angie's not back yet?" She stepped forward to take a closer look at the ovens.

"No," he said, watching her closely as she opened and shut the oven doors. "Rogan insisted on the three ovens." It was obvious he had no idea why.

"I guess so I can bake red velvet cake and bread pudding at the same time."

"Probably," Stefan started but his cell phone interrupted them again. While he took the call, Jen went down the three steps to the keeping room off the kitchen. She stood by the French door looking out at the landscaped back yard, actually large enough for the lap-style swimming pool and completely surrounded by a high brick wall. A wood pergola teeming with vines covered a patio. There was a small stone pool house that looked like an English potting shed. It was perfect. She could imagine all their friends over for a barbeque or just laying out by the pool with Lizzie. They could get a dog. Jen's heart squeezed so painfully she thought she might actually pass out.

Not only did Stefan expect her to live here, he expected her to love living here. It wouldn't even occur to him that she wouldn't. Her breath caught in her throat when he stepped up behind her and put his arms through hers, clasping his hands low on her stomach. Overwhelmed by the heat radiating off him all she could think was that he smelled so good.

"Why are you fighting me so hard on everything?" he whispered against her ear, causing all the tiny hairs on her body to tremble. "Tell me what's going on, Jen. What made you run away to Paris?"

She lost the battle to keep her eyes open. Her stomach twisted painfully as his words reminded her of all the reasons she should not be in this house with him. She definitely shouldn't be standing this close to him dreaming about dogs and barbeques. Home. It just hurt too much.

"Pastry school," she lied softly.

He kissed the delicate place where her shoulder and neck met and her skin shimmered. If he ever really tried to seduce her, Jen knew she wouldn't have a chance. Not that she wanted a chance. She wanted him. All of him. So much it was killing her. So much she didn't dare move, knowing he would stop if she made the slightest attempt to kiss him or touch him. Her fingertips burned and the ache inside her deepened. Jen knew life wasn't fair. She'd learned that at a young age. She didn't expect things to be fair. But this, this with Stefan, was just cruel.

"Eventually, I will find out what happened."

"Don't know what you're talking about." When she couldn't take another second of his breath against her skin and his hands on her, she turned around, reaching up to kiss him. He did exactly what she expected and stepped back. Knowing he would back off didn't stop more cracks opening up inside her chest when he did. At some point, she had to start getting used to it. Proving again she was an idiot, because she couldn't possibly live long enough to get used to this kind of pain.

"Keep looking around," he said gruffly. "I need a shower."

"Me too," she said, then almost smiled at the way he stiffened.

"I'll take a guest room," he said. "Master bedroom is at the end of the hall."

She watched him walk out, then heard his footsteps on the stairs. It was a few minutes before she could move. She wished desperately that she was brave enough, or brazen enough, to strip off her clothes and get in the shower with him. It had totally crossed his mind. She'd heard it in the gruffness of his voice and seen it in how quickly he'd left the room. What would the high and mighty Stefan Seller do if she did?

She sighed. He'd laugh himself silly.

CHAPTER THREE

The size of the kitchen and open living room should have prepared her for the master suite. The master bathroom was incredible. They had taken in a bedroom to create it. While it flew in the face of the history of the house, one look at the huge custom shower, and she forgave Rogan. There were at least ten different jets in it and a complicated control panel that she didn't know where to start with. There was also a deep tub with whirlpool jets that she stared at wistfully for a minute. She hadn't had a hot soak in forever. The tiny apartment in Paris had had a closet sized bathroom with the smallest shower she'd ever seen.

She stared doubtfully at the control panel for a minute. How hard could it be? She pulled the dress over her head and slid it down her arms.

"It's already preset," Stefan said, surprising her. "Just hit this button." An arm brushed her back, reaching around her to press the panel.

Jen went cold, then hot, and realized two things at once. She hadn't heard him come in, and she was standing there in a sheer black bra and leggings and nothing else. It didn't matter that for just about every summer until her senior year, she'd lived in a bathing suit around him when they spent weeks at the beach house. Now she felt exposed and off balance. Vulnerable.

"Don't you knock?" she hissed, scrambling to pull her dress back over her head.

Warm fingers curled around her upper arm, stopping her. "Not on a door I'm paying for, no, I don't. And it occurred to me you wouldn't know how to work the shower."

Her head fell forward and her stomach clenched. He was too close.

The heat from his body burned along her back. He was wearing running shorts and nothing else. She should have kept her mouth shut. She gasped when the back clasp on her bra released. She could not wrap her brain around him undoing her bra. Then one warm finger slowly traced the line of her spine down to the small of her back to slip under the waist band of the leggings. It was like having a live wire caress her. She lost her breath and she arched her back? as he trailed his finger back up.

Her whole body lit up. She felt like the head of a match someone had just dragged across flint. *Step away from him.* One step would break the contact, before the rest of the match caught. Of course, he read her mind again. He was shockingly good at that. His hand shot around and flattened against her stomach bringing her back against bare skin and hard muscles that scorched her. He pushed the thin bra straps down over her arms. She crossed her arms to cover herself.

"Don't," she whispered, her voice trembling. There was only so much she could take.

"What?" he asked, his breath warm against the curve of her neck. "Don't help my fiancée get into the shower before she collapses from exhaustion?"

"I don't need any help," she insisted, wishing he would just leave before she swung around and threw herself at him. Of course, if she did, he'd walk away.

"Be still." He pushed her hair away from one side of her neck and kissed her. She just melted. Just absolutely dissolved into a puddle of jet fuel. The match hit the puddle and she went up in flames. Her lacy bra slid to the floor and he caught her wrists and pulled her arms up and back over her shoulders where they wound around his neck. She turned her head so he could cover her mouth with his. It was a scorching, erotic, carnal kiss she was certain she could live on for the rest of her life. And since she might actually have to, she went with it. She at least wasn't going to make it easy for him to walk away this time.

He turned her in his arms without breaking the contact of their mouths, and crushed her against him. He was burning up. She slid her hands down to flatten against his chest, on the sculpted pectoral muscles she fought herself not to lick every time she saw them. It went on and on. He devoured her until she didn't even remember who she was, who he was, or where they were. Words like *beautiful, amazing, sweet,* drifted through the haze. Then his right hand slid down her back and past the knit waistband of her leggings to discover she was wearing a thong, and the sound that rumbled out of his throat told her he didn't want to stop. Not at all. Something close to triumph surged through her and she pressed closer, pushing her arms around his neck so he could lift her to get her closer. And just as her legs went around his hips, Prince Charming kicked in and Jen really *really* wanted to kill somebody.

He set her back from him, not as roughly as he had in the car, but it hurt just the same. And pathetic as she was, she tried to step forward, but he just moved farther away. And because her humiliation would not be complete without them, hot tears blinded her as he left. He wasn't even breathing hard. She hated him. Hated him. Hated him. Hated herself.

Stripping off the rest of her clothes, she could not get under the hot water fast enough. Her skin burned under the steaming jets of water as she tried to stop shaking. She ached everywhere, her body screaming for him to come back. Scorched inside and out, she still couldn't get the water hot enough to wash the feel of his mouth off hers, or the feel of his hands off her skin. It was ironic, really, that he kept breaking her into smaller and smaller pieces when she knew he believed he was protecting her.

Stefan stood two doors down, his forehead leaning against cold tiles as he waited for his erection to go away on its own. Despite the freezing cold water, it didn't budge until he did something about it, but doing something about it didn't even begin to help. He let the water catch his hoarse cry, then slid down to sit on the cold floor and catch his breath.

She had been wearing a thong. His hands shook as he pushed his fingers through his wet hair. He wondered faintly what color it was. He suspected not white.

He could sleep on the couch in his office on the first floor. That would work. He slowly released the breath he was holding. He definitely couldn't sleep up here. There was no telling what he would do. Not seeing her in so long had made him sloppy.

Another deep breath. Another exhale. Still not really helping.

Who was he kidding? He'd never felt like this around her before. Out of control. Primitive. Starving. He'd never felt like this around anyone.

And he'd never once in his life gotten off thinking about her and all that soft, warm heat he'd finally let himself get near. He closed his eyes.

Sloppy.

But somehow not feeling guilty. Not like he'd expected to feel.

Should feel.

No, just a lot of frustration and aggravation, and he really needed to run and soon. His fingers curled into fists and he forced himself to get up and try to get clean. Because that's what he really felt like. A drug addict and she was skimming through his blood stream at an alarming rate. He definitely needed to run.

He shouldn't have kissed her earlier. She was upset, exhausted, and overwhelmed. He just hadn't been able to stop himself. Now he beat himself up remembering how pale she'd looked, and how much weight she'd lost, and how she'd gone up like kindling and burned every shred of common sense he had right out of his mind. He still wasn't sure how he'd walked away from her. He didn't actually remember letting her go. He just remembered her muffled cry of protest when he did and his next memory was standing in an icy cold shower trying to get his breathing under control. The moments between those two events were white, hot and blank.

He'd definitely be knocking on doors first before he walked into rooms where she could be undressed, despite what he had told her. He didn't trust himself to walk away the next time.

He heard the TV turn on in the master bedroom when he walked back down the hall to check on her. Just to check. Because he was sleeping in the office.

She was sitting up in the huge bed, flipping channels on the flat screen when he knocked on the half-open door.

"That shower is amazing," she said, her voice gentle, breaking the tension between them. He stepped just inside the room.

"You need anything?"

She shook her head.

"I'll be downstairs if you do." He turned to leave, knowing there was no way in hell he was getting any sleep tonight. Not now that he'd noticed she was wearing one of his favorite Saints T-shirts. The one that had disappeared a few years ago. It was a lot more faded now, and lightning sizzled at the back of his skull as he realized she'd probably been sleeping in it for years, naked underneath it except for maybe a thong. Probably a cotton-candy pink thong. His whole body tightened up again.

"What's going on at STI, Stefan?" she asked before he could leave. "All these phone calls and you look ready to break something."

He sighed, leaning against the door, relieved she thought it was work keeping him so wound up. He resisted his first instinct to tell her not to worry about it. But STI *was* half hers. And she was twenty-two years old now. She needed to take an interest in the company and what was going on. "Volikovneft is gearing up to drill off the coast of Cuba. They want the Taylor valve and we're also going to supply the bolts and other materials. But Maretti is trying to convince the Russians that we can't deliver the amount of valves they need. He is trying to sell them a cheaper version he manufactures in China."

"Are we going to lose the contract?"

Stefan shook his head. "It's complicated, and Alex Volikov is a pain in the ass."

"How bad do we need it?" she asked, surprised she was actually interested.

"We don't need it, but it would be a nice insurance policy for the plant in north Mississippi. But we can't cut the price in half to compete with Maretti. We're not going to. Maretti thinks if we lose this deal, we'll take the company public to raise capital. That's what he wants, not the Russian contract."

"Why does Andreas Maretti want us to go public?"

"I'm sure he'd buy in," Stefan said, rubbing his eyes. "But we're actually pretty sure Judge Robicheaux's behind all this."

"Madlyn's grandfather?" Jen said, sitting up straighter.

"The old man overheard Nic tell my father that he thought the stock would value really high for an initial offering because a lot of funds would want it for their portfolios to show they invest in domestic manufacturing. Good PR for them. An obscene amount of cash for STI."

Her fingers pushed through her hair and Stefan paused, watching her closely. When she looked up at him finally, she only looked tired. He let himself relax just a little. He never knew how she'd react when he discussed the company with her, but right now, her eyes were clear if a little confused.

"Why would Madlyn's grandfather care about STI?"

For a split second, he wasn't sure what to say to her. He could answer the question several different ways, but he knew what her reaction would be to each answer, and he wasn't prepared for any of that right now. He started to answer, when she asked,

"Do *you* want to go public?"

Grateful for the unexpected reprieve he jumped at it. "If we go public, we lose a lot of control. It will be hard to keep manufacturing domestically. We'll probably end up manufacturing overseas within ten years just to keep profits where investors would demand. It might be a lot of money up front, but it's not worth it in the end."

Jen nodded. "I agree. I don't ever want to manufacture my dad's designs overseas. He wouldn't want that either."

"No," Stefan agreed. "He wouldn't."

"So what are you going to do?"

He fought back a yawn as he wiped his hand over his face. "I've already done it. Matt is going to release a story in the morning that STI is going ahead with the expansion in north Mississippi and any contracts involving the Russians were strictly rumors."

"I don't understand."

"Yeah, but Volikov will. I just told him to go fuck himself."

"So we are going to lose the contract."

"Not a chance. Now, enough shop talk. Get some sleep."

"Stefan," she stopped him when he turned towards the door.

He paused but didn't turn around immediately. He closed his eyes and prayed just a little that she would let it drop. "Yeah?"

He turned when she hesitated. He found her watching him, brown eyes so careful. His hand tightened on the door frame. "We really need to talk," she said slowly. "About us," she added.

"Okay, but not tonight. I'm wiped, Jen, really."

He held his breath and let it out when she smiled, her face going all soft and lovely. His entire body tightened and he held onto the doorway until he was sure he would continue out of it instead of doing what he really wanted to do, which was slide under those blankets and suck that slightly fuller bottom lip into his mouth and lose the rest of himself in her.

"Okay," she said, easing down under the covers and pulling the blankets up. Her head touched his pillow and he thought he really was going to just drop dead right there. "Night."

"Night," he growled and stalked out of his bedroom while he still could.

"You're gonna punch a hole in this thing," Rogan said, coming downstairs from the apartment over the carriage house to the gym Stefan had built on the first floor. He caught the punching bag and held it still. Stefan continued to pummel it without saying anything, harder now that Rogan held it. "Ooookay..." Rogan said, "Things not working out with the hottie you came home with earlier? I didn't see her leave. Did the limo not impress her?" Rogan snickered. Stefan ignored him, hitting the bag harder.

Rogan wouldn't let up. "I admit, I'm surprised you would bring a girl here. I thought this house was for Jen."

Stefan froze, mid-punch, his eyes meeting Rogan's across the bag. "That was Jen."

Rogan laughed, then stopped when he realized Stefan was serious. "That couldn't have been Jen. Her legs went on forever."

"You don't get to notice how long her legs are," Stefan warned him.

"No way. That was Jen?" Rogan grinned. "Paris was good for her."

"Yeah," Stefan said, slamming his fist into the bag again. He could bloody his knuckles all he wanted but it wasn't going to help. He needed to run. Stefan crossed to the refrigerator, pulled out a bottled water for himself and tossed Rogan a Long Neck.

Stefan tried to change the subject. "Angie still in Houston?"

"No, Miami. Working on Nic's latest hotel."

"She file the paperwork?"

Rogan's expression went dark. "Can't file it if I don't sign it."

Stefan leaned back against the counter. "Man, we've been through this."

Rogan shrugged, finishing the beer in record time. "She's not divorcing me."

Stefan almost laughed at that. He'd known Rogan most of his life. Rogan was the third oldest of eleven kids raised in a one bathroom house. He was nothing if not patient, but Angie sent Rogan off the rails like nothing Stefan had ever seen. Until today, Stefan had never quite understood how Rogan could lose it so bad. After watching Jen catwalk towards him at the airport, Stefan was starting to have sympathy for his oldest friend.

"How are you going to stop her?"

Rogan's expression went darker. "She's my wife. I know how to handle her." He grabbed another Long Neck then stopped in the middle of popping the top. "How in the hell could that be Jen?"

"She's lost a few pounds and all her clothes are black."

"How do you lose weight at pastry school?"

"Ask her."

"She like the house?"

Stefan snorted and slammed the water bottle into the garbage can then grabbed another one. "She doesn't hate it," he said bitterly.

"What the hell does that mean? Did you show her the ovens? She should have burst into tears over that kitchen."

"Not so much." Stefan finished the second water and grabbed his gravity boots and strapped them on. He needed blood in his brain. "Nothing ever goes as planned with Jen."

Stefan reached up for the pull-up bar, then folded in half to swing the boots up until they attached. Then he dropped, letting his back stretch out before he started upside-down abdominal crunches.

"You're not human, you know that?" Rogan told him. "How can you do that without throwing up?"

Stefan didn't say anything, just concentrated on the up and down. The sit-ups weren't the same as running either, but hanging upside down usually cleared his head.

But not tonight. Nothing was working tonight.

"She really didn't like the house?" Rogan demanded.

Stefan paused mid-crunch. "She looked like she was about to be sick and she tried to run away."

"What did you do?"

"I didn't do anything," Stefan exploded. "You know, I had a plan. I had a really great plan. And before I can get it off the ground, she leaves for six months."

Rogan just shook his head. "Man, told you a long time ago you can't plan this."

Stefan's eyes narrowed. He planned everything. He didn't like wild cards and chance. He needed to know what was happening and ninety-nine percent of the time he was in complete control of his world. In fact, the only part of his world he couldn't seem to nail down was Jen. "Well, it's blown to hell now anyway. I guess I'll do like you and wing it."

"Worked with Angie."

Stefan started crunching again. "You're separated, remember?"

"No, she thinks we're separated. I'm just letting her have some time. Trust me, she'll be back. We had dinner about a week ago and she's miserable. She just won't admit it."

"You had dinner? Like a date?"

"Yeah. So what?"

"You're separated but you're still going out?"

"Yeah. A lot. We've been out more in the last few months than since we had Zack, which is the whole problem anyway. I don't pay enough attention to her. Got too busy at work and didn't realize it. It won't happen again. Same thing with Jen. You just need to be straight with her, you kept her in the background for years and now..."

"She was just a kid," Stefan snapped. "What was I supposed to do? She's still too young."

"She's always going to be too young for you. Get over that."

"Did you want to get married at twenty-two? I sure as hell didn't. She should be out having fun, doing girl shit. Shopping, buying more of those shoes. A lot more of those shoes..."

"No one says you have to get married next week. Wait a couple of years before you actually marry her."

"Uh, no. Waited six years. Not waiting any longer."

Rogan's head snapped back. "Dude, you don't have to marry her for that."

"Oh, fuck yes, I do," Stefan roared back at him, as his feet hit the floor. "You think I'd do that to Robert? You really think so? Plus, Mac, with his mind control and bullshit radar... You really think I'm going there before she's legally mine? Would you?"

Rogan's expression went dark again. "No, man, I guess not, but..."

"You guess not?" Stefan cut him off. "Seriously? You guess not?"

"She's not a kid anymore."

"Is that right?" Stefan asked, pulling the boots off and resisting the urge to slam them against the wall. "Tell you what? I'm just gonna go back inside and do her right now. How's that sound to you?"

Rogan stood up, his expression like pitch and his green eyes even blacker. "Point taken," he grumbled.

"Don't like that idea, do you?" Stefan smirked when his best friend shook his head slowly. "I promised him," Stefan said in a low voice, watching Rogan flinch. "Can't break that promise."

"You're not breaking it," Rogan assured him. "You've waited until she's twenty-two. You've quadrupled her trust fund. And you're running a company to protect her interest in it. I think you're slick with Robert, man. What else could he expect?"

"Yeah, whatever. Enough of this shit. I appreciate it, man. I do. But now I gotta go back into that house where I know she's asleep in my bed and try to force myself to stay out of that room. It was easy to do that before when she was all quiet and sweet. Now she comes back from Paris all sleek, in those shoes and skin tight clothes and fuck me..."

Rogan paused at the door that led upstairs to his apartment. "I don't envy you. But I know you. She's safe as houses."

Stefan shook his head. Safe? Not even close.

CHAPTER FOUR

The next morning, Jen found Stefan in the kitchen blending one of his notorious protein shakes. The blender masked her movements as she sat down at the island and just enjoyed the view for a moment. He was wearing jeans that were so faded they were white in places and one of the knees was missing. The tan T-shirt had once been brown with a sailboat on the back. He'd cut the sleeves out now and it clung to the muscles of his back.

He barely reacted when he turned around and faced her. Nothing seemed out of the ordinary. Maybe she had imagined that kiss after all. It wouldn't be the first time. She'd dreamed he'd kissed her after her prom and there was no way that was real. He'd looked at her like she smelled funny when he'd seen her coming down the stairs to meet her date. And last night she'd been really tired. Maybe the jet lag had her mind playing tricks on her again.

"Protein shake?" he offered.

She relaxed just a bit, unsure if she should be terrified or relieved that her mind was still playing tricks. There was no way this human iceberg in front of her had kissed her like that last night. And even if he had, she was following his lead and acting like nothing was wrong. "Do you have any real food?"

"Yogurt, fruit. That's real food."

"Eggs?" she asked.

"Hard-boiled," he said, because anytime he bought a dozen eggs he boiled them and put them in the fridge. Sometimes she wasn't sure he was human.

"Can I borrow your car?" she asked.

He went very still. "Excuse me?"

"Can I borrow your SUV?" she corrected. "I just want to run up to the grocery store and get a few things." She'd promised Lizzie pancakes. Stefan wouldn't eat them of course, but Rogan and Lizzie would.

"You don't drive."

Jen stiffened. "Yes, I do."

"Since when?"

"Since Jared taught me how last year."

"The hippie taught you how to drive?" She watched as his blue eyes frosted over.

"He's not a hippie, and now that I'm back, I should probably get a car."

"You want a car?"

"Yeah, I want a car." She definitely wanted a car now with him acting like this. "You got a problem with that, Stefan? Lizzie has a car. You have two cars and a motorcycle and three bicycles that cost more than the other three combined. Why can't I have a car?"

He stared at her, blinking slowly. "What kind of car do you want?" His patronizing tone got all over Jen. And, of course, she had no idea what kind of car she wanted because she had just decided thirty seconds ago she wanted one. But now, she really wanted one.

She slid off the bar stool. "Forget it. Jared will be home in a few days. He can go with me."

"He going to buy you the car too?" Stefan asked, his voice taking on a dangerous quiet that should have sent her flying back to the bedroom for cover.

But it didn't. "Why are you so angry?" she asked, her eyes narrowing on him. His reaction was way out of line. She found herself wanting to see just how low and quiet his voice could get. "You should be relieved I got over my fear of driving, not acting like I've just stolen your favorite running shoes."

The doorbell rang, interrupting their chilly confrontation. She headed for the door and when she opened it, she completely forgot to be upset. Lizzie stood grinning at her and holding up two grocery bags. "Hint, hint."

Jen hugged her despite the bags, then took one and found everything she needed for pancakes and groaned in relief.

"I know," Lizzie said. "He has yogurt, hard-boiled eggs, fruit, and bottled water. He's not human."

"I love you, you know that?" Jen grabbed the other bag and headed towards the kitchen.

"What's this?" Stefan asked as she unloaded the bags on the counter.

"Breakfast," Lizzie said. "Or it will be in a few minutes. You should stick around, Stefan. Jen makes the best pancakes in the world."

"Pancakes?" Stefan echoed. "I'll pass." He'd poured the protein concoction into a travel glass and was drinking it slowly.

"I'm not making you any," Jen assured him.

"Why not?" he snapped back.

"White flour," Jen announced, setting the bag of flour down too hard on the counter. "Refined sugar." The sugar also hit the counter. "Your nemeses, remember? Useless carbs. Ooh, blueberries. Good call, Lizzie." She grinned at her friend. "Text Rogan and tell him to come down."

"Rogan gets pancakes?" Stefan demanded, his glass slamming down a little too hard on the counter.

Jen swung around at him, her hands on her hips. "Rogan gets whatever he wants. Red velvet cake, brownies, bread pudding, and pancakes."

Stefan took a step closer to her forcing her to back up against the island. His eyes weren't frozen anymore. "Is that a fact?"

"Yep," she tried to stand her ground, she really did. But the counter top pressed against her waist as she eased back away from him. "Everyone gets pancakes but you," she informed him, her chin going up so she could keep eye contact with him.

His eyes narrowed. "What do I get?"

"Protein powder and yogurt," she told him, completely forgetting that Lizzie was in the room. "And a boiled egg."

"If you're making pancakes in my kitchen, then you'd better make enough for me too," he warned, his voice so low and quiet she could hardly hear him.

She looked up at him, her whole body alive with the angry knowledge that she had not imagined that kiss. And now she really wanted him to kiss her again. *No, no kissing.* She was furious at him. Her fingers caught hold of the granite counter top behind her in an effort not to grab hold of his shirt and jerk him down so she could kiss him. But if he stepped any closer to her she wasn't going to be responsible for what happened next. "You won't eat them."

"We'll see about that," he leaned down, brushing his mouth across her startled lips. "I seem to be developing a taste for sweet things."

"Uh, hey, guys," Lizzie interrupted suddenly. She pointed at the door. "Do I need to leave? Cause I can just pop next door and see Rogan so you two can work out whatever this is."

They both turned to her at the same time, both a little stunned and confused.

Lizzie grinned, her blue eyes dancing with humor. "I mean, it's just pancakes."

Stefan straightened up and stalked out of the kitchen without another word.

Jen watched him leave, then looked back at Lizzie, who was about to fall off her bar stool she was trying so hard not to laugh. "Don't you dare say anything," Jen warned her, but she was fighting laughter too. "Not if you want pancakes."

Lizzie zipped her fingers across her lips, but she was still smiling.

Mixing the batter turned out to be an excellent outlet for all of Jen's frustration. "What is the matter with him?" She just couldn't hold off asking any longer.

"With who? Stefan?"

"Don't be cute. You know what I mean."

"Okay, first, I can't help being cute. Second, he's been like this since you left. All frost giant crazy," Lizzie said. "And not in a sexy Tom Hiddleston kind of way either. More like a I'm-not-sure-how-to-function-because-Jen-went-to-Paris-with-the-hippie kind of way."

Jen stared at Lizzie, the spatula forgotten as it dripped batter into the bowl.

Lizzie finally noticed her staring. "What? You thought he wouldn't notice you were gone?"

"Well, I didn't..." But she had no idea what she didn't, or what she thought. "That's crazy."

"No, what's crazy is that you two were all set to sail off into the sunset, and suddenly you leave for Paris, and no one is exactly sure why, and Stefan goes from serious, controlling guy to insane, mega-controlling frost giant. What happened?"

"Nothing," Jen flipped on the griddle. "I got accepted to pastry school."

"And it had nothing to do with the fifteen minutes you were alone with Madlyn at Rogan's birthday party."

The spatula started stirring with a vengeance.

"Jen," Lizzie said carefully. "I haven't said anything to Stefan but I know it was her. What did the Red Queen say to you?"

Jen shook her head, dropping perfect circles of batter onto the hot griddle. "Nothing."

"I'm your best friend. I know better."

"She didn't say anything that I didn't already know, Lizzie."

She let the pancakes bubble, then started on a blueberry sauce. She knew the likelihood of Stefan actually eating her pancakes was pretty slim, but just in case he did, she was sure he'd like the blueberry reduction much better than maple syrup.

Rogan walked in just as the first batch were finished. He always had great timing like that. "It's good to have you home," Rogan said, hugging her tight but not tight enough she couldn't fix him a plate. "We've missed you."

"You've missed my brownies."

He pressed a kiss to her forehead. "And your bread pudding."

"Well, Stefan is making me stay here so maybe I'll do some baking just to piss him off."

Rogan laughed, snagging a blueberry. "Give him a break, *cher*. He's still trying to recover from those shoes."

She flipped the pancakes. "Really?" she asked, trying to sound casual.

Rogan joined Lizzie on the other side of the island. "When you walked in with him last night, I didn't recognize you."

"Rogan," Lizzie laughed, pushing her shoulder against his. "That's horrible."

"Am I that different?" Jen asked, suddenly serious.

Rogan shrugged. "You look older."

She flipped the pancakes over again, and when they finished she slid two onto Lizzie's plate and two on Rogan's. She poured up more circles as Stefan walked back in.

"Where's my plate?" he asked, when he saw Rogan and Lizzie eating.

"I ate yours," Rogan announced.

Stefan slid onto the bar stool next to Lizzie and stared at Jen.

"Stefan says he'll eat pancakes," Lizzie explained to Rogan.

"Bullshit." Rogan laughed.

"Watch me."

Jen took another plate down, dished up two pancakes, drizzled them with blueberry sauce, added a handful of fresh blueberries, and set it all down in front of him. She gave Rogan the other two pancakes without taking her eyes off Stefan. He stared down at the plate.

"Well?" she asked.

He looked up at her and grinned. "Am I supposed to eat them with my fingers?" he asked, sweet as pie, and Jen decided she might actually be capable of murder. Resisting the urge to stab him in the eye with it, she grabbed a fork out of the flatware drawer and handed it to him.

"Thanks," he said, and sank the edge of the fork into the fluffy stack.

Jen watched, mesmerized, as he actually put them in his mouth and chewed. Something warm started to swirl deep inside of her. He was eating her pancakes. She could not believe it, but she was seeing it with her own eyes. He actually had closed his eyes while he chewed. Lizzie snapped a picture with her cell phone.

"Best pancakes on the planet," Rogan said.

Stefan nodded, swallowing. "Delicious," he agreed, "Marry me and I'll let you cook for me every day."

Lizzie snorted, almost choking on her pancakes.

"I don't even know where to begin," Jen told him. "I think your arrogance has finally peaked," she said, but she was smiling. She couldn't help it. The audacity of it was just too much, but that was Stefan. Arrogance on him was almost adorable.

"Maybe it's the syrup I don't like, normally. I like this blueberry sauce," he admitted, rewarding her with one of his heart stropping grins. All the air fled her lungs and none came back to replace it. "I'm going to want more of these," he warned.

"Banana pancakes next time," Lizzie requested.

Stefan's cell phone rang then, but he didn't stop eating when he answered. She put two more pancakes on his plate, gave Rogan two more, and Lizzie one while Lizzie swore she was going to an extra spin class. Then she put two on a plate for herself. Stefan reached across the island, grabbed her plate and set it next to his so she would have to sit down next to him to eat.

He turned to her when he ended the call. "I've got to go to the office."

"On Sunday?" Lizzie breathed. "Seriously?"

"Seriously." Stefan said. "Rogan, you got a minute?"

Rogan nodded, and took his plate with him as he followed Stefan out of the kitchen.

"Things are better." Lizzie smirked, trying not to laugh.

Jen smiled at her best friend. "He ate my pancakes," she said, still stunned by the reality of it. She knew it was dangerous, but she just couldn't help the tiny flare of hope that sparked inside her. "I didn't think he would actually eat them."

"Jen," Lizzie said, "He loves you. I don't know why you think he doesn't."

"He feels responsible for me. He worries about me," Jen admitted. "And he does apparently want to have sex—"

"Okay, no!" Lizzie shook her head, wild curls flying as she threw out her hand. "Stop right there. T.M.I. I do not want to hear that. It's just too weird and gross. Sorry."

Jen laughed, and dropped her fork. "You started it."

Lizzie waved her hands around. "I won't make that mistake again."

Jen cut her some slack and changed the subject. "Why didn't you tell me about the house?"

Lizzie shrugged. "He made me promise not to, but if it makes you feel better, I spent a fortune on that furniture. He almost had a heart attack when he got the bill, but all I said was 'Jen will love this', and he was fine with it. And you do, don't you? Love it, I mean? You've always loved this house."

"Yes," Jen admitted. Because she did love it. It was everything she could have ever imagined in a house.

Lizzie sighed. "I am totally a hundred percent on your side whatever you decide to do. But if you really don't want to marry him, you need to tell him."

"I have told him. Over and over."

"I just don't understand," Lizzie said, suddenly sounding sad. "You've loved him since we were kids, and you were so happy last year. What happened? Are you not in love with him anymore?"

Jen took a deep, steadying breath. There were so many things she wasn't sure about, but how she felt about Stefan was not one of them. "I don't think I know how not to be in love with him, Lizzie. I've never not been. At least, I can't remember not loving him, but you know everything is so patchy from before the accident, and I'm never sure what's a memory or what's just wishful thinking."

Lizzie gave her a sad smile. "You don't remember when you first came to live with us?"

"Bits and pieces." She did remember Mac coming to get her from school and trying to tell her about the accident. The first real clear memory she had was after she'd been with them a year and they'd spent Spring Break at the beach house. She could remember how hot the sun was, the sound of the ocean and watching Stefan run on the beach. He ran every morning. She'd followed him down there and sat in the sand watching him disappear down the beach and later reappear again. She had no idea how long she'd been out there. She remembered when he slowed down because he saw her sitting in the sand.

"Hey, kiddo," he'd said, "You're up early."

"I had a bad dream," she'd told him, and she could still remember the startled look on his face as he dropped down next to her in the sand. All she had understood was that the sand was warm on her toes, the sun sparkled silver on the waves, and everything was going to be all right as long as Stefan was sitting beside her.

"I didn't speak for a year, did I?" she asked Lizzie, the memory of that perfect moment causing a painful lump in her throat. It had been enough just to be next to him. Why couldn't that be enough anymore?

"No, you didn't," Lizzie said. "Not until we were at the beach. I think you told Stefan you'd had a bad dream. You were traumatized, and you'd been in the hospital for such a long time."

"Hospital?" Jen sat up suddenly, not understanding what Lizzie was talking about.

Lizzie moved closer to her. "Hey, Jen, let's talk about something else. We can go shopping or swimming, but don't worry about all this right now."

"It's too cold to swim," Jen said, her heart rate rising. Was something burning? Did she smell smoke? She jumped off the bar stool. The floor tilted under her feet. She caught hold of the cold metal on the back of the bar stool. "Lizzie, why was I in the hospital?"

"Oh, honey," Lizzie reached out for her. "The accident."

"But, I was at school. Mac came to the school and told me." There was a low-pitched hum behind her left ear and everything suddenly came into really sharp focus. "Oh, wait. Lizzie," Jen looked at her, stepping back as Lizzie reached for her again. "No, wait. I was." It was right there. Just out of reach.

The principal had gotten her out of class and walked her up to the office where Mac was waiting for her. Something was burning. Smoke was filling her nose, sliding down her throat and burning her chest. She heard someone crying.

"Don't cry, Lizzie," she said softly, and everything went gray.

When Jen opened her eyes, Stefan was watching her closely, his fingers stroking across her forehead and into her hair. She hadn't seen that look in a long time. It was his be-careful-she's-about-to-break look. "Lizzie," she said, worried. "She was crying."

"She's okay, Jen, just relax. You fainted."

"Fainted? That's ridiculous. I don't faint." Then she realized she was in the downstairs guest room. Damn. "You're supposed to be at work."

"Come to the office with me."

"So you can keep an eye on me?" she asked, and closed her eyes. Had she really fainted? Damn it. She was so tired.

"No, so my silly sister doesn't do anything else to upset you."

"Leave Lizzie alone."

He brushed a stray hair behind her ear. His fingertips felt so good sliding over her skin. All the bitter cold was gone out of his expression.

"Do you remember what you were talking about?"

Jen nodded. She was lying. She had no idea what they'd been talking about. She still couldn't believe she had fainted. But she liked the way he was touching her. Maybe if she stayed still, he wouldn't stop.

"Tell me what it was," he said gently. Of course, he knew she was lying because he could read her mind.

She remembered making pancakes. She remembered Stefan eating pancakes. Of course, she could have dreamed that part. What were the odds Stefan had actually eaten pancakes? She vaguely remembered Lizzie crying. She sat up. He was the last person she wanted to know that her memory played tricks on her.

He took a deep breath. "You were talking about the accident," he said, and she cringed. "Do you remember now?"

The entire morning snapped back into place. Lizzie was telling her that she had been in the accident, but Jen knew that wasn't true. She remembered the day Mac came to her school to tell her about the accident. He was so tall. She knew him but had always been afraid of him. She could remember him telling her that everything would be okay. Her parents were in heaven. He was going to take her home with him and she could stay in Lizzie's room until they got a room fixed for her. He had made her feel safe while her entire world crashed down around her.

"Do you know what happened the night of the accident?"

"Yes," he said grimly. "Most of it anyway"

She took a deep breath. "I very clearly remember Mac coming to my school to tell me about the accident. But Lizzie says I was in the car."

He cursed under his breath.

"No, I'm tired of everyone protecting me," Jen said. The words came out stronger than she expected.

She watched him struggle with something. Protecting her was second nature to him, but then blue eyes leveled with hers. "Do you know what time the accident happened?" he asked.

"Around 8:30," she answered automatically. Everyone knew that. "Oh," she whispered, her breath hitching in her throat. The accident had been at night. There was no way she'd been at school. The world tilted on its axis and she closed her eyes. Why had she never put those pieces together? She had always known the accident had happened at night. Why did she remember being at school? Maybe she really was crazy. "I was in the car," she said, the words skittered over her like bugs. Her skin crawled and the bottom of her stomach dropped out. "I was in the car."

"Yes," Stefan said. "The car flipped and caught fire. You hit your head. You were in and out of hospitals for six months."

She shook her head, sure that he was telling her the truth but unable to call up a single memory of being in a hospital. Six months of her life was just a blank. And some rabbits. Her mind always wandered towards rabbits when she tried to remember the accident. Proof that she was crazy, so she never, ever mentioned that to anyone.

Something cold slithered around her. Brain damage. Was that why her memory played tricks on her? All these years, she'd just believed she was a little loopy. No wonder they all treated her like she would break at any minute. She hadn't considered that she might actually be broken.

"There's nothing wrong with you now," Stefan told her. "There wasn't any brain damage if that's what you're worried about." Damn, she'd forgotten how he could read her mind.

"I want to know what happened." And for the first time, she really did want to know. "I can't remember any of it."

"No need for you to remember it," Stefan told her, wishing he didn't remember it. The image of her so small in that hospital bed covered in bandages, with Lizzie curled up next to her, was seared into his brain. The doctors had finally relented and let Lizzie stay with her because Lizzie would start screaming anytime they tried to make her leave. And Jen rested better with Lizzie in the room. They spent weeks in the hospital with her. To this day he hated *Alice in Wonderland* because Lizzie had made him read it to her while she lay next to Jen, trying to pull Jen out of the rabbit hole. When Jen finally did wake up, it still took days for her to recognize anyone. And then she still didn't speak for almost a year.

That day was seared into his brain too. They were at the beach house and he'd gotten up really early for his run. On the way back, he'd spotted her sitting on one of the dunes, watching the waves. She'd been twelve by then but still so small. Her scars had almost healed and her hair had grown out and had just started to brush past her ears. The doctors had said no more surgeries unless something unexpected happened and everyone was looking forward to things finally getting back to some sort of normal.

He'd stopped a few feet from her, watching her closely but she just seemed to be enjoying the early morning sunshine and the breeze. Her toes were digging into the sand and that half smile that played at the corners of her mouth lately meant she was fine. He relaxed and dropped down in the sand next to her. "Hey, kiddo, you're up early."

Then she'd turned to him, and sighed. "I had a bad dream," she told him, as if it hadn't been almost a year since anyone had heard her voice.

He'd caught his breath but tried to act normal. "Zombies?" he'd asked, because she and Lizzie were terrified of zombies.

She shook her head. "Rabbits," she'd said. "White rabbits chasing me."

"Did they have big, sharp, pointy teeth?" he asked, standing up and pulling her to her feet.

"No, silly, pocket watches." Then she'd looked up at him and said, "Race you!"

And she'd taken off towards the beach house. It was the only race he'd ever been happy to lose.

Stefan shook his head, envying her the memory loss. He was glad that she didn't remember. "You were eleven. I don't remember everything from when I was eleven. You were sedated for most of it so I'd be surprised if you could remember any of it."

"I think I remember the smoke. I dream about smoke. Sometimes I'm wearing it like a dress. It's weird."

"As long as it's not a wedding dress," he said.

She laughed, at that, and Stefan watched the tension drain out of her shoulders. Her color was back in her cheeks and her eyes were much clearer now.

"No, I think maybe a prom dress." She lied, trying to pick up his attempt to lighten the mood.

He surprised her with an exaggerated groan and threw his head back. "No, your prom dress was definitely pink."

"I do remember my Junior Prom," she informed him. "Especially how rude you were."

"Rude?" He sounded offended. "How was I rude?"

"You looked at me like I smelled funny." She shivered. It had been one of the worst moments of her life. She would never forget that look on his face. It had been all she could do not to run back upstairs and cry.

He was just shaking his head. "That dress looked like cotton candy. I wanted to lick it off of you."

"You looked like you wanted to choke me," she shot back.

"I did. You should have asked me to the prom. I wanted to strangle that boy."

"Really?" she interrupted him. "I should have asked you to the prom? You would have laughed in my...wait, licked it off?" Her breath caught.

He nodded, his eyes bleak. "I still dream about that dress. Bad dreams. You have no idea how that dress has tortured me, all that pink floating around you and it shimmered..."

"I was sixteen!" She was shocked. He'd been home that weekend but had been anything but nice to her. She and Lizzie had walked downstairs so excited about their Junior Prom. Stefan had walked out of the living room and stopped dead. The murderous look on his face was branded onto her brain. He'd never been anything but easygoing and fun until that point and she just hadn't been able to cope with the brunt of his anger.

"You were jail bait," he agreed, jerking her back to the present again. "But you aren't anymore." His smile turned sly.

Her eyes narrowed as she remembered all that dark intensity on his face and the tension rolling off him that night. He hadn't been thinking about murder at all. Something dark and sweet bloomed deep inside her now. She slanted her eyes up at him, lightly licking her bottom lip. "You know, I still have that dress."

His eyes closed and Jen would have sworn that he shivered. "Don't tell me that. I really have to go to the office," he grumbled.

"You're serious, aren't you?" she said. The rest of the conversation was forgotten now. "You wanted me when I was sixteen?" Something curled up her spine and around to pool low in her chest. It was warm and sweet and felt almost like hope.

"In the worst way imaginable," he admitted. "Not much gets past Mac. He pulled me into his study that night and told me in no uncertain terms that you were off limits."

Hot color streaked her face. She'd had no idea. Mac knowing was too embarrassing to contemplate. "He didn't."

"Yes, he did. He handed over your trust fund to me that night and told me to see how fast I could double the principal. And when you turned eighteen, he might let me take you out. Why do you think I wasn't around much after that night?"

"You were in training."

"I needed somewhere to focus my energy."

"This isn't funny," she said. "You focused your energy on plenty of girls before we got engaged. Very tall, very pretty girls." Until Rogan had married Angie, Stefan and Rogan had gone through girls like crazy. Jen had lost count of the movies, football games, and dinners she'd sat through with some chick on Stefan's arm darting nasty looks at her every chance she got. Now Stefan was telling her that he'd wanted her when she was sixteen. Well, he must not have wanted her too badly because it certainly hadn't curtailed his social life.

"Never said I was a monk," he teased.

"Just stop, Stefan."

"What? You don't believe me? Then how do you explain that absolutely no one was surprised when I gave you that ring?"

"I was."

"Well, you were the only one."

They'd had a twenty-first birthday party for her. Jared's band, Sugar Coma, had played. Elliot Carter had catered it. There were floating candles in the pool. Stefan had walked her out on the pier behind his parents' house, pulled the incredible ring out of his pocket, and slid it on her finger before she realized what it was.

"We'll get married at Christmas. You can decorate as many Christmas trees as you want. Just no construction paper, please," he had told her, kissing her then, and she had just stood there like an idiot thinking all her dreams had come true. Looking back, she now knew the kiss had been restrained. And he'd been way too quick to walk her back up to the party that had suddenly morphed into an engagement party with champagne everywhere.

Everyone had known but her. And no one had questioned her agreement. What if she'd said no? But he hadn't actually asked her, had he? He just said *we'll get married* and she'd smiled like a little fool. She cringed as the sweet memory lost a little luster. How could she have been so gullible? Now she understood why Jared had avoided her for most of that week prior to the party. And when he danced with her at the party, he'd just cut her off when she'd tried to tell him it was what she really wanted. "You know where to find me when you need me, Jen," he'd said, then gone back to play with the band again.

"You know, you never asked me if I wanted to marry you," she said.

Blue eyes narrowed on her, but his expression didn't change.

"Were you afraid I'd say no?"

"You're feeling better," he announced, changing the subject.

"Yes, actually much better." She felt steadier and clearer than she had in a long time.

"Good," he said, "Change. Office." And he was out of the room before she could say anything else.

She knew she was right. He hadn't asked her because he hadn't been sure she would say yes. And he just hadn't wanted to risk her saying no. Maybe he couldn't read her mind after all.

CHAPTER FIVE

Even an hour later, riding in the passenger seat of the Range Rover on the way to Sellers Tower, she was surprised at how good she felt. Her skin felt light. Everything was sharper. Brighter. Like the sun had come out from behind a cloud. She had no idea why finding out that she'd been in the accident made her feel better but it did. Because it was the truth, she guessed. And it explained so many things.

She rested her head back against the leather seat and watched him drive. She'd never let herself look at him for this long at one time before, but now her eyes drank him in. There wasn't much left, in the hard angles of his face and the unbearably sexy hollows under his cheek bones, of the beautiful boy she'd grown up with. But every line was familiar. The angle of his jaw was more refined. But there was strain around his eyes. He looked tired. He looked worried.

Worried? Jen shivered as she identified the unfamiliar expression she'd seen flickering around his face in the last twenty-four hours. It took her breath away. Stefan was worried. If she hadn't seen it for herself...

"If you keep looking at me like that, we won't make it out of the parking garage." he told her. She smiled to herself. She was starting to believe that he didn't see a child when he looked at her now. And she was still reeling from that whole prom–dress-cotton-candy comment, and the fact that he had not been sure she would say yes if he had bothered to propose on her birthday. The idea that Stefan wasn't one hundred percent in control of things was disturbing, but it was also exciting.

"You didn't have to bring me, you know," she said. "I actually feel better than I have in a long time."

As soon as he cut the engine, he turned in his seat. "I can't think straight when you're out of my sight. And I need to think straight today. So you are going upstairs with me, and we aren't going to argue. And you aren't going to start up about not marrying me. Got it?"

"Got it," she echoed, a strange little thrill curling up inside her. She leaned forward and brushed her fingers across his face. He covered her hand with his and leaned into the caress, pressing his face against her fingers and sending hair line cracks running all over her belief that he was not in love with her. He cared about her. She had no doubt about that. But he wanted to marry her because he felt responsible for her, responsible for the company their fathers had built. He didn't want to risk losing control of STI. She understood that, had proof of it. It was just so hard to believe it when she was with him, especially when her heart looked for every possible excuse not to believe it.

STI occupied the top three floors of Sellers Tower in the New Orleans business district. Stefan's office was spartan, to say the least. He had a desk, with a big chair behind it and a couple of chairs in front of it. There was nothing on the walls. No other furniture.

"Come here often?" she asked.

"Not if I can help it."

"Well," she looked around. "Lizzie is better at this than me, but I think you have room in here to put a treadmill or elliptical machine if you want. You could mount a small flat screen there." She stopped. "Why are you looking at me like that?"

He smiled. "Because you're a genius."

She smiled back. She understood him much better than he realized. "You don't want to be up here because you feel trapped. You just need to make the space yours. I know you don't really like to run on a treadmill but it would be better than..."

Her words trailed off into the heat of the sudden kiss that caught her completely off guard. So much so that she wound her arms around him without thinking and kissed him back. All those little curling sizzles she had been feeling suddenly flared hot all through her. She moved closer as his fingers curved around the nape of her neck. And it just seemed to go on forever. Especially since when he tried to lift his head to end it, her arms tightened around him and pulled him back down to her.

He shuddered, then went completely still. His fingers closed around her wrists to pull her arms back down. She actually cried out in protest when he broke away from her and stepped back, his chest heaving as he tried to drag air into his lungs.

And she really just couldn't help herself. The harsh words flew out of her mouth before she could stop them. "Will you stop trying to protect me!"

He laughed, sounding almost strangled. "Protect you? That's a joke. You *need* protection from me, Jen. I have no business being around you." That last bit came out so savagely that she shrank back. "I can't keep my hands off you for fifteen minutes in a row."

"But I don't want you to keep your hands off me," she said softly.

He stared at her, his eyes wild. "Don't say things like that to me, I'm warning you." He turned his back on her and headed towards the desk.

"What? Things like I'm not a little girl?" she flung at him and he stopped in mid-stride but didn't turn around. "Or, that I'm not a fragile butterfly that you're going to crush? Or that I know what it's like to feel trapped in a glass box?"

He still stood there, tension coiling him tighter and tighter. And she was doing that to him, twisting him into knots. She'd had no idea she could do that to him and the knowledge was heady. It made her reckless, so she just couldn't help herself when she pushed harder. She wanted to grind that protective instinct into the dust and she might never get another chance. So she went for it. "Or maybe, that I can still feel your hands and your mouth on me and I like it so much I'm burning up. And it hurts like hell when you stop touching me."

And then he was coming for her. She fought a smile. Fear and excitement swirling up inside of her. She actually laughed out loud when he slammed into her and walked her back up against the wall. Stefan unbound. Finally.

He unleashed himself on her full force, crushing her mouth, effortlessly lifting her off her feet. He caught one of her legs and pulled it up around his waist and Jen forgot how to breathe. He pushed against her until she was in no doubt how much he wanted her, while, the entire time, his mouth devoured hers. She loved it and she wanted more. If she lived a hundred years she would never get enough of him.

And maybe because it raged so hot so fast, he suddenly eased off the kiss, but he didn't move her. She moved her hips just so and loved his swift intake of breath. "I will strangle you if you don't stop moving," he ground out.

She pressed her mouth against his jaw, the stubble prickling against her sensitive lips and rasping across the tip of her tongue. He groaned and she just could not stop herself from raking her teeth down his neck. How could anyone taste so good?

"I'm serious, Jen. Be still."

"Oh," she whispered. "Like this?" She rocked against him. "Or this?" She moved just a shade differently. He didn't just want her, she realized. He needed her. She could feel it rippling through him, making her feel indestructible.

"You're playing with fire," he told her, pinning her harder so she couldn't move.

She leaned forward and kissed his forehead this time. Then she lowered her mouth to his and ran her tongue along his bottom lip. The groan that came out of his throat almost didn't sound human. He dropped his forehead to her shoulder. She tightened her leg around his waist. "Stefan," she whispered against his ear. "Look how hard you're holding me. Your hands are nearly white around my wrists. And I'm not close to breaking."

He covered her mouth again. This time it was slower, deeper, and made her forget the whole world. He swept into her mouth, the kiss turning hungry and stoking the flames licking through her body, threatening to rage out of control. He made several attempts to lift his head, but each time she bit at his mouth, or slid her tongue across his until the kiss turned savage. When he finally broke it off, he turned his face sideways and Jen opened her mouth against his temple, then smiled when he shuddered. "Not here," he was pleading with her now, his voice ragged. "Just, not here, like this. I don't want our first time to be in this damned office."

The raw sincerity in his voice resonated through her. She didn't want that either. She'd actually forgotten where they were. She nodded and other than her arms around his neck, she didn't move until he gained some control back. But it was hard for her too, because he was burning hot and she ached to move against him.

He loosened his hold and groaned as he let her slide down his body. He kissed her one more time before separating himself from her, taking at least two layers of her skin with him, leaving her raw and shaky.

"You might need to think about a sofa too," she suggested. "It could come in handy."

He almost laughed at that. She watched him put some distance between them. His hands were still shaking. She liked that. She was getting to him.

"You are driving me crazy on purpose," he told her. "Don't think I don't know it."

Her heart was beating so fast that she was sure it would fly out of her chest. All that delicious hope was in full bloom. "Is it working?"

He swung back around to her. She could see he had one of his comebacks ready, and she watched it die on his lips. He looked like he was seeing her for the first time. A spark ignited. He shook his head, and closed the distance between them. "Make me understand," he asked her, closing his hands on her shoulders and lowering his head to meet her eyes. "Make me understand why you don't want to be my wife." The words sounded like they had been wrenched out of his chest.

She shrugged, trying to turn away from him. "Why *do* you want to marry me?" she asked, unable to meet his eyes.

"Seriously?" he asked, voice all low and quiet, but, this time, flat. Ice started to form between them. "I am so tired of this."

The nerve endings on her body burned then froze. She took a step back, gasping at the unexpected sharp edge of pain that sliced through her. She watched him walk out the door. More doors opened then closed in a distant part of the office. She stood there a few minutes then sank down to the floor. She pulled her knees under her chin and held them with her arms, resting her forehead on her knees.

Part of her had been clinging to some desperate hope that Madlyn had been wrong and that the things Madlyn had said to her that night were motivated by jealousy. Jen closed her eyes. She should have known better. Madlyn Robicheaux was never wrong, and frankly had nothing to be jealous of. And why shouldn't Madlyn want her to know the truth? If Jen's brother hadn't been killed, Robert and Madlyn would have married.

She'd pointed that out to Jen at Rogan's birthday party seven months ago when Jen had slipped outside to get some air. "I'm not your enemy, Jen. I never have been," Madlyn had told her, when Jen had refused to acknowledge her when she approached. "We would have been sisters if Robert had survived."

Jen had finally looked at her. "What do you want?"

"I just want to help you," Madlyn had said, reaching across the table to cover Jen's hand. Jen had watched her so closely for any signs of insincerity, and while she had no doubt Madlyn was a grand master of deception, she couldn't detect a shred of dishonesty in her that night. "You need to think very hard before you marry him, Jen. He cares about you. Just not the way a man loves a woman he wants to marry."

Jen had pulled her hand away and clasped it into her other hand in her lap as Madlyn spoke her deepest fears out loud.

"Has he really kissed you yet?"

The weight on her chest had started pressing down harder on her and she could only stare at Madlyn. It was all true. All those sweet good night kisses came back to haunt her and the fairy tale started to unravel. Madlyn was right. She had stared down at the diamond flashing on her finger, and for the first time it didn't take her breath away. "But why would he marry me if he didn't want me? It doesn't make sense."

"Surely you aren't that naïve? The Sellers keep you wrapped in cotton wool but you have to understand, there's a lot at stake when it comes to your trust fund."

That's when the ice had started to invade her system, crystallizing in her blood stream, even as the puzzle pieces started to fit in place. "My trust fund?" she echoed, feeling suddenly very tired. "But Stefan doesn't need the money."

"Not the money, Jen. The stock."

Jen had gone very still, unable to do anything but listen to the brutal words Madlyn was delivering with such compassion. It all suddenly made really nauseating sense. She was a first class fool. There was no such thing as dreams coming true.

"Don't be too hard on yourself. He's very good at getting exactly what he wants - no matter what he has to do to get it," Madlyn had said, the picture of sympathy and concern. But it didn't reach her eyes, Jen noted absently. Madlyn's eyes were dead, like a shark's. She was a cold, deadly predator and as Jen finally grew up in the space of those seconds, she knew without a doubt that Madlyn had her own agenda for telling her these things. But it didn't make her wrong. Oh no, everything Madlyn said was absolutely correct. And Jen had started to understand why Lizzie called her the Red Queen. Madlyn was calm. She was helpful. She might explain the rules of the game, but only because it would make winning even sweeter for her if Jen knew exactly what was going on and still lost. Everything Madlyn had said was the raw, painful truth.

"You think I don't know what you're doing?" Jen had whispered.

Madlyn had eyed her carefully, then slowly gotten to her feet. "My motivations don't matter, Jen. Only the outcome."

"He may not really be mine," Jen had admitted slowly. "But he's not yours either."

Madlyn had leaned down, her black eyes making Jen shiver. "You still don't get it, Jen. I can still have him anytime I want."

Jen had glanced down at the solitaire flashing fire at her in the moonlight.

"Are you really that desperate, Jen?" Madlyn's smile had been so sympathetic, bile started to rise up Jen's throat. "Ask yourself why would a man like Stefan Sellers ever want to attach himself to a broken little girl? He wouldn't. And if he really desired you, would he have paraded his girlfriends in front of you the way he has all these years? He doesn't see you that way."

She'd stood up then, smoothing the lines of her red skirt. "If you go through with this marriage, Jen, he'll grow to resent you. Is that what you want for him? If you really love him, you won't let him trap himself in a marriage he will only regret one day."

Jen had watched her walk away and join the party. Madlyn had headed straight for Stefan. He'd leaned in to tell her something and she'd laughed and laughed. Jen had watched them together for a minute. They were perfect together. Both tall, handsome, intelligent, and powerful. And what was she? A mousy little broken doll.

But even mousy little broken dolls didn't enjoy being made fools of. So while her heart had slowly broken into sharp, jagged pieces, the rest of her cringed in humiliation. She'd lost track of how long she sat there, watching but not seeing the party inside.

"Why are you out here by yourself?" Stefan had asked, when he found her later.

"I'm sorry. It was just too loud," she'd said, wondering where the calm words came from. Part of her had just died. She must have been running on auto pilot. "Can you take me home? I'm really not feeling very well."

Later, when he'd dropped her off at his parents' house and walked her to the front door, Jen had turned quickly towards him when he'd leaned to kiss her good night. Desperate to prove Madlyn wrong, Jen had dived into the kiss with an urgency that surprised him. He'd set her back from him and she'd realized with icy clarity that he did still see a little girl. He might never see her as anything else. He wasn't in love with her. Not even close.

"What's going on?" he'd asked her, laughter teasing the edges of his mouth.

"Just tired," she'd lied, as the rest of all her girlish hopes and dreams floated away. Funny, she was so numb by then, it didn't even hurt anymore.

The numb feeling hadn't gone away. She'd called Jared the next morning and met him for lunch. He'd just passed the bar, finishing the last of his father's requirements for freedom. He wasn't actually going to join the Marshall Law Firm, because his father hadn't been specific enough when he'd said, "You can do whatever the hell you want as soon as you pass the bar."

"I guess he just assumed that if I passed it, I'd go ahead and buy the three-piece suit too," Jared had laughed. "Imagine his surprise when I told him about Paris."

Jen had smiled but it hadn't met her eyes.

Jared's smug expression flickered to real concern. "You gonna tell me what's happened or do I have to beat it out of you? What did Prince Charming do now?"

She'd shaken her head.

"Did you tell Sellers about Paris? I'm guessing it didn't go well."

"No, not yet." She hadn't told Stefan that she'd been accepted to pastry school because she hadn't planned on going. She'd been trying to think of a way to tell Jared she couldn't go, knowing he would be furious with her. Now, she was relieved she'd been such a coward. It seemed like a lifeboat in the middle of the Arctic sea. "But I will."

Jared had pulled his chair closer to the table and had leaned across, reaching out to gently tap her jaw with his knuckles. "Buck up, fairy princess. Your white knight will wait for you."

Jen's eyes had narrowed and her spine materialized out of nowhere. "Screw you," she'd hissed at him.

Jared had sat back, throwing his head back and laughing like crazy. "That's my girl. One day we're going to exorcise that princess gene completely. Now, unless you're here to tell me you aren't going to Paris, tell me what the fuck happened. Oh, and just a warning, you are going to pastry school even if I have to hogtie you and hold you down on the plane."

"I'm going," Jen had assured him.

"Good, because there is no way you can marry him, Jen. Have you looked in a mirror? There will be nothing left of you to put in a dress." He'd shoved his strawberry napoleon across the table at her. "Put it in your mouth, chew, and swallow," he'd said impatiently, looking like some demonic angel. "Stall, tell him you need time. Because, sweetheart, you do need time. You need to get your head straight, and you can't do that with him around. When we get back, we'll be so busy opening our bakery, he'll have to give you more time."

"You're right," she'd whispered, cutting a corner off the Napoleon and forcing herself to eat it.

"I'm always right. Here." He'd pulled a piece of paper out of his jacket pocket, unfolded it, and laid it on the table between them. It was a sketch of a cupcake with a big swirly top. The cupcake had a zombie face and there was a big chunk bitten out of the frosting swirl. Jared had surrounded the cupcake with the words *Jen's Voodoo Snacks and Sweets.* "What do you think?"

"I love it," she'd whispered, wondering if normal people got all misty eyed at the sight of a zombie cupcake. Further proof that she was broken. "It's perfect."

"It's happening," Jared had said. "We are going to rock the pastry world. They won't know what hit them."

She'd nodded, let him brow beat her some more, then done exactly what he said. Two days later, she told Stefan that she'd been accepted to pastry school. Listening to Jared had probably saved her sanity. Jared was the one person she knew who didn't treat her like she was about to fall apart. He could be overbearing and bossy, but never mean. He was funny, and sometimes too crude—okay, usually too crude. But he never told her to get down off a ladder and had no qualms about handing her a heavy box to carry. She loved him. He was the closest thing she had to family and the one real, steady friendship in her life that had no connection to any of the Sellers. He was just about the only one she could really trust.

"Let's go," Stefan snapped from the office doorway, dragging her back into the present.

Jen looked up, shaking off the memories.

"Elliot is holding a table for us."

She nodded, pushing herself to her feet. She was stiff and the light was fading outside. How long had she been sitting there? She'd lost time. That hadn't happened in a long time. When she reached him in the doorway, he tossed his car keys at her. "You drive," he barked and spun around, leaving her to follow him out of the office.

CHAPTER SIX

Jen stared at herself in the mirror and swallowed hard. The dress was worse than she remembered. What had ever possessed her to buy it? She turned in the mirror and looked over her shoulder and cringed. The draped back was open all the way to her waist where the suddenly tight skirt stopped well above her knees. The front draped too but not nearly as dramatically. It was suspended by two razor thin jeweled straps that looked ready to break at any minute. She loved it and hated it at the same time.

The dress made her feel exposed and, if she were honest, just a little reckless. She stepped into the Manolos and took a deep breath. She didn't have another dress to change into. Elliot's restaurant wasn't formal but he didn't allow jeans after six.

Telling herself Stefan probably wouldn't notice, she took the stairs carefully in her heels, then stepped into the living room where she heard the flat screen on a game. Half-expecting to find him on the sofa talking on his cell phone, she froze when he stepped into the room from the guest room and stopped dead.

"Oh, hell no."

"What?" Her eyes narrowed as she watched him walk into the room.

"You're not wearing that," he told her, stopping a few feet from her. The frost giant was back. "Go change."

Her jaw dropped slightly. Had he really just said that to her? "You can't tell me what to wear."

"You're not going out with me dressed like that," he amended.

"We're not going out," she reminded him. "It's just dinner."

"Go change," he said, his voice short and his eyes just a little mean.

Something snapped in Jen. And whatever it was crawled right up her spine and went ramrod straight. "No," she said, not as loudly as she wanted to, but not so softly that he didn't hear her.

Apparently he had only been about half frost giant, because his expression went subzero and his face turned so hard it could have been carved from marble. "You aren't going out with me dressed like that," he repeated.

Her fingers curled into small fists at her side. "Like what?" she demanded.

"Like some..." he stopped, something breaking in his expression. "Fuck it. Wear what you want."

"I will," she told him, blinking back hot tears as she imagined him finishing that sentence in all sorts of horrible ways, "cheap tramp" being her top vote.

The silence raged between them as he slipped on his jacket. He headed towards the door without a word, jerking it wide and holding it open until she finally crossed the room and walked through it. Whatever was locked into her spine kept her head held high and her face calm as she moved past him.

Fuck, there were little bows on the ankles of those sheer black stockings. He noticed them as she swept past him out the door in a light cloud of perfume that almost made his knees buckle. Then he looked up and knew he'd made a huge mistake. The dress had no back. The slinky black material draped all the way to the base of her spine where it suddenly went skin tight. If he got through the next few hours without breaking at least three laws, he would be the luckiest man alive.

Maybe the wrong plane had touched down in Kenner after all. It made a lot more sense that this was evil Jen. His Jen would never have tried that dress on, much less worn it out in public. She'd have turned beet red at the very idea. The sexiest thing he'd ever seen her in was her skinny jeans and a white cotton blouse she hadn't realized was so sheer that the blue lace on her bra showed through it. And that hadn't lasted long because he'd spilled something on it the first chance he'd got, forcing her to change into a T-shirt. Even the bathing suits she wore didn't affect his blood pressure like this scrap of black fabric. All he could think about was pushing her down and the dress up. He'd make her leave on those stockings with the tiny black bows. And the shoes.

"You do a lot of shopping in Paris?" he asked, not meaning for his voice to sound so nasty but for once he just couldn't help it. He wasn't used to being so lightheaded and he couldn't quite feel the tips of his fingers.

She didn't even glance at him. "Not really."

"Good."

Caramel eyes swept up to his. He'd expected regret, maybe some groveling, and her asking him to take her back upstairs so she could change. What he got was the polar opposite. She was furious and she wasn't backing down. And the only thing that shocked him more than her reaction was his reaction to her defiance. He loved it. His whole body burned hotter watching her spitting fire at him. He clenched his fingers into fists to keep from grabbing her and showing her what he really thought of that dress, those shoes, those tiny black bows, and her attitude.

"Nothing's wrong with this dress."

"I can give you a list of things wrong with that dress."

They were back to the raging silence as he opened the door to the SUV for her, then slammed the door a little too hard as she tugged her skirt down. He took several deep breaths as he rounded the car to the driver's side. He didn't let himself glance at her when he got in. He couldn't afford to see the way the dress had ridden up her thighs so the lace at the top of those stockings peeked out to torture him.

"You wouldn't take me home," she finally exploded. "It's the only dress I have and you can't wear jeans at Elliot's after six."

Stefan turned the key in the ignition. "You could wear jeans."

"Fine," she snapped. "I'll go back and change."

She was reaching for the door when instinct took over and he reached across and stopped her. He surprised himself by not wanting her to change. He might not be crazy about anyone else seeing her in the dress, but no way was he letting her take it off now. "No, you want to wear it, you wear it."

"I don't see what the big deal is. I know it's short, but I've seen your girlfriends pour themselves into shorter dresses."

"Yeah?" He had no good argument for that, but he still heard himself say, "Well, you aren't one of my girlfriends, are you?"

He heard the sharp intake of breath and felt it hit his gut as he realized she'd completely misunderstood him. He was just about to explain to her that she was a whole lot more important than any of those girls she'd seen him date, when she repeated, in a suddenly small, hurt voice that almost crushed his chest. "Nothing's wrong with this dress." Then she caught her breath and turned on him, no longer small and hurt as she launched at him. "Just like there was nothing wrong with my prom dress, but you ruined that, too."

At the mention of her prom dress, Stefan felt lightning slam into the back of his head as everything suddenly went cotton-candy pink and every single red blood cell in his body headed south with a vengeance. His mind replayed in high definition the image of her walking downstairs on her prom night. It was burned in his brain so he could see every detail of that pink cloud of tulle that had made him lose his mind. "I have a list for that dress too."

"You have a list for everything."

He turned to her, really hating the flash of raw pain he saw cross her face. Then he watched her blink it away. If he hadn't turned so suddenly he never would have guessed she was feeling anything but anger. It made him wonder what else she was good at hiding from him, and that was something he never expected to have to deal with. He'd known Jen all her life. Why was she hiding from him?

"I like this dress."

"Why are we still talking about this?" he demanded, not at all satisfied when she turned away and stared out the window.

Elliot Carter's restaurant was on Barracks Street at the edge of the French Quarter, just a few blocks from the French Market and around the corner from Trick's. Elliot was waiting at the front door when they arrived.

"Jen?" Elliot was more than a little surprised when he saw her. She blushed, because if Elliot thought the dress was surprising then it really must be over the top. She was going to kill Jared. "Jared take you shopping in Paris?" he laughed, ignoring the storm raging on Stefan's face.

"For my birthday," Jen said, loving the way Stefan's nostrils actually flared as he put two and two together and came up with the hippie.

"Well," Elliot laughed nervously. "Jared has never been subtle, has he?"

They followed Elliot past several people waiting for tables to the small table in the back Elliot always kept available for his partner.

"So we still training for April?" Elliot asked Stefan.

Stefan shook his head, "I doubt it. I'll know more next week."

"That's going to make Jackson happy. I guess his time is safe for this year."

Startled, Jen watched disappointment flicker across Stefan's closed expression. Lizzie had said that Martin had pulled him off a bike yesterday. She only now put her own two and two together. The New Orleans 70.3 was in a few months. He would need a really fast time to qualify for the Iron Man World Championship. She took a deep breath. Until he got the Volikovneft deal done, he wouldn't have time to train.

"Did you get a chance to look at the space?" Elliot was asking her, as Stefan sat down.

Jen froze, her eyes darting back to Stefan who was once again on his cell phone. Elliot had found a coffee shop on Royal that was moving out. He thought it was the perfect spot for the bakery and had emailed Jen all the info a few weeks ago. She had begged him not to tell Stefan. "Not yet," she said now, "Waiting for Jared to get back."

"Well, let me know when I can order your secret weapon cakes. I want to put it on the menu. I'll send out the fish, it's amazing," he said, and disappeared into the kitchen.

"Secret weapon cake?" Stefan asked, setting his phone down on the table.

"It's a joke," she said.

His already stormy expression darkened. "You and Elliot have a private joke?"

"No, it's not a private joke. It's my triple chocolate layer cake. He wants me to make them for the restaurant. He calls it my secret weapon."

Stefan looked blank. "Your triple what?"

She leaned across the table. "You may find this hard to believe, but a huge percentage of the human race actually likes sugar, Stefan. And they love chocolate. And just about anyone who has tried my chocolate cake says it's the best they've ever had." She sat back and crossed her arms. She had complete confidence in her baking. So what if Stefan was oblivious and avoided sugar like the plague? Even the instructors in Paris had been impressed with the crazy things Jen could do with sugar.

"So, why haven't you made it for me?" he asked.

She shook her head. She had made it for him. She'd invented it for him. He just hadn't eaten it. He'd taken it back to the frat house just like he had all her other experimental baking attempts. At least his fraternity had appreciated it. At thirteen, Jen had thought it was the coolest thing in the world when his frat brothers started emailing her requests. She'd learned to make bread pudding and red velvet cake for Rogan. Carrot cake for Jackson Napier. Snickerdoodles for Matt Hansen. Brownies and cowboy cookies for Elliot. She'd come up with a bittersweet chocolate cake for Stefan, not that he'd ever tried it. But after Elliot had a slice a few years ago, he'd told her she needed to go to pastry school and had gotten her the information on the school she and Jared had attended.

"You do not eat cake," she reminded him. "It's just one more reason why we shouldn't get married."

He laughed out loud at that. "Because I don't like white flour? What has that got to do with anything?"

"I'm a pastry chef," she said, as if it were obvious.

"I ate your pancakes."

She opened her mouth to make a comeback but just had nothing.

Stefan grinned when she closed her mouth again. "And I had seconds."

She sat back in her chair and changed the subject. "You were planning on qualifying for the Iron Man this fall weren't you?"

He shrugged. "Just wanted to shave a few minutes off my time. No big deal." He dismissed it but she knew he was downplaying it. He'd never been happy with his time when he raced in 2004. He'd qualified for the next year but when Katrina blew up the Gulf Coast he had stayed home to help with the clean up. He hadn't had a chance since then to go back to Hawaii, but this was his last year in this age class.

"There's always next year," she said.

He shook his head. "No, it's done." He'd made up his mind, and that hurt. She knew how much he loved it. She couldn't imagine him actually giving it up. That was almost as bad as the suits she suspected she would be seeing a lot more of.

Their salads arrived. The spring mix topped with artichokes and figs looked gorgeous on the plate, but Jen doubted she was going to get any of it past her throat.

"So what space are you supposed to be looking at?" he asked, almost succeeding in sounding casual.

The world dropped out from under her and her fork clattered against her plate. Had she really thought he'd missed Elliot's question? Would she never learn? Stefan didn't miss much.

"You said you were waiting for the hippie to get back to go see it?" Stefan prompted, looking deceptively relaxed as he leaned back in his chair.

She opened her mouth, completely caught off guard.

She watched his face go solid granite and the whole frost giant thing worked across his eyes, down his jaw and thinned out his mouth. "What kind of space do you and the hippie need?" he bit out, and she was surprised his teeth didn't shatter, his jaw was so tight. She doubted he even realized he was tapping his knife against the table.

She swallowed, wishing the floor would open up and drag her down. She really was not prepared for this right now. "We're opening a bakery."

He blinked, a couple of times. "A bakery?"

She nodded. "Elliot told us about a space around the corner that's becoming available. There's a coffee shop in it now..."

"Elliot?" Stefan interrupted her. "Elliot found you a space? In the French Quarter? For a bakery?" His voice was so quiet, so cold, she almost couldn't hear him.

"Yes."

He lifted his water glass and she was surprised the water stayed liquid. He took a sip, set the glass down, and leaned forward. "No fucking way," he hissed across the table.

Pre-Paris Jen probably would have jumped up from the table and tried hard not to burst into tears. Pre-Paris Jen would've caved in and accepted his unreasonable reaction as the final word. But not this Jen. This Jen got angry. Fast. And when she answered him, her voice was as quiet as his and he really should have paid attention. "You haven't seen our business plan."

He lifted one arrogant eyebrow and for once it was not adorable. "I heard hippie, bakery, and French Quarter. I don't need to see your business plan."

"You can't say no without at least looking at it," she told him, amazed at how calm her voice sounded.

"Just did."

She stared at him a minute, drowning in the ice cold knowledge that she really did not know him at all. And he certainly didn't have a clue about her. "It's not your call."

"We'll see about that."

"Stefan," she said carefully, "I want fifty thousand dollars out of my trust fund first thing Monday morning."

He took another sip of water and just stared back at her. He was waiting for her to dissolve into tears. He was waiting for her nerves to give out. She could see it in the smug expression on his face and the glittering light in his eyes. He was so sure he was going to win, he wasn't even trying to make her understand why he was being such a jerk. Suddenly, it became the most important thing in the universe that he not win this argument. She had no idea where the words even came from. But she heard them coming straight out of her mouth in a strange mocking tone that she hadn't known she was capable of. "It doesn't matter. As soon as Jared gets home, we're getting married and you'll have no say over anything to do with me anymore."

She had about ten seconds of victory before the world blurred. He moved so fast she never even saw him coming. Fingers closed around her arm. Her chair upended and hit the floor. Shocked gasps surrounded them as he hauled her back to the kitchen. Before her next breath, she was pinned against the wall in Elliot's office, staring up at a complete stranger she was sure was going to break her neck.

"Say that again," he dared her.

"We're getting married," she said, her voice still calm even though her whole body was threatening to shake apart.

"Take it back," he growled at her, a vicious desperation in him that she'd never seen. "Take. It. Back." he repeated slowly.

She wasn't going to. No way. She just stared at him, not quite believing that he was buying it. Some perverse little spark egged her on. "I love him," she insisted, determined to push Stefan over the edge. If it was the last thing she did, she was going watch him fall all the way to the bottom.

"You're lying," he said, going very quiet which would tell any sane person to back off.

"I'm not lying," she said, not backing off. "I love him," she insisted again and met Stefan's blue eyes straight on when she said it, trying not to love the flare of undiluted fury that made his mouth fall open. Well, it wasn't a lie. Not exactly. She did love Jared, just not the way she loved the selfish bastard pinning her against the wall. The selfish bastard she was dying to kiss again. The gorgeous bastard she was suddenly having a ball torturing. He'd asked for it, she assured herself. He deserved it.

Then he leaned in to her, bringing his face very close to hers. Her lips ached, her throat went dry as everything turned to liquid heat below her waist. "If you think for one minute I'm letting you marry that hippie musician, you really have lost your mind."

"You can't stop me," she shot back, fighting to keep her smirk in place. He was so close she could almost taste him. Her whole body screamed for it. Even the muscles in her legs started to burn. She wanted to grab him by the hair and kiss him hard, but only after he was on his knees.

"Really? You want to test that theory."

"Yeah," she said, the word a dare.

He pressed her harder against the wall, leaning one forearm close to her head as he moved even closer to her. "What'd I tell you when you were sixteen?" he demanded.

Her eyes widened. All these years she'd thought she'd dreamed that. He really had found her on the back porch while everyone else was asleep and she was trying to get over the worst prom night in the history of civilization. Stefan had ruined it before it started with one look and she'd spent the entire night sorting through crushed hopes and damaged dreams. She'd cringed when he'd joined her on that swing, afraid of what he'd say. He'd shocked her silly by kissing her. A sweet fairytale of a kiss that she still wasn't convinced was real. Then he'd made her promise no more boys.

"Did he fuck you, Jen?" Stefan demanded, tearing her away from the sweet, treasured dream she now knew was a real memory.

Her whole body jerked with fury. He had not just said that to her. So she nodded, but found she couldn't meet the wild look in his eyes when she did it, and her dark lashes swept down as she closed her eyes. This was not so exciting anymore.

"No, you lying little witch," he snarled at her, his hand on her jaw as he tried to turn her face to his. "You open your eyes and tell me to my face that you gave him what was mine." His hand clamped down on her face. "Open your eyes."

She shook her head because she knew she just couldn't do it. She'd lost. She should have known better. How could she possibly go up against him and win? She actually loved him. She only ended up hurting herself. "Let me go," she whispered.

"Open your eyes or I will find out for myself if you let him touch you."

Her eyes snapped open and the look on his face made her blood run cold. It had honestly never occurred to her to be really afraid of him. But it should have. She'd pushed him way too far. Part of her reveled in it. Part of her wanted to crush his mouth with hers and see what happened. But the part that really loved him knew she had to diffuse this situation before he did something he would never forgive himself for. The weak, pathetic, stupid part of her that loved him won.

"Are you sleeping with him?" he asked, his words so soft and quiet, her lungs seized and her heart actually slowed down.

"No, of course not," she said softly, still unable to meet his eyes as hot color swept over her cheeks. She'd thought she had dreamed making him that promise that night. She'd believed all these years it had just been a fantasy, but she'd kept the promise anyway. It hadn't been that hard to keep since she'd never actually looked at another man. She'd never wanted anyone but Stefan.

He closed his eyes and his chin dropped as he apparently tried to rein himself in. But he didn't loosen his hold on her. Then he looked up and his eyes snapped open and he was completely back in control. The Sellers calm was back in full force. It broke her heart.

Then he leaned his face in closer to hers. "The only man you are going to marry is me. You got that?"

"No," the broken parts of her hissed. "No, I don't 'got' that."

"You're mine, Jen. You've always been mine."

"No," she whispered, opening her eyes and meeting the blue fire of his straight on. "I want a pre-nup. I don't want a big wedding. No dress. No cake, no big party. We can go to Vegas or to a judge, I don't care. I'll only agree to six months and then we can separate until the divorce is final. But I will not live with you in that house."

The calm drained right out of his expression, and she finally understood the definition of livid. "Is that all?"

She knew she had gone too far. Again. She still didn't care. So she went even further. "Yes. No. I mean. No sex. I'm not sleeping with you."

"Are you done?" The words dripped from his mouth like frozen chips of steel.

She nodded, knowing the only way out was straight ahead even though she already knew she'd seriously miscalculated. She braced herself for shouting, but what came out was so deadly soft, so amazingly lethal that it was the equivalent of a bunker-busting bomb when he spit it out at her. And it was only one word. "No."

His blue eyes were glacial. Her bones turned to ice and threatened to shatter. He got as close as he could, forcing her to flatten against the wall. His mouth hovered over hers, but all she could see was simmering glacial blue ice. Who knew ice could burn?

"There will be a huge wedding and you will wear an obscenely expensive white dress, and you will dance with me at the big party afterward. You will live with me and you will sleep with me. And you will never ever mention divorce to me again. Do you understand?"

She nodded, drowning in something she just couldn't describe. She ached everywhere. She wanted him to kiss her. Damn it, why did she always want him to kiss her when he was angry at her? What was wrong with her?

"I want to hear you say it."

She opened her mouth but nothing came out. She hadn't even known he could get this angry. Her heart was about to come out of her chest and she was inexplicably burning up. Maybe she should kiss him. *No.* No kissing.

"Don't you dare start crying," he warned her.

"I'm not," she shouted back at him even as one hot, tear escaped down her pale face. "I'm not crying," she said, dashing back the tears. "I hate you. I am not marrying you."

The curse that cut out of him as he backed up had her sliding down the wall. He caught her and pulled her back up. He started to say something else, but she just closed her eyes and turned her face away from him. "I am not going to marry you. Why can't you just let me go? I'll sign whatever you want. You don't have to marry me."

"Fine," he snapped. "If that's what you want Jen, forget the wedding."

"What?" she whispered, her focus snapping back to him.

"You win," he hissed. "No wedding."

She nodded. She'd won? What?

She was completely unprepared for the dull blades that started spinning in the pit of her stomach before slicing towards her heart. She'd been so focused on trying to get him to let her go, she hadn't really considered how it would actually feel if he did. Things would just be so much better if she had one shred of pride where he was concerned. Then maybe her face wouldn't have shattered into the devastated tears that had been lurking on the edge all day. How was she supposed to know it was going to hurt even worse if he gave her what she claimed she wanted?

He dragged her up against his chest and wrapped his arms around her. "As long as I live. I don't think I'll ever understand what goes on in that beautiful head of yours."

She pressed closer to him, hiding her face in his neck. Wanting to disappear. What was she going to do now? She really never imagined he would change his mind. He'd never changed his mind about anything before. Not ever. It only proved he'd never really wanted to marry her at all. Not really. She really was just an unwelcome responsibility.

"Why do you do this?" He growled against her hair. "Are you trying to drive me crazy? Because it's working."

The door opened suddenly as Elliot finally broke into his own office. "Sellers, what the hell?"

"Is there a back way out?" Stefan asked, ignoring Elliot's anger.

"Jen," Elliot called. "Are you okay? Say the word, and we'll walk him out of here."

She pressed deeper into Stefan's arms. "My fault," she said hoarsely. His arms tightened even more. Was he really going to leave her? Humiliated and terrified at the same time, she'd never even suspected he would actually give in.

"It's been a really bad couple of days, Elliot. We're both exhausted. She just likes pushing my buttons."

Elliot wasn't convinced, but he had known Stefan a long time. "Wow, who knew you had buttons? Two minutes and we'll have your car around back. Give me your keys."

Stefan tossed his keys at Elliot. Then he slid his arm under her legs, lifted her up, and carried her through the kitchen.

Too angry to let himself enjoy the feel of her curled into his chest, Stefan set her on the front seat of the Range Rover and slammed her door a little too hard.

"And the legendary Sellers calm bites the dust," Elliot snickered behind him. He was holding bags with food boxes. "I don't remember her driving you crazy like this. She was always so quiet."

Stefan nodded and took the bags. "Thank you." He ignored Elliot's comments and put the bags on the back seat, then ran his hands through his hair and over his face. He had lost it tonight. He couldn't ever remember losing it like that. He really needed to go for a run. Soon.

"Try not to break her, man. I'm going to get rich on her cake. I think I can sell it for twelve bucks a slice." Elliot clapped him on the back.

"About that," Stefan turned around. "You think you might've mentioned the bakery disaster to me?"

Elliot's grin faded. "Disaster? It's not a disaster. It's a great idea. The space is one block down and the foot traffic from the French Market alone will keep them in business."

Stefan stared at one of his oldest friends in complete shock. "I don't want her working down here."

"Geez, Sellers, what're you thinking? She's going to stay home and have your babies? Grow up. She does crazy things with sugar. You want her to waste that talent on birthday cakes you won't even eat?"

"You think I should give her fifty grand to partner up with that hippie so they can open a bakery that probably won't last six months?"

Elliot shrugged. "That hippie has an MBA from Tulane and a law degree from Loyola. Although why he didn't go to LSU beat me. Marshall and Marshall out of Baton Rouge? Maybe you've heard of them?"

"Grant Marshall's brother?" Stefan asked, suddenly very tired.

"Yeah, asshole. Grant's younger brother. I guess Tulane was his form of rebellion. Otherwise you might've been his big brother seeing how he would've been a fourth generation legacy."

Stefan took a deep breath and pushed his fingers through his hair. "I can't believe Grant thinks this is a good idea either."

"It doesn't matter what Grant thinks or what you think. They have a solid business plan, a great location, and the financial means to pull it off. You need to get out of her way."

Stefan glared at Elliot, not recognizing him for a minute. Elliot was always so easy going. Stefan had never seen him quite so determined before. "She's that good?"

"Yeah, man. She's that good. Rogan calls it Voodoo, and he would know. Now that you aren't in constant training, you should live a little and have a cookie."

Stefan laughed. "She made me pancakes this morning," he admitted.

"And you ate them? Did anyone take a picture?"

"Ha. Ha."

Elliot grinned, then. "Seriously, she'll be right around the corner, Stefan. I suggested the location so I could keep an eye on her. And you know Jackson will camp out there for carrot cake. She'll be fine."

"I'll look at their business plan, but I'm not making any promises."

"She wants this, Stefan. You stop her and you'll lose her."

"She told me she's in love with the hippie, that they're getting married."

Elliot's jaw dropped, then he practically spun completely around as he burst into hysterical laughter. "No shit? She said that?"

Stefan nodded. "I don't think it's funny."

"You must have really pissed her off."

"What?"

Elliot laughed again. "You don't know her at all, do you? Absolutely no clue. It's hysterical. She's got you on your knees and you don't even know it. You'd better pray *she* doesn't realize it."

"Again with the not funny."

Elliot sobered. "Let me tell you something about the future mother of your children, Sellers. If she wanted Jared Marshall or any other man in the state of Louisiana, she'd already have them. She would not be putting up with your overbearing control freak self. Hell, I'd switch teams if I thought I had a shot."

"Fuck you," Stefan grinned. "I'm telling Jackson you said that."

Stefan rounded the car to the driver's side.

"Jackson would switch teams too if he had a shot. Get smart, brother. Give our girl whatever she wants."

When he slid behind the wheel, he was in much better control. Jen, however, was huddled up against the passenger door, as far away from him as she could get.

"Seat belt," he said gruffly, and when she didn't respond he reached across her, grabbed the strap, and pulled it across her.

Her scent wrapped all around him, but he didn't let himself linger too close to her. She was chalk white and very careful to stay back as he clicked the seat belt into place. He'd scared her.

Hell, he'd scared himself.

He took a deep breath. He really wished he'd run this morning instead of cycling. Of course he was pretty sure that he could have run around the world a dozen times and her threat to marry Jared Marshall would still have sent him into caveman combat mode.

Marrying the hippie. Over his dead body. Or better yet, over Jared Marshall's dead body.

"We need to set a date," he said, turning the key in the ignition. He pulled up the calendar on his phone and tossed it onto her lap. "Pick a Saturday in April."

He didn't have to glance at her. He actually felt her stiffen up, and her sharp intake of breath cut him in places he didn't want to think about.

"But you said...Stefan," she cried, and his brain switched on as he braked for the red light he'd almost blown through. Yeah. Definitely going for a long run as soon as possible.

"I lied," he said, sounding harsher than he meant to.

This was not the way things were supposed to be. She was supposed to be happy. She was supposed to have missed him. Damn it. Jen was supposed to love him. She'd loved him her whole life. Until that exact moment Stefan hadn't actually comprehended how much he'd always counted on that. Taken it for granted, even, using the excuse that she was still a kid not to do anything about it. Now that she was old enough, she looked horrified by the idea of even being with him. Never mind that she went up like a roman candle when he touched her—the rest of the time she was guarded, prickly and—fuck him, because this was the worse fucking part, the part that ripped his guts out and danced all over them—she looked sad. Sad! Unhappy. Even frightened. It was killing him.

"Pick one," he finally snapped, unable to keep the frustration out of his voice. "Now. Or I'll choose Halloween and you can wear black, that way it'll look and feel like the funeral you act like it is."

She looked up at him, her expression stunned. He cursed, wishing he could just rewind to the airport and start completely over with her. Now he was emotionally mauling her.

Then something completely unexpected happened. Something that reminded him of why he wanted that ring on her finger sooner rather than later. She smiled at him. Her beautiful mouth spreading into a wicked grin that was so out of place on her but so very much Jen. His Jen. The Jen he'd let fly away from him six months ago.

"Can we make the bridesmaids and groomsmen dress like

zombies?"

Relief washed over him like spring rain. Finally, something felt normal, as a familiar impish light that he hadn't seen in such a long time flashed in those gorgeous brown eyes. He missed this girl. This beautiful, sweet girl who looked like a storybook princess who should be picking wild flowers and singing to little woodland creatures. But underneath that candy coated exterior, she loved zombie movies, the more gruesome the better.

"Yes," he agreed, "Lizzie will hate that."

Horns went off. The light had turned green. His cell phone rang and he watched the little bit of color that had returned to her face drain right out again. She practically threw the cell phone at him and turned towards the window, but not before he saw the light go out of her eyes.

Jen absolutely refused to cry. Her teeth bit down hard on the inside of her lower lip as he answered his phone. Closing her eyes, she rested her head against the cold windshield and tried to picture a black wedding dress. Because black would really be appropriate for their wedding. What had she really expected, after all?

His voice was so warm as he spoke on the phone. Jen wanted to open the door and jump out before he had a chance to slow down. Hitting the pavement and feeling her skin rip off could not possibly hurt as much as sitting next to him, listening to him talk to Madlyn Robicheaux. They had some weekend plans that they needed to reschedule. Familiar bile crawled up the back of Jen's throat. She swallowed it down but she could do nothing about the jagged pieces of her heart that started to break into even smaller pieces. She wondered how long before it just turned to dust. Sometimes she wished it would just go ahead. She was so tired, it hurt.

A Halloween wedding would be perfect. She closed her eyes and imagined a black wedding dress again with layers and layers of black tulle swirling around her, smothering her. It wasn't even really black. It was dark gray. It wasn't even made out of real tulle. It was just billowing smoke. And it was choking her, trailing into her nose lightly, tickling at first before it started streaming down to steal the air from her lungs.

Then Stefan was yelling at her. Calling her name. Shaking her. But she just couldn't breathe. "Jen, wake up, we're here." And she realized he had not been yelling at all.

She sat up, dusting off the familiar nightmare that never failed to call on her when she was the most stressed. She could still taste the smoke and feel it trailing into her nose and crawling down her throat to burn her lungs. The smell and taste left her ice cold and terrified no matter how many times she had the dream. And she had been having it since she could remember. But this was the first time the smoke had come to her as a wedding dress. Appropriate, really. As much as Stefan hurt her these days, it was still nothing compared to the games her own mind liked to play with her.

Her car door opened. The cold, ruthless businessman was back and impatiently waiting for her to get out of the car. His face was hard and his expression impenetrable. This man would never agree to a zombie wedding party. She swallowed down the hysteria threatening to choke her and slid out of the SUV.

Rogan met him in the driveway. "Elliot sent me a steak," Rogan informed them, and Stefan handed him the to-go bags as they followed Jen inside.

Jen started to go through the kitchen but Rogan snagged her around the waist and pulled her down onto a bar stool. "No, you don't," he teased. "Sit down and tell me how much you love this kitchen. You do love your kitchen, don't you?"

"You know I do," she admitted, smiling at Rogan the way she should have smiled at him when he first showed her her new kitchen.

Relieved and irritated at the same time, Stefan watched them banter back and forth and found himself relaxing. Jen was smiling and there was color back in her cheeks. Rogan actually got her to eat.

"I special-ordered those ovens, you know. They are huge."

Jen's smile doubled in wattage, amping up Stefan's frustration with it. "They're amazing. The marble on the island is perfect and I love that you raised up the dishwasher like that."

Stefan listened as she said all the things to Rogan that he'd wanted to hear her say. He told himself he wasn't jealous. How could he be jealous of his best friend? His married best friend who definitely considered Jen his little sister. He'd thought Rogan was crazy and going to extremes when he'd designed the kitchen. Now Jen went on and on about how cool it was the pantry light came on when the door opened. And she loved the big copper sink because she could actually get a gumbo pot in it. And she couldn't decide if the pot filler or the pasta rest was the bigger bomb. Rogan had gone all out and she loved every single detail.

Stefan took a bite of fish and it tasted like ash. He dropped his fork and walked out of the kitchen, leaving them behind laughing and talking. He had a hot date with a punching bag and he didn't want to be late.

The side door slammed and a minute later the carriage house door closed. "You gonna tell me what happened or do I get to guess?"

Jen shook her head. "I may have screwed up big time."

"I doubt that."

"Elliot mentioned the bakery space before I had a chance to say anything to Stefan."

"Ah," Rogan said, cutting more steak off and putting it on her plate. "How'd that go?"

Jen dropped her fork, her throat refusing to let anything else pass as a lump formed. "He said no before I had a chance to really explain things. He refused to read my business plan and well, I kinda lost it."

"And..."

She looked away, looked anywhere else actually. "I told him Jared and I were getting married."

Rogan's fork hit the marble counter. "You didn't really tell him that, Jen. Tell me you didn't really say that."

She sipped the water, trying not to choke on it. "I couldn't help it. He's been unbearable since he picked me up at the airport."

"As long as you didn't tell him you slept with Jared, because if he believes that, you need to call the hippie and tell him to keep his ass in Paris for at least another six months." Rogan's green eyes widened in disbelief when she didn't immediately deny it. "No, Jen. Please tell me you didn't tell him that. I'm not sure any of this is fixable if you did."

"No, I let him think it for a second but I... He just dismissed the whole idea without giving it a second thought. And earlier when he saw my dress, he was so rude. You have no idea how much that hurt."

Rogan laughed then. "Didn't like your little black dress, did he?"

"No," Jen snapped, "He basically said I looked cheap."

"I do not believe that."

"He thought it," she insisted.

"I'm pretty sure that's not what he was thinking." Rogan laughed again. "How much do you need for the bakery?"

She told him, trying to choke back tears.

"I can loan you the money until you get access to your trust fund.

I've already looked at the space with Elliot. It's not going to be that much work to get it ready, and the location is good."

"I can't let you do that," she said.

"I'm not giving you the money. It'll be a loan with paperwork, interest, just like the bank, but I'll hold the paper for you. Oh, and free brownies for life."

She smiled. It was so sweet of him to offer, but she couldn't let him do that. "Thanks."

"You aren't really going to marry the hippie, are you?"

She sat up and pushed away from him. "Maybe. We've talked about going to Vegas and getting married so I can get access to my trust. Then we'd go to the Dominican Republic and get a divorce and a tan."

"You have got to be kidding me."

"We were joking about it, and you know that's not what I want."

Rogan hugged her again. "I do not understand you and Stefan. You want to marry him and he wants to marry you. Why is there a problem?"

"He's not in love with me," Jen whispered the words out loud. "You know he's not."

"You need to talk to him, kiddo. Really talk." Rogan's phone rang and he pulled it out of his pocket. "Speaking of talking, it's Angie. Gotta take it," he said, shaking his phone.

Jen nodded, finishing her water as Rogan stepped over to the keeping room to talk to his wife. Jen decided to give him some privacy and because she was a complete idiot, she followed Stefan out to the carriage house. Just to poke the bear some more.

Of course when she opened the door, she nearly choked on air. He was shirtless, hanging upside down in another doorway doing abdominal crunches. More evidence that life wasn't fair. Her throat went dry, and the rest of her got hot and wet really fast. She leaned against the doorjamb, enjoyed the show of rippling muscles in his legs and abs as she tried not to burst into flames. After an eternity, he paused, dropped down, and opened his eyes.

"Can I help you?" he asked, upside down, the nasty edge back in his voice.

She shook her head, pushing away from the doorjamb. There was no help for her. She was the biggest idiot on the planet. "I'm sorry about earlier," she said, wishing she didn't sound so hoarse.

He stared at her a minute, swinging slightly. Then he reached up and released the boots. She watched him swing down. There wasn't an ounce of body fat on him anywhere. His feet hit the floor. He pulled the boots off then grabbed a water bottle out of the refrigerator.

"Elliot seemed to think it's a good idea," he said, his voice calm and steady. He wasn't even breathing heavily. The whole human thing was still seriously in question. He was just too beautiful to be real. "I just don't like the idea of you in the French Quarter. It's not safe."

"I'm not trying to open a strip club."

His eyes swept her from head to toe. The slow appraisal sent wildfire racing under her skin, especially when he lingered on her legs. His eyes burned but the rest of his expression was blank.

"Will you just read our business plan and keep an open mind when you do? That's all I'm asking."

He watched her another half a minute, then gave her a curt nod before turning to the punching bag. Jen watched him throw a few punches at the swinging bag, then went back outside. He hadn't said no. Maybe the nod meant he'd consider it. Maybe. But she seriously doubted it.

Hours later, Stefan lay on top of the duvet in the downstairs guest bedroom with a low carb beer balanced on his chest. He'd given up on sleep several hours ago and was forcing himself to focus on an infomercial for a blender that he was sure he had to have. He sent Martin a text with the phone number and website for the blender so he could order three tomorrow. It had four blades and they claimed it would juice. He didn't care if it juiced. He cared that it was sharp. He went through blenders like crazy. He sipped the beer, and refused again to let his mind wander to the business plan. He'd read a few pages of it earlier and honestly it had potential. But there was no way he was letting her open up a bakery in the French Quarter. None. Damn it. It wasn't safe.

The beer nearly upended when he heard her scream. He sat straight up, waited a moment, then heard her cry out again. He headed upstairs. He was prepared to knock the door down, but the few functioning brain cells he had left checked the door knob. She'd left it unlocked, a habit from childhood when the bad dreams came. Mac had taken her bedroom doors off the hinges more than once until they'd finally just replaced her doorknob with one that didn't lock.

He found her thrashing on the bed, and caught her before she screamed again. He hadn't known she still had these dreams. She never remembered them, thankfully. He slid under the covers and hauled her back against him.

"Jen, you're dreaming, baby. Settle down."

And she did, just like she always did. She moaned his name, then broke his heart when she said, "You've got to stop Robert."

"I know," he told her, even though she was still asleep.

"Stefan, stop Robert," she whispered, sounding like the lost twelve year old he would have done anything to keep safe.

He covered the back of her head with his hand and held her tight until the demons finally turned her loose and her breathing evened out. She curled into him and he knew he'd made a huge mistake. She didn't feel like a lost twelve year old as she relaxed against him. She smelled like oranges and sunshine and her skin was like satin under his fingers. Definitely not twelve any more. He pulled her tighter to him, drank in the feel of her pressed against him. He'd wanted to hold her like this for so long he didn't remember not wanting it. She fit against him like she'd been made for him.

One long smooth leg eased between his, and Stefan groaned as quietly as he could when his whole body came to attention. She whispered something else but this time she didn't sound distressed. He let himself enjoy the feel of her against him, allowed himself to nuzzle slightly at the back of her neck, drawing the clean scent of her hair into every part of him. His arms tightened around her and he sighed as she nestled deeper against him. He could forget about getting any sleep now, he thought, as he yawned and gave up the fight with his eyes lids just before drifting off as he relaxed back into her.

CHAPTER SEVEN

Jen opened her eyes and wasn't sure where she was at first. The shower was running. She glanced at the alarm clock next to the bed and froze. There was a wrist watch on the bedside table in front of the alarm clock. She'd dreamt that she slept in Stefan's arms last night. That he'd curled around her and chased the shadows away. She'd slept better last night than she had in...well, she didn't remember when. So now she knew she hadn't dreamt it. She couldn't decide if she was upset because she still couldn't tell what was real and what wasn't when it came to Stefan, or because she'd been unconscious while he held her. Or maybe she really was just crazy.

She sat up just as he walked out of the bathroom. He had a towel knotted around his hips and he was rubbing his hair with another towel. Every single one of her internal organs tried to switch places as she watched rivulets of water run down six foot three inches of golden, ripped muscles. Greek gods had nothing on Stefan Sellers, and she decided she was going to stop ragging him about avoiding carbs, because whatever he was doing was seriously working.

When he caught her watching him, he stopped short. "Hey."

She just stared at him, wondering where all the oxygen in the room had suddenly gone. She could still feel the warmth of all those muscles pressed against her back, his arms around her. She could smell the spicy lime scent of him. It hadn't been a dream.

Because he could read her mind, he said. "You had a nightmare."

"Oh." She didn't remember having one, but hey, she didn't remember lots of things these days. Except their fight. She remembered it in Technicolor and full stereo surround sound. Now looking at him mostly naked with his blonde hair in adorable spikes, she realized she really was crazy. Any sane woman would be throwing themselves at his feet. She'd certainly watched it happen before. But not Jen, oh no. The most eligible bachelor in Louisiana wanted to marry her, and she was worried about why. She tried to swallow but her mouth was like sandpaper. If she had any sense at all, she'd quit worrying about why and start concentrating on when. As in soon. Preferably, now.

"I've got to go into the office, but I'll try to get done by lunch and we'll see about finding you an SUV. Martin is already doing some recon."

She nodded, watching as he disappeared into his closet.

She was still sitting up in bed, shell-shocked, when he walked back out dressed in a dark charcoal suit with micro-thin pinstripes, a gray shirt, and blue silk tie. It didn't seem possible, but he was even sexier dressed. "Stefan," she said, her voice hoarse and her throat sore. She must have really had a nightmare. Her throat felt like she'd been at a Saint's game.

He grabbed his watch off the bedside table. He shook his head, warning her not to say anything. "You can have an SUV. It's safer in the city and I'm sure you can use the cargo space. And I'll look at your business plan. But you are not marrying the hippie. Are we clear?"

She nodded.

"And you are marrying me," he added. "I had a plan, but you've blown it all to hell, and I can't help that now. New Plan. First step, we find you a vehicle."

She looked up at him and met his eyes. He was still angry but he had it under control. She had so many things she wanted to say to him that she wasn't even sure where to start.

"Last night you said I didn't have to," she reminded him.

He groaned, the corners of his mouth going south. "I said no wedding, Jen. You should pay better attention. We're still getting married. I'll see you around noon."

She nodded, and watched as he walked out of the room. She rolled over, burying her face in the pillows, trying not to notice that they smelled like him, spicy lime and sandalwood. Relieved that the marriage she claimed she didn't want was still on, she wondered how she was going to marry him when he talked to her like that. Okay, so he was right about the SUV, but she wasn't about to admit it.

A dart of pain smashed into the center of her chest and radiated out. She closed her eyes and just absorbed it. Maybe, if she hadn't gone to Paris, she would never have noticed what an arrogant ass he was. Pre-Paris Jen worshipped Stefan. Anything he'd said had been all right with her. But the Jen who'd come back from Paris just wanted to tear strips off him. And then kiss them and make them better.

She sat up. Brain damage or not, she absolutely was crazy. There was no other explanation.

She rolled out of bed and walked downstairs. The house was quiet except for the clicking on an antique grandfather clock that echoed through the silence. She stopped on the last two steps and sat down. She stared up at the massive chandelier. He'd bought this house for her. He'd spared no expense putting it back the way it should be. Jen could close her eyes and hear music and see ladies in long dresses sipping punch and dancing with handsome young men.

And her kitchen. She walked to the refrigerator and grabbed a yogurt container, shaking her head in awe. She smiled at the blender upended on a dish towel, the only evidence that Mr. Neat and Tidy had been there. No loose ends. Every box ticked. She stood in the kitchen, ate the yogurt and thought of ways to warm everything up. There was a perfect spot for her cookbooks. She needed a coffee maker. Her every instinct was to start turning this place into her home. Their home.

It was unbearable. There was no way she could just stay in this house. The longer she did, the more attached she got. This was Stefan's house. This was not her home. Her home had been destroyed by the flood waters after Katrina. But even then she hadn't lived there since her parents were killed years before. She'd lived with the Sellers at their house, then later at the lake house Mac had built for his wife when she refused to cross the Pontchartrain to rebuild. But none of those had ever been home. They were just places she'd lived.

Her throat got so tight even the yogurt wouldn't go down. She dropped the cup in the garbage can under the sink. Washed the spoon and laid it by the upended blender. Tears blinded her without warning. Great, now she was crying over flatware and small appliances. It was just that she really wanted this to be home. She wanted to make this into a home for both of them. She wanted that happily ever after he'd promised her. She wanted to forget what Madlyn had said that night.

"He'll regret it one day. If you love him, you won't let him make this mistake."

Jen really didn't know what to do. But she did know that she simply could not wait around this house all day feeling little pieces of her heart shrivel and die. So she showered and refused to cry anymore. She changed into her favorite jeans and a simple blue shirt and comfortable shoes.

She felt much more like herself when she caught the St. Charles streetcar and rode it up to Canal Street, then walked the rest of the way to the tall, glass building that housed her father's legacy. Mac had added a fountain to the entrance when they'd remodeled after Katrina, and Jen spent some time sitting in the lobby on the edge of the fountain trying to come up with an excuse to go upstairs. Wait, she owned half of this damned company. She didn't need an excuse and she headed straight for the elevators.

Martin was not at his desk when she reached the top floor, but the door to Stefan's office was not closed either. She heard voices before she stuck her head in. The deceptively friendly, sugar sweet drawl started acid brewing in Jen's stomach. She braced herself then took a deep breath. Madlyn Robicheaux only looked venomous. She didn't actually have fangs. Jen hoped.

Jen pushed the door open and stepped in without knocking. And there she was. The Red Queen herself. Sleek, jet black hair to go with dead shark eyes. Red power suit, black Pradas, and a red Birkin sitting neatly in the chair next to her as she and Stefan went over paperwork. She was the very picture of elegant business and class, as long as you didn't mind the stench of decay. Jen was pretty sure there wasn't another human being alive that she despised more.

Madlyn and Stefan had dated in college. She'd been his attorney since the moment she passed the bar. But even better, they remained very good friends. Very good friends with very good benefits. Jen might be Stefan's go-to girl if he needed a silent sidekick at a business dinner when he was between girlfriends. But Madlyn was his go-to for sex when he was between girlfriends or even when he wasn't. While everyone believed Stefan and Madlyn had ended things after college, Jen knew they hadn't. She'd discovered firsthand what kind of relationship Stefan had with Madlyn. And unfortunately it was one of the few memories Jen had that she was absolutely sure was real, beyond a shadow of a doubt. Because Madlyn never let her forget it.

She'd seen them together once, the night she and Lizzie graduated from high school. Lizzie had skipped a grade so they had ended up graduating together. Mac and Nadine Sellers had thrown a huge party at the new house in Slidell. When everyone had left, Jen had gone looking for Stefan. He'd disappeared sometime around midnight, but Jen had wanted to tell him goodnight. His car had still been in the driveway.

She should have realized that Madlyn Robicheaux's car was still in the driveway too. So it was really her own fault when she found them in the boathouse. Madlyn's red bikini top on the floor, Stefan's cut offs at his ankles. Jen could still feel the way the icy shock had rolled over her, freezing her feelings for Stefan so hard and so deep inside her that most of what she felt for him was still buried there. She'd told herself repeatedly that she was too young for him. That her feelings for Stefan were wildly inappropriate considering he saw her as a little sister. Still, she hadn't been able to tear herself away from watching them for a few stolen seconds before she couldn't stand not breathing any longer. Afraid that expelling the breath she was holding would alert them to her presence, she'd backed away from the door. But not before dead black eyes razored in on her from over Stefan's shoulder. Scarlet nails had dug into Stefan's hair and back as Madlyn spotted her. Terrified Madlyn was about to tell Stefan she was there, Jen had fled. She didn't even remember how she got away. And Madlyn evidently had not said anything to Stefan, because he'd never so much as hinted that anything was up when she saw him at supper the next night.

But she'd never looked at him the same way.

And she'd never hated anyone the way she hated Madlyn.

They both turned towards her now, but Madlyn was the first to speak. Jen met those shark eyes straight on. Madlyn knew exactly what Jen was remembering. The sly cat smile curved scarlet red lips. "Jen, your ears must have been burning. Stefan and I were just going over your pre-nup agreement."

Jen kept her face calm and did not react. Pre-Paris, she probably would have turned purple and run straight out of the room hyperventilating and dying of embarrassment. But today the girl that had come back from Paris just smiled her very best nice girl smile straight at Madlyn, then turned to Stefan.

"Sweetheart, you made Madlyn draw up our pre-nup?" She pretended to pout. "That's kinda cold, don't you think?" She bit back asking if they'd included an adultery clause that allowed them to enjoy their benefits even while he was married to Jen. She wouldn't put it past Madlyn, since the other woman had always treated her like an extra stupid piece of furniture despite her insincere claims of sisterly affection.

Stefan didn't even blink as he met her straight on with laughing blue eyes. Jen crossed the room to him and sat down on his lap, giving him a sweet kiss on the cheek. He went very still but his face gave nothing away. She could tell he was enjoying himself though. A little too much.

"I can't believe you would even ask her to do that," Jen said, then smiled sympathetically at Madlyn. "He's so insensitive sometimes."

Jen fought not to let her smile go wild when she watched Madlyn blink too hard and the lines of her mouth flatten out. Hard fingers clamped down on her waist but she didn't react. He shifted her slightly. She turned towards him, her eyes flashing fury at him while her back was to Madlyn. But her voice was all pampered princess when she said, "You promised to buy me a car, remember? Can't you two finish this up later?"

"You're right, Stef, Paris was good for her," Madlyn said, no more indication that anything Jen had said or done had affected her at all.

Stefan dragged his eyes away from Jen's suddenly brilliant smiling face. "You have no idea," he agreed.

"Is this it?" Jen asked, diving forward suddenly to grab the paperwork on his desk before he could stop her. "Let me guess," Jen announced. "In the event of divorce, Stefan retains all STI stock."

Fingers bit harder into her waist.

"Not exactly," Madlyn assured her. "Just control of it."

"Even better," Jen said, as if that made her even happier.

"But your settlement is very generous," Madlyn purred, not letting Jen score another point. The shark eyes flared to life, but unfortunately with amusement instead of anger.

"Oh, I have no doubt Stefan plans to make sure I am well provided for," Jen gritted out, anger turning her stomach inside out, and suddenly this game wasn't fun anymore.

"Madlyn," Stefan finally interrupted. "I'll read this over tonight and email you any changes. I did promise to take Jen to lunch."

Madlyn smiled. "Of course. You two love birds have fun." Madlyn gathered up her paperwork as she stood. "It's nice to see you, Jen. We should do lunch."

"Absolutely," Jen lied.

As soon as the door clipped shut behind the Red Queen, Jen started to move, but strong fingers gripped the waist band on her jeans and stopped her. She yelped as he actually flipped her around so she was straddling him. She started to protest but she kind of liked the strain that flashed across his face as she settled her weight against him. That little move had clearly backfired on him. It was all she could do to keep from grinding down against him.

And of course he read her mind, and his hands went to her waist again, this time under her shirt, and warm fingers held her still as he laughed, sounding just a little strangled. "Oh no, you don't. You stay right where you are," he warned. "I think you actually scored a point. That doesn't happen very often with Madlyn."

"Pre-nup?" Jen said, ignoring the backhanded compliment. "You have her drawing up a pre-nup for us?" She should move her hips just to punish him.

Stefan nodded. "I believe you were the one who demanded one. It's to protect you. Not me."

"You just keep telling yourself that," she sniffed. She stiffened when one hand left her waist to lace into her hair.

"She's right, Paris was good for you," he said, pulling her head down until her hands pressed into his shoulders, and her lips hovered right over his. "Maybe we should go there on our honeymoon."

He didn't kiss her. He just brushed his mouth across hers. It was worse than a kiss, because it made her ache to kiss him. Her eyes closed, and she slid her hands from his shoulders up the strong column of his neck.

"Kiss me," he whispered.

"No," she told him, sighing as his lips brushed against her jaw.

"Why are you spoiling for another fight?" he asked, sliding his mouth down her neck. "You can't be jealous of Madlyn. She's ancient history. You know that."

"You're drawing up a legal contract that plans our divorce, and you haven't even bothered to ask me to marry you," Jen told him. "You can't even be bothered to take me on a date."

"A date?" he laughed against her throat. "You think we need to get to know each other better? We've been on plenty of dates."

"We've never been on a date," she told him, furious that he thought this was funny. "But it's okay, Stefan," she assured him. "There's no need for candlelight and violins anyway. I already agreed to six months."

He moved so fast she didn't even have time to cry out when she found herself flat on her back on his desk, with him looming over her. He leaned down, pinning her hard against the smooth wood. "I've had just about enough of this, Jen."

"I am not marrying you," she said, slowly pronouncing each word. "You got that?"

Blue eyes skimmed all over her, heating up her insides even more. She wanted to kiss him. No, no she didn't. He had her pinned to his desk. How could she possibly want him to kiss her?

Then his face changed, as something dawned on him. "Why six months?" he asked.

"What?"

"You said you'd agreed to six months. Why would we only want to get married for six months? Where did that come from?"

"I'm not stupid," she bit out at him. "I know you think I am, but I'm not."

"Actually, I never thought you were stupid until now. You said you'd agreed to six months and I could have the stock." He let go of her suddenly and backed away from her as if she'd burned him.

She sat up on the edge of the desk and watched as he crossed the office. He stopped in front of the huge bank of windows that overlooked the river. His fists slammed into his pockets. He had a fabulous view of the Mississippi but she could tell he wasn't seeing any of that. Jen had a really bad feeling, deep in the pit of her stomach.

"You think this is all about your trust fund," he said, his voice rough, but he didn't turn around. He rubbed one hand across his face then pushed it through his hair. Jen watched as he stood there another minute, his shoulders stiff. The entire atmosphere in the office had chilled, and she almost shivered. "Don't you?"

"Not just the trust fund."

"I already control your trust fund. Try again."

"The stock. The stock that can't be sold until I'm thirty or..."

"Married," he finished for her, as if it were the most obvious thing in the world. For a split second, Jen thought maybe she'd been wrong. Then he turned to her, absolutely no emotion on his face. "So let's go get that SUV."

She nodded, no longer really hearing what he was saying. All she could hear was the distance in his voice and that nasty little voice in her head saying *See, he didn't deny it.*

He stayed on his cell phone for most of the drive. They pulled up at the dealership and he didn't even stop his conversation, just waved to a row of SUVs and said, "Pick one."

She stared at him for a minute but he was ignoring her again, talking on his phone. She turned to the salesman who was looking increasingly uncomfortable. She smiled slightly. "I like the car over there," she said, pointing to a red convertible BMW instead. "Can I see it instead?" she looked at his name tag. "Jim?"

The salesman smiled at her. "Absolutely. I'll just go get the keys."

She followed him over to the car, and she made it as far as the driver's seat before Stefan stopped her. "What did we talk about?"

"You said pick one." She slid behind the wheel and waited for Jim to come back with the keys. "I like this one."

"This is not an SUV."

"Really?" she asked, trying to sound shocked. "I had no idea."

"Get out of the car," he said.

She just shook her head and wrapped her hands around the steering wheel. She really did like the shiny red car. It was gorgeous. She knew it was completely impractical, but there were all kinds of gadgets and bells and whistles. "I want this one."

"You want another fight," he told her. "You need an SUV. You need the cargo space and it's safer in the city."

She looked up at him, smiling slowly. "I'm tired of safe. Admit it. I look great in this car. Even better if I had on my black dress. What do you think? Oh, wait, I've got a great idea. Let's buy this car, take it back to your place, I'll put that dress back on and maybe you can pin me down to the hood this time?"

She watched as most of the color drained out of his face and his eyes caught on fire at the same time. He went very, very still. And because she had completely lost her mind, and because that shadow of hurt had blazed out of his eyes, she continued. "Or maybe I could just wear the shoes...and my stockings. Did you notice the little black bows? They're my favorite."

Jim stepped up with the keys, and Stefan looked up at him quickly. "We'll take this one."

"You don't want to drive it first?"

"No," Stefan barked before Jen could say yes. She smiled to herself and flipped her hair back. She knew she was going to regret everything she'd just said, but until he got her alone, she was going to enjoy it.

Then Stefan was hauling her out of the convertible and dragging her into the dealership, where he disappointed Jim by not financing the car, but then delighted the middle-aged salesman by not negotiating either. He just wrote a check and handed it over.

"You didn't even try to get them down on the price?" Jen said, when Jim left them alone in his office to finish the paperwork.

"I don't negotiate," he said, not looking at her.

"What do you mean you don't negotiate? It's a car. Everyone haggles over a car."

"I don't," he said.

Jen's jaw dropped. "You're serious."

"Yes, I'm serious. I can afford the car. I don't have to prove anything. And when some joker brings me a low ball offer on a property we're flipping, I don't negotiate that either. They either pay what we want or they find something else."

She just shook her head. "You're unbelievable."

"I don't have time for games. But I have to admit, I'm looking forward to the car being delivered. I think we'll make another stop and find you the right lingerie to go with those shoes first."

Prickling heat rushed all under Jen's skin, but she told herself he wasn't serious. He couldn't be serious. She looked back at him and one sandy eyebrow lifted as he dared her to say another word. For the first time since her plane touched down in Kenner, she kept her mouth shut.

Jim saved her when he walked back in with paperwork.

"Can you have it ready today and deliver it before five?" Stefan asked, not taking his eyes off Jen. "I have plans for it this evening."

"Absolutely."

A few minutes later, he stood in the passenger doorway of his Range Rover and waited for her to clip her seat belt. She turned back to him when she realized he wasn't moving. Her breath caught on the cool, flinty-eyed look he was giving her.

"You going to keep playing this game with me?" he asked, his voice scarily quiet again.

She licked her lips, noticing how his eyes riveted to that movement. "I think so," she admitted, wondering why she was determined to provoke him at every opportunity. She knew it was crazy but she couldn't seem to help herself. It was too delicious.

He took a deep breath. "The hippie tell you I was after your stock?"

"No," she said quickly. "Of course not."

"You came up with that all on your on?" he asked.

"It makes sense," she insisted. "I'm not an idiot."

His mouth flattened into a grim line, and he just shook his head and slammed her door.

"I already vote your stock and control your trust," he reminded her when he slid behind the wheel.

She crossed her arms and turned her face away from him. "You demonstrated that when you just wrote a check and didn't bother to negotiate."

He laughed, but it wasn't a pleasant sound. "I didn't write that out of your account. Happy late Birthday."

She swung back around at him. "You can't buy me a car for my birthday."

"Just did."

"Stefan, you can't just..."

"What?" he demanded sharply, turning suddenly in his seat when he braked at a red light. "Buy a hot car for my smoking hot fiancée so I can pin her to the hood while she wears her fuck-me shoes and black stockings with bows?"

"Stefan," she gasped, ribbons of heat streaming through her central nervous system without warning.

"Stop playing games with me," he warned. "You'll lose."

He pulled back into traffic and Jen stared out the window watching the city rush by. Wait. Had he just called her smoking hot?

"Jen, I don't have to marry you to get control of your trust fund. I just have to make sure you don't marry anyone else."

"I told you I'd sign whatever I have to sign."

"Good, then you'll have no trouble signing our marriage license."

"Why do you even want to marry me? I just don't understand."

"I really hate that for you, Jen. I do. I might have spelled it out for you this morning, but now, you're on your own. When you figure it out, let me know."

She decided to regroup. Tactical retreat. She wasn't going to give him any excuses, but she wasn't going to let him win either. And she definitely wasn't going to feel all warm and gooey because he'd called her smoking hot. He couldn't have meant it. Except he hadn't sounded sarcastic about that part.

"You think I'm smoking hot?" she asked out of the blue, not even beginning to understand how she'd said it out loud.

She let herself glance at him when he didn't answer. She smothered a laugh. He didn't know what to say. He actually didn't know what to say to her. He was having to think about it, and for once he wasn't thinking fast enough.

His phone rang, saving him, and he answered it before it could ring twice. Jen bit back the laughter bubbling up in her as she let herself feel just a little warm and gooey.

"I'm dropping you at the house," he said gruffly, when he ended the call. "I've got to meet Rogan at a job site."

"Fine." Definitely warm and gooey.

CHAPTER EIGHT

Jim wasted no time delivering her new car. She slid behind the wheel and just sat in the driveway unable to actually get back out and go inside. She thought about driving out to the lake house to show Lizzie. Lizzie would absolutely die.

Her phone rang and the caller ID had her grinning from ear to ear. "Jared," she nearly screamed into the phone. "I really need you to come home, so I can kill you."

He snickered on the other end of the line. "In Atlanta about to board my flight," he said, sounding smug and proud of himself but she was so relieved she didn't care.

"You're almost home? Why didn't you tell me you were coming?"

"I got a standby flight. Didn't want to say anything until I was sure. Can you pick me up in a couple of hours?"

"Absolutely," she said.

"Gonna need a place to crash until my apartment is ready," he said.

"Stefan bought a house. It's huge. Wait 'til you see the kitchen."

"A house?" Jared asked.

"On St. Charles Street."

Jared snickered again. "I guess all those business dinners really paid off."

"If I weren't so glad you were coming home, I'd leave your butt at the airport. You have no idea how wrong you were about that dress."

Two and half hours later, she watched her rock god come gliding through the airport. She smiled at the women who watched, biting their lips and fanning themselves as he passed by. He had his guitar slung over his shoulder, he hadn't shaved, and his wavy black hair was all over the place. He was totally lapping up the attention, but not a soul could tell that but Jen. He was the picture of bored casual. Until he spotted Jen. Then his face split into a grin, and he lifted her off her feet and spun her around. She kissed him on the forehead and hugged him tight. "I'm so glad you're here," she said, holding him much tighter than usual.

When he set her down, he caught her hand. "What the hell?" he demanded, taking a long look at her engagement ring. "He didn't waste any time, did he?"

Jen pulled her hand back. "I just..."

"Hey," Jared cut her off. "You want to marry him, marry him. It's all good. Maybe you'll get the asshole out of your system."

"I got a car," she said, changing the subject before she got all emotional.

He whistled when they reached her new car. "Keys," he demanded holding out his hand for them, waving his fingers impatiently.

"I never said you could drive."

"You really think I'm not driving this cherry, you are crazy. Keys!" Then he grinned that devil grin at her and she caved, tossing the keys at him. He caught them easily, stowed his guitar and bag in the back, then vaulted over the driver's side door.

"Be careful, it's her first day out," Jen warned him.

"I'll be gentle." He grinned shamelessly, turned the key in the ignition, and groaned with pleasure as the engine roared to life. He cranked up the radio and screeched out of the parking garage.

"We need to stop for groceries. There's nothing at Stefan's but protein powder and boiled eggs."

Jared shivered. "Are you sure he's human?"

They stopped off at Whole Foods and immediately forgot that they were in a hurry. Jen went a little nuts in the produce department, while Jared headed straight for the deli where he chose no less than ten different types of cheese. One was a cave cheese and Jen threatened him if he tried to open it inside the house.

"I'm not sure all this will fit in the convertible," Jen said, as they unloaded the buggy at the checkout line. "I'm not sure it will even go back in the buggy."

"Should've got an SUV," Jared teased her, winking at the girl scanning their groceries, trying to distract her so she didn't notice some items didn't scan. Jen watched her swoon and just shook her head.

"You will never grow up," Jen said, handing the girl back a ten dollar jar of olives she'd missed. Jared shrugged and started stuffing bags in their buggy.

Then Jared stuffed everything in the trunk and the back seat and they headed for the house on St. Charles. Stefan was sitting on the side porch when they pulled in and the irritated look on his face turned grim when Jared jumped out of the car.

"Hey, Sellers, long time no see," Jared said, grabbing two handfuls of bags and handing them to him when Stefan reached the driveway. "Dinner's in an hour."

Stefan took the bags and headed inside without a word. Jared smirked at her. "Surprise," he said under his breath and Jen couldn't help the nervous giggle that escaped. She grabbed a bunch of bags and followed Stefan. She stayed in the kitchen and unloaded all the groceries while Jared and Stefan brought them in.

Then Jared joined her in the kitchen and started seasoning the steaks. "You do eat steak right?" he asked Stefan.

Stefan nodded. "Sure. I'll be in my office."

Jen watched him disappear down the hall.

"So, he's not really happy to see me, is he?" Jared asked.

Jen did laugh then. "Probably not," she admitted. "But he'll get over it once he tries your steak."

Jared raised his eyebrows quickly and grinned. "Where's that cheese?"

"Don't you dare open that cheese in my house!" she said, refusing to admit how comfortable she was calling it her house.

About an hour later, she stood outside his office door trying to work up the nerve to knock. She leaned her forehead against the door wondering if trying to have Stefan and Jared under the same roof would ever be anything other than a bad idea. She knocked and a second later he growled "Come in."

"Hey," she stuck her head around the door. "Dinner's almost ready."

He looked up from his laptop, and watched as she moved into the room.

"Shut the door," he told her. Then, "Did you know he was coming back today?"

She shook her head. "No, he caught a standby flight. I didn't find out until he was in Atlanta."

"Still plenty of time to maybe drop me a text and let me know we're having company."

"I didn't think about it," Jen said and watched his eyes darken even more. "I'm sorry. I should have."

Stefan sat back in the leather chair, his eyes frosting over. "I've been reading your business plan."

"And…" she prompted, but already knew by the set of his jaw what was coming.

"It looks good except for the location."

She closed her eyes briefly and when she opened them again, she faced him straight on. "The location is important."

He shook his head slowly. "There are some spaces on Magazine Street."

"Magazine Street?" she repeated. "That isn't what we're going for at all. We want the foot traffic from the French Quarter."

"Magazine has foot traffic."

"We want to make small king cakes, Stefan. They're the size of a cinnamon roll or a pretzel. You can hold it in one hand and eat it. People are not going to walk down Magazine eating a mini king cake. But tourists in the French Quarter will."

He leaned forward and snapped the laptop closed. "If you want me to invest in this, you'll rethink…"

"I never asked you to invest in this. I asked you to give me *my* money to invest in this."

"That's not going to happen."

"What?" she demanded. "That makes no sense at all."

"Oh, you think I'm going to let you hand over that much money to your hippie friend? You've lost your mind. At least with me on board, he has someone to answer to."

She opened her mouth and closed it again. She turned away from him before she said something she really regretted and yanked the door open. She paused in the doorway. "Forget I ever asked you about this. I'll figure something else out."

Stefan was on his feet before she could leave. "Do not go to Mac with this, Jen."

She held onto the doorknob to keep from leaping across the room and smacking him. "Stop talking. I don't want to get any angrier than I already am. Dinner will be ready in about ten minutes."

"He's not staying here tonight," Stefan told her.

She swung around to find herself face to face with the frost giant again. "Why not?"

His expression went even colder and his eyelids were barely open. When he didn't answer her right away, she realized it was because his lightning quick brain just couldn't come up with a good answer. She kinda liked that. Twice in one day.

She stepped further into the room, just completely unable to leave it alone. "The bed in the guest room is queen-sized. Plenty of room for both of us."

Stefan stood up and Jen couldn't help the instinctive step back she took. "What?" she said, slicking her tongue across her bottom lip. "Did you really think we could afford a two bedroom apartment in Paris?"

"Still playing games with me, Jen?" he whispered.

She nodded. "I can't seem to help myself."

"Why do you think that is?" he asked, slowly closing the distance between them.

She shrugged, trying her best to stay calm. "No idea."

He stopped in front of her, his hand reaching out to slide around her neck as he pulled her forward. "I know why," he said, his head dipping, and Jen's toes started to curl.

"Why?" she asked, sounding breathless.

"Because of this," he said, gliding his tongue across her bottom lip.

"That could be it," she agreed, letting him press her back against the wall.

He raised his head slowly, smiling as her mouth followed his and she stepped forward. He shook his head. "Oh, no," he warned her, pressing her away from him despite the tiny, distressed cry that escaped before she could stop it. "You want that, all you have to do is walk down the aisle."

She closed her eyes and leaned back. "Wanna bet?" she whispered, turning away from him and reaching for the door.

He grabbed her then, and pulled her back up against him. "Absolutely. What are the stakes?"

"I win, you give me my money, I sign whatever you need to give you permanent control over the stock and you call off this whole farce of a wedding."

His arms tightened around her as he buried his face against her neck. "And if I win?"

"If you win, we'll already be married, won't we?"

"True, but I need a sweetener."

"You don't like sugar," she reminded him.

"That's where you're wrong." His tongue lapped along her throat and Jen almost came unglued. "Very sweet."

"What do you want?" she asked.

"You move the bakery location out of the French Quarter."

She tried to wrench away from him. "You realize this means war?"

"I was hoping you'd say that, baby."

"The Seller's Calm is going down," she promised him.

"Can't wait." His voice was like silk against her ears. "Deal?"

"Deal," she snapped.

"Excellent," he whispered. "Even if I lose I still win."

"Proving you really don't want to marry me at all."

"See, you have got to start paying attention. You said wedding not marriage."

She wrenched away from him and jerked the door open.

"I warned you not to play with me," he reminded her.

"You'd better come eat before I spit on your steak!" She stalked out of the office, furious when she heard him laughing.

Stefan's victory was short-lived. Sitting at the table watching her with Jared Marshall turned out to be an exercise in pure, white-hot masochism. Oh, he had no doubt that they were just friends. There wasn't even a hint of a spark of anything between them other than silliness. They acted like a couple of kids around each other. He couldn't even hate the younger guy because it was so clear that Jared Marshall had the unique ability to make Jen radiantly happy.

Stefan had known Jen all her life but not once had he ever seen her like this. She was completely relaxed, meeting every crazy thing Jared said head on. They laughed. She giggled and teased him viciously. Stefan was seeing the real, unguarded Jen Taylor for the very first time. His gut twisted painfully. He should have seen this side of her way before now. Why had she been so guarded with him all this time? How much more of herself was she holding back? He'd had glimpses of her wicked sense of humor before, and he had been learning first hand over the last few days that she could cut him to ribbons with her smart mouth. Her little declaration of war earlier in his office had almost brought him to his knees. He had no idea how he'd kept from dragging her down to the floor of his office and letting her win.

Now he wasn't sure he really knew her at all. He'd thought she was shy, quiet, and timid. Timid? Ha! She wasn't even close to that when she let herself go. And she was letting herself go tonight. She was telling Stefan in great detail all about Jared's patented seduction technique.

"He'll sing that John Mayer song about your body is like Disneyland," she crowed and Jared almost flung potatoes at her with his spoon.

"Wonderland, freak. It's Wonderland," he corrected her.

"Right," Jen nodded. "Wonderland. I guess I get confused because you're like Peter Pan with an oversexed libido. Then, when he finishes the song, he'll take a break, unplug his guitar, and leave Adam to do all the work. He'll hop off the stage, grab the girl, and disappear into the back with her. He's got a make-out spot in the back of Trick's. It's his lair."

She was oblivious to the fact that Stefan wasn't laughing, because she was too busy making faces at Jared. The hippie grinned like an idiot and didn't deny a single thing she said. "And if they manage to resist him, he invites them over for a quiet dinner and cooks them pasta and feeds them his chocolate cheesecake, and before sunrise there's another notch on his guitar case."

"You are so full of it," Jared told her, sitting back in his seat. "I would never notch my guitar case. Are you crazy?"

She turned to Stefan and her smile dimmed. It might have been kinder if she had just stabbed him in the eye. Because he didn't want the light going out of her smiles when she looked at him. He wanted her to glow and shine like she had been. He wanted her. All of her. And for once, he wasn't quite sure how he could go about getting what he wanted. He didn't like that at all.

"What kind of guitar?" he asked Jared.

"Oh, don't get him started on the real love of his life," Jen said, standing up suddenly and clearing dishes. Then she did something that Stefan was pretty sure he would remember and treasure for the rest of his life. She leaned down and kissed him on the cheek, pausing before she raised her head. "I made dessert, so I assume you're having some?"

He turned his head and found her smiling at him. A real smile. "Absolutely," he said, and watched her smile finally meet her eyes for him. He absolutely loved that.

While Jen was in the kitchen, Jared leaned back in his chair and downed the rest of his wine. "You've never seen her like this, have you? Really happy, I mean."

Stefan shrugged, sitting back in his chair, watching her move around in her kitchen. The house was starting to feel like home now that she was in it. Stefan hadn't felt at home in a very long time.

"I've seen her happy," Stefan told him. "Just not giddy, unguarded, and relaxed."

"She was like this every day in Paris," Jared informed him.

"Your point?"

Jared shrugged, looking older and very serious. Stefan finally understood what it was about the other guy that he'd never been able to put his finger on. Jared reminded him of Robert. Robert had been wild and crazy and full of laughter and life the way Jared Marshall was. Maybe that was why Jen was so attached to him.

"Jen is special," Jared said, keeping his voice low. "I just hope you appreciate what you have. Because she loves you, and does not believe for one single second that you feel the same way for her."

Stefan nodded, feeling his lungs starting to seize up.

"If you hurt her," Jared warned, "if you really hurt her, I won't have to beat the shit out of you, Sellers, because losing her will devastate you. She might not think it now, but eventually, she will get over you. She can do so much better than you. But that beautiful girl in there," Jared told him, nodding his head towards the kitchen. "You will never do better than her. You really lose her, you won't ever recover."

Stefan stared at the younger man a long time. The deadly serious brown eyes staring back at him were so like Robert's, Stefan had to remind himself that Robert had died a long time ago. "I like you," Stefan said finally, fighting a smile at Jared's confusion. "I'm glad you have her back." He meant it too. So, Jared Marshall wasn't a complete fuck up. Whatever. Granted, he should have known that anyone Jen was that attached to wouldn't be, but he wasn't about to admit to himself or anyone else that he resented the time she spent with Jared.

Jared nodded, then smiled reassuringly at Jen when she looked up and watched them closely. She gave them a wary look then went back to putting strawberries in bowls.

Stefan downed the rest of his wine and set the glass down a little too hard. "You know, you remind me so much of Robert it's scary."

"Robert?" Jared asked, his brows narrowing.

"Her brother," Stefan explained, and the surprise on Jared's face gave Stefan a tinge of satisfaction. "She doesn't talk about him?"

"No," Jared admitted, his eyes going back towards the kitchen. "She never talks about her family or the accident."

"Because she doesn't let herself think about it, and most of it she can't remember. I'd like to keep it that way."

Jared nodded, surprising Stefan by not arguing with him. The hippie might be irritating, but Stefan accepted that they were on the same side when it came to Jen. He could live with that.

Jen stepped up with three bowls of berry shortcake. "Are you two bonding over here?"

"Not even a little bit," Stefan assured her, noticing that Jared got his bowl first. "I'm going to beat the shit out of him as soon as you go to sleep."

"As if," Jared sputtered around a mouth full of whipped cream.

She grinned. "There's no sugar in it," she said, as she set Stefan's bowl down in front of him. "I used Stevia. See what you think."

Jared made a face. "Stevia?"

She turned to him. "I put sugar on yours, idiot."

"Has she made you pancakes yet?" Jared asked, shoving a huge spoonful of berries and pound cake in his mouth.

"Yes," Stefan said, wondering if he should mention there was no pound cake in his bowl. Just berries and whipped cream. He didn't really want to get into another white flour argument.

"They're not as good as my waffles," Jared insisted and Jen threw a blueberry at him, which he caught with his mouth.

Stefan watched as they started up again with their craziness. This time he smiled, and even started to enjoy it. And even when he tossed Jared out to bunk on Rogan's couch in the carriage house, Jen was radiating so much happiness that Stefan was almost drunk on it. Rogan grumbled until Jared announced he had leftovers. Stefan suspected Rogan would get pound cake too. He had no idea why he resented that.

"Admit it," she shouldered him as he shut the door. "He's not so bad."

Stefan gave her a doubtful look. "I admit nothing."

"You finished your steak," she pointed out.

"Okay, yes, I admit the hippie can cook."

"Thank you," she said softly, and he stopped, turning back to her. "For what?"

She nodded. "For looking at our business plan."

"It's solid. I just want you to pick a different location."

"I'm not going to do that." Her smile went out completely. She sounded so tired and resigned. He couldn't take his eyes off her. The set of that delicate jaw and the steely determination in her eyes undid him. Rogan and Elliot were right. This was important to her and he had no right to stand in her way. Besides, her refusal to back down was turning him on like crazy. They'd never clashed about anything before and Stefan was still shocked at just how sexy she was when she was spitting fire at him. He loved it. A lot. So for a minute, he was tempted to not tell her what he'd decided because, damn him, he was enjoying her refusal to give in.

But he wanted her light back more than he wanted the sexual tension that came with the arguments. He wanted her smiling and dancing on air for him. He just wanted her happy more than he wanted to take his next breath. And if the bakery would do that, then she would have the best bakery the city had ever seen. And if it had to be in the French Quarter, well then, "I get complete control and approval over your security system and during Mardi Gras you agree to let me hire security guards."

She hit him so fast, he almost lost his balance. Long arms and legs wound around him and he was rewarded with more kisses than he could count. He caught her easily and walked the few steps back to the sofa, thinking that ecstatically happy Jen was a helluva lot sexier than angry Jen. He sat down before he could fall down and allowed his fingers to trace through her hair. He pulled her head back so he could see her face. She smiled at him, really smiled, even brighter and more beautifully than she did for the hippie. And gravity lost all its hold on Stefan Sellers as he gave up part of himself he hadn't even known he was still holding on to.

"And I get pancakes," he told her, his voice pure gravel again.

"Definitely," she agreed, leaning to kiss him, and he let her. Let her explore his mouth, slick that pink tongue along his bottom lip and tangle with his. He lasted about thirty-seven seconds before he seized control of the kiss and tried to lose himself in the sweetness of her.

And as usual it all started raging out of his control, but a part of him he just couldn't seem to stop wouldn't let it happen.

She was pulling at the buttons on his shirt but her fingers were trembling too hard to work them loose. Finally, he caught her hands, eased her back, wincing at her cry of protest. He raised her hands to his mouth and kissed them. "Slow down," he told her. "We've got plenty of time."

All the air left his lungs when she batted his hands away and got the buttons loose this time. Then her hands were on him and Stefan could feel his hinges coming loose. Why had he ever believed he was in control? Was he insane? Control and Jen could not occupy the same space for him. If she ever really called his bluff, he was in big trouble.

"Jen," he hissed, then laughed and choked at the same time when her mouth opened against his stomach. "Baby, hold on," he gasped, not believing how hot her mouth was on his skin. Also not believing he was actually trying to stop her. Yes, he was crazy. Unfortunately. Or just plain stupid.

"No," she breathed against him.

He couldn't remember what they should hold on for. In fact, he didn't actually have a good reason for stopping her. Her mouth ran havoc up his throat, across his chest, and further down until she was tracing the lines of his abs with her tongue. He groaned, his head going back on the couch as he closed his fingers into tight fists telling himself just one more minute and he'd stop her. Thirty more seconds and he'd slow this down. His belt buckle clinked and the alarm bells won. He caught hold of her frantic hands.

"Stefan," she groaned in protest.

He pulled her back up so she was facing him, cupped the back of her head and pulled her down for another raging hot kiss. She straddled him, rocking against him until he was forced to flip her onto her back or lose control altogether. He lifted his head. She was so unbelievably beautiful. Her caramel eyes were dilated, and her lips were swollen. He liked that he'd done that. He liked that she was dazed and trembling beneath him. He couldn't wait to see her face when he was finally inside her. His whole body shuddered and something ravenous awoke. He wasn't quite ready to give into it yet. Who knew what he'd be on the other side.

"Slow down," he repeated, his voice so hoarse he didn't recognize it.

She shook her head, but her eyes were still smiling. "This is war," she teased.

"We're still not rushing this." He heard the words come out of his mouth, but he had no idea where they came from. He didn't actually agree with them. And he really didn't like the pain-filled expression that darkened her brown eyes before she shut them. She hadn't even tried to hide it from him this time. He honestly wasn't trying to hurt her. This just meant too much to him to blow it. He wanted it to be perfect. And right now, his definition of perfect was not two minutes on his sofa. He just didn't seem to have enough blood or oxygen in his brain to form the words that would make her understand that.

She pushed against him, only opening her eyes when he moved away. She scrambled back, trying to think of something clever to say, but she just had nothing, less than nothing really. All she could think was maybe he didn't really want her that badly after all.

"Hey," he said, catching her before she could fly out of the room. He pulled her back into his lap. "Look at me," he said softly.

She swallowed hard and braced herself for whatever mocking comment he had for her. But when she finally did look at him, she didn't see even a trace of laughter anywhere.

What he did say took her completely by surprise. "We need to set a date."

"A date?" she echoed.

He nodded, pushing her hair away from her face. "In April."

"April," she repeated, nodding, trying to come to terms with what he was saying. April was only a few months away. Not nearly enough time for Nadine Sellers to put together the wedding she would insist on. "So soon?" Jen said.

"Not soon enough. I want to do this right," he told her, and she could see his mind was made up. And once Stefan made up his mind, there was no changing it. She could try to wear him down, keep playing her silly games and pretend she had a chance at winning. But she wouldn't beat him. But she wasn't going down without a fight. No way.

"That's crazy," she finally managed to say.

"We've waited this long, what's a few more months."

Jen closed her eyes and took a deep breath, then pushed out of his arms. She told herself she should be flattered. She also tried to tell herself that it was sweet. But instead she just got angry and really, really frustrated. "You aren't the one who promised no more boys."

"I think that's understood, Jen," he laughed, making her even madder.

She got off the sofa, not sure why she was so angry. It wasn't like she hadn't been aching like this for years. What difference did a few more months make? But she found it made a lot of difference to her. He wanted her, she knew that. Just not nearly as desperately as she wanted him. And it was humiliating.

It really is just about the stock. It's just a bonus that he doesn't find you repulsive, that sadistic little voice whispered in her ear and that second of self-doubt was like ice water rushing all over her. Then the part of her that rejoiced in jumping up and down on his buttons roared to life. She turned back around and faced him. "Where do you keep the extra batteries?"

His eyebrows narrowed in confusion. "Kitchen drawer on the end. Why?"

She didn't answer, just marched straight past him into the kitchen, grabbed some batteries at random. She could feel his eyes tracking her movements. She could also tell the exact moment the light bulb went off. He was stunned, shocked, horrified, and definitely turned on if the blaze in his eyes was anything to go by. He honestly looked like he was having trouble breathing.

Her smile suddenly went all Mona Lisa. "See you in the morning," she assured him sweetly, waved the handful of batteries at him, then disappeared down the hallway. Then she did something she hadn't done in years. She locked the bedroom door.

"Wait on that, Sellers," she smiled to herself, dropped the batteries down on the dresser, and went straight for the coldest shower of her life.

What the hell did she need batteries for? No. No way! His brain shorted out. Just went blank. Actually unable to connect even the easiest dots for a full second. She smiled at him, all slow and knowing. Then the dots slammed into each other and detonated as lightning hit the back of his head again. Her smile transformed into a provocative smirk and Stefan's imagination went off the chain. Just snapped it in half. It was stone cold shock and not control that kept him pinned to the sofa as she flounced out of the room and stomped up the stairs. Was she actually whistling?

No. She was bluffing. His Jen would never have a sex toy. Not ever. But she wasn't his Jen, was she? This was the Jen who argued with him. This Jen dared him to pin her down on the hood of her red convertible and teased him with black stockings with little bows on the ankles. She tricked him into eating pancakes. Even fed him strawberries and made him want pound cake, which was one of the worst things you could put in your body. And she had almost gone down on him like she'd been doing it for years. Fuck him! This was not his Jen. This was evil Jen from the evil alternate universe. She was killing him.

And he loved it.

CHAPTER NINE

Jared may have been sleeping on Rogan's couch in the carriage house but he still seemed to spend every single moment in the house. He and Jen had set up headquarters on the new dining room table and Stefan had been forced to actually go over the business plan with the little shit, although he refused to admit out loud that he was impressed and the hippie did actually have a brain for business.

"Tell me something," Stefan said, tossing some sketches back on the table. "You passed the bar. You have a real knack for business law, but you want to make pastry?"

Jared grinned and leaned back in his chair. "Chicks dig pastry."

"Please," Jen groaned. "Jared only sat for the bar exam so his father would loan him the money for the bakery."

Stefan just shook his head in disbelief. "Just seems like a waste."

"Nah," Jared insisted. "Grant's carrying on the family tradition. Now he's exactly what you expect from an attorney. Very serious, very boring, and you never see him coming. I would just drive him nuts if I joined the family firm."

"I thought that's what you lived for," Jen teased him.

"I'm starting to understand why Grant was so supportive of this whole bakery idea," Jared laughed. "See, you never see him coming."

Still not believing that Jared would actually take the bar exam just so he could open a bakery, Stefan finally said, "This all looks good, but I think you've underestimated how much money you really need. But I'm in."

"You're in?" Jen repeated. "I told you..."

"Jen," Stefan cut her off. "The money isn't coming from me. The loan is coming from our investment company. I emailed Nic the business plan and he thinks it's solid too. Rogan has already offered to write you a check."

"Business loan?" Jared interrupted. "That'll work."

Stefan nodded, and named a number that was larger than Jared's original estimate. "If you're going to do it, do it right."

Jared grinned. "Deal," and Jen watched in horror as the two men shook hands.

"What just happened?" she demanded. "That did not just happen."

They both looked at her, apparently surprised that she wasn't ecstatic.

"You two just cut me completely out of the equation."

"How?" Stefan asked. "This is what you wanted!"

"I asked you for my money, Stefan, not a loan," she gritted, feeling inexplicably betrayed by the two men she loved most in the world. And why were they all suddenly so buddy buddy? She liked it better when they were spitting at each other.

"That's not going to happen. You want the bakery, these are my terms."

Jen stood up, pushing her chair back. "You don't get to set the terms either. It's my money."

"I know it's your money," he shot back. "But you're not using it for this. In fact, there's no reason for you to use any of it at all. As soon as we get married, it's all going into a new trust for our kids."

She opened her mouth, then closed it again. She was so angry she couldn't even form words. But then he'd mentioned kids. Kids? Something burst inside her and went to war with the anger and Jen wasn't even sure how to feel about anything. It was the way he said *our kids*. It was so sweet it hurt.

"Jen," Jared tried to calm her down and it was exactly the wrong thing to do. She turned on him then.

"Don't," she hissed at him and left both of them gaping at her.

"You should go after her," Jared smirked.

"You're her best friend," Stefan reminded him.

Jared stood up and grabbed the empty beer bottles. "Dude, this is all you. Sorry."

He found her sitting on the edge of the guest bedroom bed. "There are tax advantages for us if we loan you the money," he said.

She nodded, not looking up at him. "It's fine."

"You also get Nic Maretti," Stefan reminded her. "He makes money in his sleep, Jen."

"It's okay, Stefan."

He sat down next to her. "It doesn't make it less yours."

She nodded again.

"So can we cease with the hostilities now?" he asked, shouldering her, trying to make her laugh. "I'm really trying here. I'm even playing nice with the hippie. Cut me some slack."

She smiled, pushing her hair behind her ears. "I feel like I got off the wrong plane."

He slid his arm carefully around her shoulders and relaxed when she leaned into him.

"C'mon," he told her, tightening his arms around her. "I DVR'd all the *Walking Dead* episodes while you were gone. You up for zombies?"

She nodded.

"Any chance of getting rid of the hippie while we watch them?"

She laughed. "Doubt it, he loves zombies too."

"Just my luck."

"Can we just watch *Shaun of the Dead*? I'm not up for a serious zombie apocalypse."

"You got it."

So Jen found herself sandwiched between Stefan and Jared with a huge bowl of popcorn they were demolishing on her lap as they both howled at the movie. The oven dinged. Jared grabbed the popcorn and announced, "Brownies are ready. You go, Jen, you don't like the next part."

Apparently, Stefan's anti-white flour and refined sugar diet did not stretch to brownies. And when he found out they were black bean brownies, he and Jared almost ate the entire batch. She watched them laughing from the kitchen as she fetched more beers - because you needed a cold beer to go with the warm brownies, according to the rock god.

Her two favorite guys. They were supposed to be sniping and arguing. Instead they looked like old friends. It was just so wrong. Stefan glanced back over the couch at her and nodded his head for her to come back. "There's a girl in the garden, you're missing it."

She couldn't help but smile back at him, then headed back to the sofa. Stefan's arm slid around her and she curled into his side as if she had been doing it for years. The side door opened and Rogan stalked in.

"You assholes, I knew I smelled brownies and you're watching *Shaun* without me?"

He already had his own beer, so he grabbed one of the last brownies and dropped down in the oversized chair. "I love this part. She's so drunk."

"I saved you some brownies," Jen said. "They're in the kitchen."

"That's my girl," Rogan grinned.

"Ah, no," Stefan said, sending Rogan's grin into orbit. "Mine."

There was something so delicious in the way he said it. She really shouldn't like it so much.

My boys, she sighed as the warmth from Stefan's body lulled her into relaxing even more against him. Her eyes fluttered shut and she was dimly aware of them laughing at the movie. Her last thought was that maybe this wasn't so bad. Stefan brushed the top of her head with his mouth, and pulled her tighter against him. No, it really wasn't bad at all.

Later, she roused just enough to find him sliding into bed next to her. He pulled her against him, tangling his legs with hers.

"Don't want to wait 'til April," she said dreamily, settling into his heat and sighing when his mouth pressed against the curve of her neck. "War is still on."

"We're waiting," he grumbled against her tingling skin, "Unless you want to show me what you needed those batteries for."

She smiled, laughing softly. "Dream on."

"You're bluffing," he insisted.

She shook her head. "Nope."

"I can't believe my sugar-sweet fairy princess would even know what one of those was."

She stretched, then settled back, not so accidentally rubbing against him so he might share the ache she wasn't sure how she could keep living with. "Not a princess," she insisted.

"Oh, really," he chuckled this time. "What color is it?"

"Pink," she sighed. "With sparkles."

He pushed his face against her shoulder and the groan that rumbled out of his chest told her that he did in fact share her pain.

Stefan sat in the boardroom the next morning, trying not to wonder if Jen really had a pink vibrator with sparkles. Sparkles? Fuck! She was bluffing. She had to be.

Damn.

His whole body tightened and he sighed, a little too loudly. The suits on either side of the table paused in their arguing to look at him. He looked back, keeping his expression slightly bored. They squirmed in their seats a little. Had he actually worried that he wouldn't be able to handle this? Hell, he'd seen frat meetings that were more difficult than this mess.

"The Russians are under control," he assured them.

There was a collective sigh of relief, until somebody grumbled about Andreas Maretti and then the board started bickering again. Stefan let them go. Maybe they would exhaust themselves. He caught Mac's conflicted expression across the table. He looked proud but also a little nauseous. Stefan knew this meant Mac no longer had any other excuses to avoid the cruise Nadine had been threatening him with.

The conversation going on around him was pointless. His mind wandered back to Jen. She'd had coffee and homemade blueberry muffins waiting for him when he came downstairs ready for work this morning. He loved blueberries, but he'd still hesitated about the muffins. He'd just grab a protein smoothie through a drive-thru because he was pretty sure she would get upset if he pulled out the blender.

"Relax," she told him, as she continued to set up a strange assortment of gadgets on the kitchen island. "I baked them with your protein powder and they have flax seed in them."

He had no choice but to try one. She smiled at his involuntary moan of pleasure. Elliot was right. She was a genius. Another bite of the muffin and Stefan decided the bakery could not open soon enough. "Is this your recipe?" he asked.

She nodded.

"Do you have any idea how hard it is to find high-protein foods that taste this good?" he asked.

She smiled. "No." He didn't quite believe her.

He dropped a kiss on her mouth, then stuffed the rest of the muffin in his. "We're going to make a fortune. Internet sales alone. You come up with a high-protein cookie we can mass market, and I know athletes who will sell parts of their soul for them."

"I can only do that in the French Quarter," she said smoothly, and Stefan couldn't help the grin that warmed his entire body.

He kissed her again, trying to keep it light and failing miserably. They were both breathing heavily when he finally stepped back, but for once, Jen recovered first.

"Have a good day at work, honey," she teased him, and for the first time in his life Stefan had almost been late.

Now, he picked up his cell phone and sent her a text.

"Gentlemen, if you'll excuse me," Mac said quietly, standing up and bringing a sudden halt to the conversation. Stefan looked up from the text he'd just sent Jen to find the entire board staring at him as Mac walked out of the room.

The heavy door snicked, and the silence in the room was deafening as Stefan faced the board alone for the first time. He'd known most of these men since he was a kid. Some of them he liked. Several were there as a necessary evil. All of them were waiting for him to say something.

So he said the first thing that came to mind. "I had Matt Hansen release a story on his news blog that STI was going ahead with expansion on the north Mississippi plant and those plans had nothing to do with rumors that a Russian company was expanding into Cuba. Alex called a few hours after it hit the internet to say he'd see us this afternoon. The deal is done."

There was a collective sigh of relief and general agreement around the table that Volikov was indeed a pain in the ass and there had really been nothing to be alarmed about. Stefan knew then that he absolutely had this. Adrenalin snapped through him, not unlike crossing a finish line after punishing your body for ten hours, but this had been easy.

Jen sat in the kitchen brushing delicate gum paste flowers with paint and gold dust. She was making lilies and doing her best not to think about anything. Just concentrate on the flowers. She loved making them. It was soothing in a way, something perfectly ordinary and normal to do. And she needed normal and ordinary right now.

She had finished the lilies and started on orchids. Her phone buzzed. She set the intricate flower down before picking up the phone. Nothing could have surprised her more.

It was from Stefan. *Show me your flowers.*

She took a picture of the tray of pear blossoms she had finished that morning then sent it to him. Just as she finished the orchid, her phone buzzed. She made herself count to twenty before she picked it up.

Are you sure you didn't cut that out of a magazine?

She smiled. He had to be incredibly busy. She almost didn't like how warm and good it made her feel that he was thinking about her. She smiled to herself and took one of the delicate lilies. She held it between her index finger and middle finger so it was next to the engagement ring that not even the gloves she wore could dim. She snapped another picture and sent it to him.

She got one back a few seconds later.

You take my breath away.

The lily dropped out of her hand, cracking one delicate petal. She squeezed her eyes tight and admitted to herself finally that she did not want to give him up. Despite everything. Even if he ultimately just wanted her trust fund, she didn't care. She didn't even care if he regretted marrying her one day.

Her phone buzzed again.

Make me that cake. The secret one Elliot wants.

K :-)

And she could make him happy. He'd even said he wanted kids. Talked about them like they were a foregone conclusion. Part of her just couldn't give in. Part of her wanted to win, to prove that she could and show him that she wasn't weak and broken. That he didn't need to protect her. That she wasn't his responsibility. She wanted him to love her because he couldn't help himself. Not because he thought it was the right thing to do.

She just had to figure out a way to push him over the edge. She didn't think the chances were very good that she could actually find a pink vibrator with sparkles in time. She still couldn't believe he fell for that. But then, he seemed to have a weakness for pink.

Jen caught her breath, then a really sly, super-wicked smile curved her mouth. "Pink," she said out loud, and she knew exactly what she was going to do. She grabbed her phone to call Lizzie. She almost felt sorry for Stefan.

Jen ran to answer the door, nervously watching the time. "Do not ask any questions," Jen warned Lizzie as she took the wardrobe bag out of Lizzie's arms.

"Can I at least come in? We need to see if it fits."

Jen pulled her inside, checked that the coast was clear, then shut the door. Stefan could be home any minute and she wasn't ready yet.

"I wonder if my brother really understands what he's getting into," Lizzie said as they rushed upstairs. "He's only ever seen your sweet and fragile side."

"Shut up," Jen hissed, but she was laughing. "I am not fragile. And trust me, he's seen my stubborn, bitchy side now."

"I steamed it," Lizzie said, as Jen pulled the floating cloud of cotton-candy pink tulle out of the bag. It was a pretty dress, but she didn't see what the big deal was. It wasn't low cut, just tightly fitted to her until it exploded in tulle just below her waist.

"I think I hate you," Lizzie said as she zipped the dress up for Jen without a single hitch.

Jen almost didn't recognize herself in the mirror. The pink did something for her skin. She always had a natural tan but the rosy shade of pink made her skin even warmer. It fit her perfectly except now it accented the soft swell of her breasts. At sixteen she probably had looked like a fairy princess, but now there was very little princess about it. The dress made her sleek and alluring. "I think it looks better on you now that you actually have boobs."

Jen swatted at her. "Shhh."

"I'm sorry, I have to ask."

"No, you don't," Jen assured her.

"He isn't going to know what hit him," Lizzie laughed.

Stefan was lost in thought when he finally pulled up in the driveway at St. Charles. He was still blown away by the pictures of the sugar flowers Jen had sent him earlier. He'd had no idea she had that kind of talent. And he was having a hard time understanding how he'd missed that. Just like he'd missed her temper. How the hell had that happened?

He'd decided when Jen was sixteen that he was going to marry her. He'd watched her walk downstairs in that fantasy of a dress and lightning had slammed into the base of his skull. He had taken one step forward, intent on breaking the boy waiting for her in half.

Jen was his. Period. No discussion. He'd taken one more step only to have Mac's hand come down hard on his shoulder. "My office," his father had warned. "Now."

Something about the tone of Mac's voice had sent Stefan to his office where he waited, pacing in front of the fireplace, and trying to stuff his inner Neanderthal back in its cave. He'd stopped when the door closed behind Mac, who looked more amused than angry.

"What do you know about that kid?" Stefan had demanded.

"Senator Waits's son?" Mac had asked, "Good kid. He'll have her home by midnight, don't worry. I threatened to remove his spleen if he didn't."

"Good," Stefan had barked, but he hadn't been satisfied.

"Your sister's date too, in case you were concerned."

"Of course," Stefan had insisted although he couldn't even remember what her date looked like.

Mac had crossed the room and rounded his huge executive desk. "So you finally woke up?"

That had stopped Stefan in his tracks. Mac had pulled a folder out and tossed it across the desk. "That's the documentation and account numbers for her trust fund. You double that value, then we'll talk. And you don't touch her until she's twenty-one, you understand me?"

"Twenty-one?" Stefan had sputtered, grabbing the folder off the desk.

"Twenty-one," Mac had repeated firmly. "You can take her out when she's eighteen, but until then, son, she is off limits."

"You think that I..."

"Off limits. End of that discussion."

"She's mine," Stefan had informed him.

"That may be," Mac had said slowly, "But not yet. And only if she wants to be."

Not once had it ever occurred to Stefan over the years that she might not want the same thing. When he'd found her sitting on the back porch swing after the prom that night, he had not been able to walk away from her. He'd startled her when he sat down next to her.

"Have fun?" he'd asked, trying not to sound like he'd been eating glass. He hadn't even paid attention to how many miles he clocked that night running on the treadmill. He didn't even like running on a treadmill. But he hadn't trusted himself to run anywhere else, knowing that he would run straight to the prom and drag her out of the dance, despite all of Mac's warnings.

She'd shrugged and smiled shyly. "I guess. It was hot and they played bad eighties music."

"Did he kiss you goodnight?"

Surprised brown eyes had snapped up to him and she'd blushed. "Yes," and the word came out a little breathlessly.

He'd slid the back of his knuckles along her cheek. Her eyelids had dropped and her lips had parted slightly. It had taken every ounce of self-control he had not to kiss her right then and there. She'd been so lovely in that pink dress swaying gently on that swing in the moonlight. Like a princess, he'd thought, a sweet fairy princess. He'd been sure she would dissolve if he really tried to touch her.

"I don't want you kissing other boys," he'd said gently, tempering back the steel running through his voice. Unable to resist any longer, he'd reached out and ran his thumb lightly across the fullness of her bottom lip.

Her mouth had curved in surprise, then slid into something a tiny bit wicked. "I won't kiss any of them, if you'll kiss me now."

He'd felt the oxygen whoosh right out of his lungs as her words knocked him completely off guard. He didn't even remember leaning forward. He just knew that his mouth brushed against hers and that there must have been some sane part of him still functioning because he'd kept it light and sweet. A fairytale of a kiss. A kiss he had never recovered from. A kiss that had ruined him for kisses ever since. He had never imagined that sunshine tasted so sweet.

When he'd lifted his head, her eyes had been closed and her lips slightly parted in protest. "No more boys, Jen. Got it?"

"Got it," she'd whispered back but hadn't opened her eyes. "Stefan," she'd breathed out his name when he'd stood up to leave. She'd opened those liquid brown eyes and stared up at him. She was so beautiful it made him ache. But the instinct to protect was thankfully stronger that night than the instinct to take what was his, and he'd managed something similar to a smile.

"Hmm?"

And then she'd broken him. "Am I dreaming?"

He'd leaned down and kissed her one more time, knowing that it was going to be a long two years without tasting her again. He whispered against her ear. "Yes. Keep it a secret and I'll make it come true."

She'd smiled, nodded and leaned back in the swing.

Now as he started to pull into the garage, a flash of familiar pink sparked the corner of his vision. He frowned. Was Jen sitting on the hood of her new car? On the hood? He was out of his SUV and rounded the front before his brain actually comprehended what the pink was.

His lungs seized as he stopped short and his mind went blank. All he could see was pink. Her wicked smile turned positively evil. "Hey, Stefan," she said slowly, leaning back on her arms, pink tulle rustling in the quiet garage. "Wanna dance?"

She was floating on the hood of the red convertible in an unmistakable cloud of pink tulle. He had no idea what it was about that dress that sent all the blood in his system south. It wasn't low cut. It was just a simple strapless dress All Stefan knew at the exact moment was that she had not looked that good in that dress six years ago.

She leaned forward again and he realized she was painting her toenails. That did all kinds of cruel and crazy things to him. His eyes followed her movements and his nostrils flared. Her nail polish matched the car, not the dress. Still leaned over, her foot flat against the hood, she turned her face to him. Had his heart actually just stopped? No, there it was, trying to beat out of his chest. She sat up straight and started twisting the cap closed on the bottle of red polish. "Here," she said, lifting one bare foot at him. "Blow."

Once again a bright pink lightning bolt slammed into the back of his skull, but this time he didn't even notice. Watching her lift one graceful foot towards him, extend delicate, red-tipped toes, and demand he blow on them shocked him worse than an entire lightning storm could. That dark and hungry, primitive part of him he'd glimpsed the other night roared to life so quickly there was no way to even begin to control it. Running around the world, twice, would not be enough.

His entire world fundamentally changed in that instant and for once, he was calling her bluff. The rest of the world could go to hell. He was done waiting. He was done being the nice guy. He was done doing the right thing. She won. And Stefan had never been so happy to lose in his life.

Jen really hadn't gotten any further in her plans than the "Wanna dance?" line, and she was pretty proud of coming up with that. She had no idea what had possessed her to ask him to blow on her toenails. She smiled and let her eyes drift up and down, taking in the hard-muscled length of him as he moved forward. She was in so much trouble. She could hardly wait.

He took four steps towards her, his blue eyes going almost gray. Jen understood what a mouse felt like backed up in the corner of a pet snake's aquarium. *He is going to devour me and I'm going to let him, because it's pretty damn useless to try and stop him.*

He did stop though, visibly struggling for a moment. She was afraid he was going to change his mind and was desperately trying to think of something else clever to say, when he spoke in a low, silky smooth voice with a dangerous edge that she'd never heard before. "I had it all planned."

Her skin started to sizzle as the words floated to her, smoky and seductive, weaving around her and holding her in place as he continued towards her.

"Music, champagne. I was going to spend hours seducing you. Kissing you, tasting you, making sure you were ready. Everything was going to be perfect."

He caught her ankle and pulled her to the edge of the hood. She looked up at him, unable to breathe. Who needed air anyway? She had everything she needed right here.

He slowly ran one warm finger across her jaw, tracing a line of heat across the delicate curve. His finger stopped at her bottom lip. "I was going to be gentle, and sweet, and make it the best night of your life. The perfect wedding night."

She was mesmerized. His voice turned her insides to lava. She couldn't feel her legs.

"Like Prince Charming?" she asked, her voice was so husky she wasn't sure he even heard her. But his finger tapped against her lips to stop her so he must have understood. Then he pressed it along her bottom lip, his eyes so focused on the movement that Jen's heart actually started to slow down and her bones started to soften. The tip of her tongue flicked out to taste the edge of his finger.

"I wanted to wait," he said, the mist getting deeper around them, the rest of the world rolling away. "Just like Prince Charming," he finally admitted. The finger was now tracing down her neck to the edge of the strapless gown.

"Stefan," she whispered, his blue eyes flicking back up to her face. Yep, absolutely everything she'd ever wanted.

"Hmm?" His fingers continued to trace along the edges of the bodice.

She arched instinctively towards him. Every single part of her ached for him. "I'll let you in on a little secret." She breathed the words out, so conscious of his hands moving over her it was hard to speak. "I don't want Prince Charming."

He caught her hands in his, leaned forward, and pressed her back against the hood. He pinned both her wrists with one hand. She caught her breath. He was really going to do this.

"I'm not charming," he assured her, his hand tightening on her wrists as he held her in place. He lowered his mouth to hers, but he didn't touch her lips. She could feel the heat from his mouth. His head tilted slightly, bringing their lips even closer without touching. She could already taste him. "Tell me what you want," he said, his lips barely brushing hers. "I need to hear you say it."

"I want you," she whispered, the words sliding like feathers across her lips, "to lose."

"You got it," he groaned against her mouth.

There was just no way Jen could've been prepared for him. She'd underestimated how much he had been holding back from her. She'd failed to factor in that Stefan was an endurance athlete. He could run for hours without breaking a sweat. He'd been in this for the long haul. While she loved being able to trip up his plans and really wanted to win their silly little war, in no way had she been ready for her prize.

She lost track of how long they were in the garage. All she knew was his mouth on hers, his hands on her. He let her arms down to curl around his neck. The kiss went deeper, and deeper until she was sure they'd never find their way back. She was vaguely aware of him guiding her legs around his waist so he could lift her up and walk them both inside. Her arms tightened around him. She was never letting him go.

He breathed against her, not really lifting his mouth away from hers as he spoke. "Our first time will not be on the hood of a car."

"Second time?" she asked hopefully, and smiled when he laughed, burying his face against her throat.

Somehow his mouth never left hers unless it was to trail across her face and down her neck. And she knew beyond a shadow of a doubt that he wasn't stopping. Not this time. Then he was tumbling her back on his bed, still kissing her. His hand slid under the dress, stroking her leg. Warm fingers smoothed up the inside of her thighs. He went very still and dragged in a harsh ragged breath when his hands continued to meet bare skin.

"Just full of surprises, aren't you?" he was hoarse but he was laughing too. She smiled up at him, she couldn't help it.

He slid his warm hand along the gentle curves under the dress. He pushed the skirt slowly up her legs. "Do you want to know what I wanted to do, when you first wore this dress?" he asked, his voice rasping against her silky skin.

"You mentioned licking."

His teeth grazed against her and she shivered.

"The first thing I wanted to do was get it off you," he explained, sliding the zip down. The tulle whispered as it landed on the floor across the room.

And then there was nothing else between them, and she was sure he wasn't going to stop now. Her eyes flew open in surprise as his fingers moved over her. He caught her protests with a kiss when his hand worked harder against her and there was a slightest sting and burn, then he pushed warm, long fingers inside her. All the air left her lungs and her body bowed tight at the delicious invasion.

"Shhh," he soothed her, keeping the seductive kiss going as he spun her body out of her control, and that deep ache she had been living with for so long started to coil into something tighter and tighter.

She whimpered, trying to move her hips. He grazed his teeth across her shoulder. "I know, baby," he groaned against her ears, her fingers bit into his shoulders. He wasn't quite steady either. "You are so tight," he told her softly, and liquid fire streamed through her. "You'll never take me like this." Then his fingers turned ruthless and he stretched her until she cried out again.

Then there wasn't any part of her he did not caress, stroke, or kiss. She lost time. She lost her sense of place. She lost herself. She had absolutely no clue where she was in the universe. Nothing else existed but his hands, his mouth, and his voice. The husky words slid all over her skin in hot waves. She fell back into reality when his mouth closed against her belly button and his tongue swept across her, teasing her.

"Stefan," she whispered, trying to sit up. His mouth was still working down to her hips, and he was pushing her legs apart again. Jen went hot then cold then something else entirely. "No," she choked out. "Oh, don't, Stefan, no." She wasn't ready for this. He was laughing at her again as she sat straight up. That delighted, hoarse laughter sent shivers all over her skin that were so delicious she couldn't see.

"You shouldn't have put on that dress."

"Don't do this," her voice was trembling. It was all starting to be too intense, but she knew there was nothing she could do to stop it.

He grinned at her, coming up and pushing her back down on the bed. He kissed her lightly on the mouth, his hand smoothing her, calming her down. She was so relieved she almost started to cry. Her eyes fluttered shut and he pressed gentle kisses to her eyes. "Now," he said in the softest, gentlest, most seductive voice she'd ever heard, as his hand trailed past her stomach to stop at her hip. "Keep your eyes closed."

His fingers clamped onto her hip and his hot, raging mouth was on her before what he had said to her even sunk in. He held her still while he drove her ruthlessly over the edge. Jen flew so fast and so hard that she didn't even have time to react. She burst into tears as he spun her up then sent her flying and the tight coils that had been aching inside her for so long finally broke free into wave after wave of shimmering light. Then, he did it to her again.

She couldn't stop shaking as he pulled her against him, soothing her with his hands. She closed her eyes and pressed deeper into his arms, her face against his throat.

"I did warn you," he reminded her, very pleased with himself.

She nodded against him, wondering if her skin would ever feel the same, if her bones would ever be hard again. Then he was pressing her back against the pillow. She couldn't open her eyes yet, but she parted her lips when his mouth touched hers for a deep kiss that was more soothing than anything else.

"You okay?" he asked. She shook her head. Okay was not even in her vocabulary anymore. He kissed her again, then trailed his mouth down her jaw, neck, and across her shoulder.

His thumb scraped across the tight pink tip of her left breast and she almost arched off the bed. He traced lazy circles then lowered his mouth to kiss the circles he had traced and started building a new fire inside of her. Then he was kissing her again, and moving over her, putting his knee between her still shaking legs.

"I don't think I'll ever forgive you for this," he rasped against her ear.

She understood what he meant. She'd ruined the romantic seduction scene he had been planning. But she wasn't the least bit sorry she'd hijacked his plans. Her fingers bit into his shoulders as she felt him ease against her. She could feel every muscle in his powerful body brace not to move yet. "Breathe," he told her, rasping the word against her ear, and she realized she had been holding her breath. Still he held on. "Relax," he soothed, his tongue tracing the shape of her ear. She did exactly as she was told, although it was difficult considering how talented his tongue was. She took another breath.

"You can still say no."

"No, I can't," the words rushed out of her.

He moved against her and then went still again. "Okay?" The soft word rumbled out, and she nodded.

Finally, she opened her eyes. He was poised right over her, watching her with intense blue eyes. He looked shattered and not at all like he was going to enjoy this. It broke her heart, but Jen discovered he wasn't the only one who could be ruthless about what they wanted. She would die if he stopped now. Cease to exist. She wasn't about to let that happen.

"Stefan," she said, clearly, surprised at how calm her voice was. "I'm not going to break."

He lowered his head and pressed his forehead to hers. "But I might," he admitted, his voice catching.

She framed that beautiful, tortured face with her hands. She lifted his head with her hands so she could see his eyes. And then she told him frankly, "I won't forgive you if you stop. Please."

"Funny that you think I could stop now," he teased, his voice breathless as he positioned himself, rubbing the swollen head of his erection against her. "Jen..."

Whatever else he'd started to say was lost as he rocked against her, taking her as slowly as he could. She tried to bite back her cry of distress, not from the pain of his possession because there wasn't any. But it was suddenly all overwhelming. Maybe she'd made a huge mistake. He'd been right after all. He was always right. What had she been thinking? They should have waited.

"Open your eyes," he said, cutting through her panic. "Jen, look at me."

She did, losing herself in the blue heat. Everything was so quiet. It was just the two of them. Nothing else existed anymore. He smiled gently, and she felt the broken parts of her heart start to knit back together. This was really happening.

"Relax," he said, "It's me, baby, just relax. You can do this."

She nodded. She'd wanted this for so long, she couldn't quit now. So she lifted one leg and wrapped it around his hip. She smiled as he groaned, as his whole body tensed.

"You feel amazing, Jen," he told her, struggling to go slowly. "That's it, let me in."

His hand slid under her hips as he angled her better and finally, finally, she had what she had waited so long for. It was so much more than she ever imagined it would be. He had stopped again and was holding still, trying to let her adjust to him. But she knew she would never adjust to having him deep inside her like this. She would never get used to this. And she didn't want to. "I'm okay," she whispered against his trembling shoulders. "Show me what you can do?" she teased, not sure how she even found the words. "You made me wait for you. Make it worth it."

Laughter crashed out of him and she was pretty sure, nothing would ever top this moment. Then he moved, and it got better. He pulled back and Jen went a little insane. He took it so slow, proving that he was slightly inhuman. But she wasn't complaining, because nothing compared to this. Nothing came even close. He moved inside of her, becoming part of her and she could hardly comprehend how right it felt. Up until this point in her life, she'd just been dreaming. Now, connected to him like this, she was awake for the first time.

Eventually, it became too much for him, and the slow, deliberate rocking inside her got more desperate. She moved her hips instinctively, taking him deeper and he lost himself. She laughed out loud when she realized his control was gone, and he moved harder and harder until she was sure she would split in two. He was so strong, but she was almost afraid he was about to break apart. She wrapped her arms around his shoulders and held him tight as a raw cry came ripping out of him. It was the most amazing thing she had ever heard.

Until that moment, she hadn't known quite how much she loved him. Hadn't realized how deeply and how dangerously she loved him. That she loved him completely and without any limits. That he was really the only other person in the world. And that if she ever lost him, she would not survive it and there would be nothing to survive for.

When he finally collapsed against her, rolling to his side automatically to keep his weight off her, Jen could only stare straight ahead. She wasn't completely back in her body yet. She wasn't sure she would even fit inside her body again. Then he pulled her up against him, throwing his leg over her, trying to pull her as close into his body as he had just been in hers. "You beautiful, crazy fool." His words were choked and she realized he was just as overwhelmed as she was.

"Okay?" she asked softly.

"No, I'm really not," he admitted. "Does it still hurt?"

She shook her head. "It wasn't that bad." And really it hadn't been. The whole thing had been so much more than she had expected, she still wasn't sure what she thought, other than she wanted to do it again. Soon.

His arms tightened. "Liar," he said, squeezing her again then moving away from her. She had expected him to be tired, to even fall asleep. But he was practically simmering with energy. It sparked off him, jumping across to her skin, making it sizzle.

"Stay here," he told her pulling the blankets over her.

As if she could move. She snuggled into the pillow, smiling at the pink dress lying on the floor. She was never getting rid of that dress.

Water started running, then he was back. He lifted her up and carried her into the bathroom where he'd filled the whirlpool tub. The water was almost too hot, and she yelped but he sat down taking her with him. He positioned her between his legs then started slowly massaging her neck and shoulders until she really couldn't move.

"Are you very mad at me?" she asked dreamily, and was rewarded with a warm, gentle kiss against the back of her neck.

"Yes," he told her, in a rough voice that did not match the kiss. "I hurt you." He trailed open mouthed kisses along the shoulder he had just been rubbing.

"Just for a second," she assured him, reaching back to stroke his jaw.

The kisses stopped and he pulled her even closer, "It was longer than a second." She was surrounded by him. It should have been overwhelming. It wasn't. It was perfect. "It will be better next time," he promised.

"Was it not good?" she asked, softly, deliberately misunderstanding him. If it got any better, she was sure she would just evaporate.

"I meant better for you," he laughed softly.

She shrugged, leaning back against him. "I don't see how."

He really laughed at that.

"You haven't declared victory yet," he reminded her.

Her hands were slowly moving up and down his forearms until he moved one hand to flatten against her stomach. He lifted her up and tipped her back so her head was resting on his shoulder. He covered her mouth in a long, lingering kiss.

She tried to turn around and his arms tightened. She moved again, and he hissed, and then she understood where she was sitting. "Sorry," she lied, and let the water lift her up so she could turn in his arms. He let go of her and rested his arms back along the edge of the bathtub. She found the bottle of lime-scented bath soap and squeezed some out in her hand.

"I'm still waiting," he reminded her.

"I'm thinking," she said, using a sponge to lather up the soap into suds. Then dropped the sponge so she could use her hand to rub the soap onto his shoulders, then down the defined pectoral muscles. His head fell back as she worked her way around then down to his stomach, dipping below the water. He caught her wrist and stopped her.

"Oh, no, you don't," he warned her, laughter dancing in his eyes. "You don't get to do that until you put a ring on my finger."

The smile that curved her lips up made him catch his breath. "I'm just waiting for you to ask me properly."

"You're waiting for me to beg," he told her, bringing her hand back up to rub his chest and shoulders.

"Would you beg?" she teased.

"Absolutely," he admitted, his voice light, but the warning edge was back.

She stopped her hand and looked up at him seriously. "Did you want me to put the dress back on?"

Feeling him zip up the dress was almost as erotic as when he had unzipped it earlier. She felt drugged. Her bones had melted into a shimmering liquid that sizzled. She watched fascinated as he lay down against the pillows. He was watching her so closely, gauging her reactions. He was still reining himself in. He tugged her forward and she understood what he wanted. Warm hands curved around her waist and lifted her up. Her dress spread all around him as she straddled him. "I can't," she whispered, suddenly nervous and shy.

"Yes, you can." He lifted her up and her whole body arched back when he connected them again in one swift, scorching move. She was still sore from earlier but it felt so good to have him back inside of her that she didn't care. She loved this. Absolutely adored it. He kept his hands on her hips, helping her find the way that worked best when she moved. Then his hands reached behind her then the zipper gave way. The bodice slipped and she had no choice but to let it go, baring her breasts to hot, hungry blue eyes. He thrust up against her, and she would have fallen back if his hands hadn't held her.

"Is this what you wanted?" she asked.

He groaned, his face almost pained. He couldn't speak, she realized, stretching and wondering how anything could possible feel this good. She loved having him inside of her, and she was starting to like being in control of their movements. And she could watch him. His eyes were closed and she was fascinated by the play of emotions across his face. He was so breathtakingly beautiful. Transfixed, she ignored what was raging inside her. Her body was going wild with pleasure but it was secondary to what she was seeing on his face. She'd seen this look before. She knew it so well. She just never dreamed she would see it like this. She moved again and he eased even deeper inside her. His lips parted on a sigh. Tears pricked her eyes. This was how he looked when he ran. Joy. Pure, breathless, singing joy. She'd never seen it any other time. She was absolutely shattered to see it now.

She couldn't breathe, but she didn't really need air for this. She found a new rhythm that hit different places and made it impossible to see. Her tears turned hot and she couldn't blink them back any longer. She'd been so stupid. So ridiculously stupid and blind and selfish. She bit her lips together, sucking back tears. If being with her made him feel like this, it would be more than enough. More than most had. And it hit her so hard, she stopped, arching over him, one primitive word screaming through her. *Mine.*

And, as usual, he read her mind. His eyes opened and he sat up without warning, stilling their movements but not breaking contact. He caught her face in his hands, "Jen," he gasped, bringing her back down. She opened her eyes and kissed him before he could kiss her. She didn't even realize she was crying. Her hands caught the back of his head, and held him to her.

He wrenched away from her, looking at her in shock. She knew she looked wild. She could feel the heat in her eyes. "No more fragile, broken princess," she pleaded, not recognizing her own voice, not even sure if he would know what she meant.

But he did and he grinned at her, "You got it," he said, almost laughing as he pulled the dress off her and threw it across the room.

And then they went places she had never even considered.

"Oh," she breathed. "Now you're just showing off."

He shuddered with laughter and kissed her. He held her tight as he drove them past madness. She blew apart in his arms, every atom in her body splitting and going in a different direction faster than light. Then she was light, but she held on until he joined her a moment later.

CHAPTER TEN

J en floated for a long time, somewhere between sleep and the space they had created. Stefan had his arms around her. His fingers trailed tiny sparks up and down her spine. "Curiouser and curiouser," he whispered, absently, pressing kisses to her neck.

The words pricked through the mist at her. At first they were sweet and she sighed. *Curiouser and curiouser.* They played through the daze she was drifting in. There was a tiny lick of something in her belly that made her press even closer into Stefan's arms. *Don't go chasing rabbits.*

Why always rabbits? Then they turned darker as they filtered into her mind, swirling around, digging up shadows, chasing shadows away she hadn't even known were there. Shadows she didn't want to lose. Sometimes the shadows were trying to keep her safe.

She went very, very still and raised her head. "Stop talking backwards," she told him, irritated.

"Jen," he said, trying to keep his voice gentle. It was not the same voice she had been hearing. "You were dreaming. Come back to sleep."

"What did you say?" she asked, a little more desperately. "I heard you say something."

"I didn't say anything," he told her, leaning to kiss her. "You were dreaming."

But she pushed back from him. "No, you said—" The words escaped her. Something about telescopes, or maybe feet. She tilted her head, not seeing him anymore. "Stop talking backwards," she whispered.

"Jen," he said, starting to sound concerned. "You aren't making sense." He caught her face in his hands again. "Don't." he said softly, trying to kiss her again and she knew he was trying to distract her.

It was right there. She could almost see it. There was something just there out of reach. It flickered just out of the corner of her eye. She knew Stefan knew what it was. She also knew he wouldn't tell her. He hadn't told her everything. Her head started to throb. She could hear him. She really could. But the words were backwards. She sat on the edge of the bed, staring down at the floor and her feet. They seemed very far away. "Who pulled me out of the car?" she asked, her voice very low and controlled. "And say it right this time."

She wouldn't let him touch her. She batted his arms away and heard him curse under his breath. He got out of bed and knelt down in front of her.

"Jen," he bit out her name, his voice really harsh but she knew he was trying to snap her out of it. She didn't want to snap out. She had finally found the rabbit hole in her head. She needed to find out where it went. And then just like that...

"Robert," she said finally, the name coming out of her gut, up her throat, and across her lips like a razor blade, stripping everything inside her. "Robert," she repeated, "Robert pulled me out of the car."

Stefan nodded, watching her closely.

"If you lie to me now," she told him in a low warning tone, "If you lie to me now."

He sat down next to her on the bed and closed his arm around her. "Robert pulled you out of the car and went back for your mother. The car exploded."

Everything went white hot as she remembered screaming for her brother.

And it all came flooding back. Stefan had been right. It was better not to remember.

"Hold on," he'd said, laying her on a patch of cool grass, and she was grabbing his hand, begging him not to leave her. "Be right back." He'd been trying to keep her calm. He'd pressed a kiss to her forehead. By the time she'd been able to push up, he had reached the passenger door and was trying to wrench it open. The fireball blew up into the sky, throwing him up and back across the pavement, burning him beyond recognition.

Stefan caught her as she tried to stand up. She was going to be sick. He got her into the bathroom just in time. When she finished, he turned the shower on and dragged her in with him until the water banished all the smoke and flames from her mind.

"He didn't die," she kept repeating, because the horror of it was too much to accept. Even ten years later, her brain didn't want to deal with it. But she was tired of shadows, and she pushed them back. "How long did he live afterwards? Don't lie to me. Say the words right."

He sank down to the floor of the tile shower and took her with him. "Seventeen hours." The words ripped out of him. "Jen, let it go, please."

She buried her face in his throat and cried. "It should have killed him."

"Yes," Stefan rasped out. "But it didn't. Not right away."

"Why didn't anyone tell me?"

He lifted her face up and held it between his hands. "How could we tell you something like that? You didn't speak for a year, Jen. And when you did, you didn't ask about him. You never mentioned him. Anytime his name came up you would just fade away. We didn't want to lose you, so we didn't talk about him either."

She nodded but tried to push away from him. He didn't want to let her go because he knew what was coming next. Robert had been a year older than Stefan and Rogan. They had all worshiped him. Stefan especially. Anything Robert did, Stefan did. If Robert jumped off a cliff, Stefan was right behind him. Except with the way things usually went down, Robert would tell Stefan to jump first. And there was nothing Stefan would not do for Robert.

"Tell me the rest of it," she said.

"He had called 911 when he got you out of the car so the paramedics were already on the way. They found you curled up next to him on the side of the road. He was talking to you, telling you everything would be okay, that your parents were in heaven. You didn't need to be afraid. The paramedics told Mom and Dad all this. No one knows how he could even speak." Stefan's voice broke.

"I remember Mac telling me all that. When he picked me up from school that day. Why do I remember being at school?"

"I think it's just your way of protecting yourself. You had a serious injury, Jen. It's a miracle you survived at all."

Stefan watched her wrap a towel around herself. How had everything gone from beautiful to destructive so quickly? She was so pale. Her eyes bruised with shadows. His stomach twisted when he saw her fingers trembling as she tried to tuck in the edge of the towel she'd wrapped around herself.

Then she turned to him, her brown eyes so vulnerable he almost couldn't breathe. "You promised him you would take care of me, didn't you?"

The accusation broke something in him. It set something loose that he was completely unprepared for. "You think I'm with you out of some misguided sense of duty. I get that. But do you really think what went on in that bedroom earlier had anything to do with promises I made to my best friend while he was dying?"

Each word ramped up his anger another notch. His fingers clenched into a tight fist when she took a step back.

"That's why you want to marry me," she said, taking another step back from him, dragging the anger farther up his throat as she moved back."

"Jen," he rasped out, wishing it didn't feel like the ceiling was about to crush him.

"No, don't. I'm trying to understand."

"Understand?" The word ripped out of him. "You're trying to understand? Why don't you try to make me understand why you don't want to be my wife but you have no problem provoking me into fucking you blind." He would have cut off his arms before he'd ever hurt Jen, but he just couldn't help what was climbing to the surface in him. He had held it back for so long. Pushed it down so deep and run and run and run until he couldn't feel a trace of it. But what had happened between them earlier had stripped him bare and he just didn't have the resources to keep the fury in check any longer. So he didn't. He did the only thing he could do. He ran.

Jen flinched as he shoved the metal vanity stool out of his way and slammed out of the bathroom. A few heartbeats later she heard the front door slam. She sat down on the edge of the whirlpool tub and just tried to breathe for a moment. She'd been so selfish, so totally oblivious to things that had been right in front of her all along.

But the bottom line was she did want to be his wife. She wanted to live in this house and have his children and build a life for them. He wanted that too. Did it really matter if they wanted the same thing but for different reasons? Could she live with that? She took a deep steadying breath. She wasn't sure if she could live with it, but she was certain that she couldn't live without it.

So, she forced herself to her feet, took another deep breath. She knew exactly what to do. She got dressed, called Lizzie, then got started on building that life.

It took Lizzie about ten minutes to reach the house. She got out of the car and stopped dead in her tracks on the front steps. Stefan was sitting on the front porch, with his back to the door. He was wearing cutoff shorts and nothing else. The heel of one hand pressed against his forehead and the other hand was shaking as it lifted a cigarette to the white line of his mouth.

A cigarette? Stefan? Lizzie closed her eyes then slowly opened them again. He blew smoke out then spotted her staring at him. He dropped his chin, resting his forehead against his hand. She almost demanded to know what he had done with her brother, but there was something so lost about him she just couldn't bring herself to give him a hard time.

"What did you do?" she asked slowly, coming quickly up the rest of the steps and crossing the porch to him.

"Fucked up. Biblical proportions."

She grabbed the cigarette out of his hands. Surprised to find that it was real. In what universe did Stefan smoke cigarettes?

"I am pretty sure you smoking is a sign of the apocalypse."

"What're you doing here?"

"Jen called me. I guess the prom dress seduction didn't go well."

He laughed bitterly. "No, it was great. The after-party went to hell."

Lizzie reached for the doorknob.

"She's not leaving."

"Stefan, you can't keep her here against her will."

"Oh, yes I can. She isn't stepping out of that house."

"Have you lost your mind?" Lizzie asked, her heart breaking. She had never seen her brother like this. His eyes were desperate and he looked like he didn't know what to do. Stefan always, always knew what to do. It was a constant law of the universe. Lizzie had done the math.

"You have to back me up on this, Lizzie."

"Let me go inside. I'll talk to her," Lizzie said, then slipped into the house.

"She isn't leaving this house!" he yelled after her.

She found Jen sitting at the coffee table, busily typing on a laptop.

"Jen," she said tentatively.

Jen looked up, and gave her an apologetic smile then turned back to the laptop.

"What have you done to my brother?" Lizzie asked, trying to lighten the mood.

Jen shrugged. "Is he still here? I thought he'd be running."

"Uh, no. He's sitting outside, guarding the door, and smoking a cigarette, or he was." Lizzie waved the butt in the air before running it under the tap in the kitchen and tossing it away.

"Seriously?" Jen almost smiled. "A cigarette?"

Jen seemed okay. She looked odd, but her voice was steady. She didn't seem to be drifting in and out like she normally did when she was under a lot of stress. "You do realize how bad it is, if Mr. Health Nut is smoking?"

"The apocalypse, I know." Jen nodded. "We had a small one earlier. I remembered Robert pulling me out of the car, and Stefan finally told me what happened." She looked back to the laptop.

"Oh, honey," Lizzie said, dropping down next to her. "I'm so sorry."

Jen clicked the button that sent a print job to a printer in Stefan's office. "I've been so selfish, Lizzie. So completely selfish. How is it possible I forgot Robert saved my life?"

"You didn't forget it, Jen. You just don't think about it."

"But that's even worse," Jen said. "How could I just stop thinking about Robert? Pretend he didn't exist."

"You're very good at not thinking about things that upset you."

"Like I said," Jen took a deep breath. "Selfish."

"Not selfish, self preservation. It's a blessing you can't remember all of it."

Jen nodded and took a deep breath. "I'm really not going to fall apart."

"I believe you," Lizzie smiled. "Tell me what happened."

"That's what I am really confused about," Jen admitted. "After the thing you and I are not going to talk about, which was amazing by the way, we fell asleep. I thought I heard him say curiouser and curiouser and it was the tone of his voice. Now I'm not sure he even said it. It's weird. I can't explain it."

"I think I can," Lizzie sighed. "But can I let him come in. He really looks pitiful."

"Not yet," Jen said. "That's from *Alice in Wonderland*, isn't it? That was your favorite story when we were little."

"You were stuck in the rabbit hole." Lizzie said, her voice breaking slightly. "I thought you were going to die, so I refused to leave your hospital room. Threw a huge tantrum until Stefan finally agreed to read you Alice in Wonderland. You finally opened your eyes a few days later."

Jen didn't know what to say. She could see it in her mind. Lizzie curled up next to her. Stefan in a chair reading. But she couldn't remember it. What else had she lost? "He misses Robert," Jen whispered, her throat threatening to close up again.

Lizzie nodded. "It was very hard for him."

"He stopped running track and started running longer distances after Robert died, didn't he?" Jen asked, puzzle pieces starting to float into place. Pieces she hadn't even known were missing.

"Because he couldn't sleep. His senior year, he would run at night, would be gone for hours, just running. Then he'd come in, go to school, come home and crash in the afternoons on the sofa. He couldn't sleep after dark. I think he started the triathlons because they pushed him so hard he could spend ten hours in a row not thinking about what happened."

Jen choked, pushing tears back. She had lost her entire family in that accident. Stefan had lost his best friend—for all intents and purposes, *his* older brother too. "This is unbearable," she whispered, her voice hoarse. "I can't believe what I've done to him."

Lizzie tried to reassure her. "None of this is your fault."

"But, when I didn't talk about Robert, all of you stopped talking about Robert, Stefan had no other way to deal with it, did he?"

"What? You think my brother was going to have grief therapy sessions?" Lizzie teased, trying to lighten the mood. "Stefan Sellers talking about his feelings. I can't even imagine."

"No," Jen said. "Of course not, but at least—"

"Jen, I think it was easier on everyone to just let it go. I know my parents and Stefan think you may break apart at any minute, but you and I know better. You are one of the strongest people I know. What happened should have destroyed you, honey. And look where you are. You have a life, you have friends, you're starting a business, you have a really annoying business partner, and you have the most eligible bachelor in Louisiana sitting on your front porch falling apart over you. He was smoking a cigarette, Jen. A freaking cigarette."

Jen laughed. "You should have taken a picture."

"I was too shocked to even think that way," Lizzie laughed. "Can I please let him in? He thinks you are going to leave him. He might start boarding us up inside any minute now."

"Stefan promised Robert he would look after me," Jen said, softly. "I think I've always known that, so when Madlyn cornered me at Rogan's birthday party—"

"I knew it. Whatever she said to you, Jen, you know how the Red Queen lies."

Jen took a deep breath and smiled sadly at her best friend. "But that's the best part. She didn't have to lie, Lizzie. Everything she said was absolutely true."

"What did she say?"

"That he didn't love me and would one day regret marrying me."

"She was wrong, Jen, and I can prove it. Step outside your front door and see what you think."

Jen smiled sadly, and got up to collect the papers from the printer. "He loves me, Lizzie. But we both know he's not in love with me. But, I've decided I'm keeping him anyway. Madlyn can't have him. If that makes me selfish and childish, I really don't give a damn. He's mine, Lizzie, and Madlyn can go to hell."

Lizzie laughed. "So why am I here?"

"To drive us to the airport."

"The airport?" Lizzie echoed, completely confused. "Where are you going?"

"Not me. We." Jen said, "All of us. Let me go take care of this first, and I'll explain on the way."

With all the shocks she'd had over the last few days, when she had time to process it later, she was pretty sure seeing him with a cigarette was in the top three. Lizzie had gotten one away from him but apparently he had a stash. He looked up when she walked out. She almost lost her nerve. But the look on his face kept her from stopping. And he had that suffering young Marlon Brando thing going on, all barefoot and shirtless on the front porch in New Orleans, smoking a cigarette while the street cars clattered up and down St. Charles. No way she could ever walk away from that.

Jen took a deep breath. There was no turning back now. Not that she wanted to. She was finally ready.

"Hey," she said, kneeling down in front of him.

"Hey," he said, blowing smoke away from her face. She shivered, thinking she might let him take just one more drag before she took it away from him.

"You have any idea how hot you look sitting out here smoking?" she asked, "I swear if you yell 'Stella', even the nuns will come running."

He just looked away from her, apparently too tired to even make a comeback.

"You can take one more drag and then you are putting it out." She smiled, but she was so nervous it didn't have the usual effect on him. He looked spent, exhausted, and lost. She'd never seen him so pale. He put it out without taking a drag, watching her warily.

"You are not leaving." he said, sounding more like a growl than a statement.

She held his gaze until he looked away first. Something that had never happened before. "I won't let you leave," he said again, softer this time.

She reached out and put her palm against his face. "I have new terms I want to discuss with you," she said, hoping that would stir him up. His breath hitched, and a moment later he nodded his head, clearly not wanting to hear what she had to say. "Are you ready?" she asked.

"I can't wait," he said, his voice ragged with sarcasm. A good sign that he wasn't totally lost.

"You said you would never forgive me for tonight," she began.

His eyes snapped to her. "I didn't mean..."

She put her hand over his mouth. "I'm talking. You're listening. It's my turn to give instructions."

His blue eyes flickered, but he relented. "Okay," he said, finally.

"You wanted to wait for our wedding night," she said.

He nodded, his eyes bleak. "I know it was stupid."

"You thought you owed that to my brother."

He nodded again. Her smile went soft as she stroked the back of her fingers across the stubble on his jaw. He leaned into the caress and closed his eyes.

She took another deep breath, then went for it. "I've booked three tickets to Vegas. Lizzie is driving us to the airport. I've already filled out our marriage license online and they are open 'til midnight. And if we get married before midnight, that will make this our wedding night." She smiled as her words started to get through to him and he straightened up, moving away from her hand. "So," she added, her voice husky around the lump in her throat, "you aren't wearing a suit. I brought you these." She dropped his favorite pair of Levi's in his lap.

He looked down at the jeans then back up at her. He stared at her like he'd never seen her before. Jen knew instinctively that he was completely stripped down to his bones in front of her right now. She had to be careful with what she said next. "We can have the big wedding later. And I will wear a great dress and dance with you. I will live with you and I will definitely sleep with you. But right now, I need you to shake this off, get dressed, and let's go."

"But," he said, catching her hand. "There's not enough time. How can we get married before midnight?" He sounded so tired. "Not that the midnight matters. As long as you marry me, the details don't matter."

"Of course midnight matters," she told him. "I don't want you turning into a pumpkin."

His laugh was harsh. She smiled, her hands covering both sides of his face. She pressed a warm kiss to his forehead, then one to his temple. She felt him sigh as her mouth slid along his jaw. She smiled when she reached his ear. She could not believe that for once she was way ahead of him as she whispered against his ear. "Time change, idiot. Step on it."

Stefan's eyes flew open as shock radiated off of him. Jen grinned at him, but she didn't have to tell him twice.

So at 11:55 Pacific time an Elvis impersonator that Jen had found on the internet pronounced them husband and wife. Before Stefan could kiss her, she swung around to Lizzie. They hugged each other, crushing the roses Stefan had bought both of them as they laughed and cried at the same time.

Stefan looked at Elvis, who was really confused. "Hey, I'm just a means to an end. They've always wanted to be real sisters." He grabbed Jen then, spun her back around. "Hello, Mrs. Sellers, remember me?" And he kissed her. Lizzie took their picture with Elvis. Stefan threatened her if she tweeted it or posted it on Facebook.

"Hey, I wanted the scoop," Lizzie said.

"There is no scoop," Stefan warned her. "Not until we tell Mom and Dad."

Lizzie grinned. "That's gonna cost you. You're gonna be in so much trouble with Mom."

"Lizzie won't tell her," Jen smiled, still not believing they'd actually gotten married. For all her claims about not wanting a big wedding, she had to admit she might have felt more married if she had walked down an aisle.

"She's not going to recognize the Church of Elvis," Lizzie assured her, reading her mind. "She's going to make you have a church wedding. You know that. Just don't make me wear pink. It washes me out. And I want to pick out my own shoes."

Lizzie chatted on about wedding plans as they walked back to the SUV Stefan had rented at the airport. Lizzie easily caught the keys Stefan tossed to her and drove them to the airport. They were just buckling their seat belts, when Stefan leaned over and kissed her without warning. It was another fairytale of a kiss, sweet and beautiful, and when he lifted his head, Jen couldn't help the soft smile that played at her lips.

"You married me," he whispered, as if she'd forget.

The gentle smile didn't flicker as she said, "I got tired of all the begging."

He grinned at her then, laughed despite himself. "What have I got myself into?"

"Hang on," Jen told him, covering his hand with hers as the plane started picking up speed. "I love this part."

"Which part?" Stefan asked, turning his palm up so he could thread his fingers with hers.

The plane left the ground. "That part," Jen smiled. "The second it leaves the ground. That's how you make me feel."

Stefan raised their clasped hands to his mouth. "We're going to be happy, Jen." She nodded, thinking that for once, she really already was.

Later, when she could barely keep her eyes open while Stefan slid the key in the door lock, Jen stepped forward only to have him catch her around the waist.

"What do you think you're doing?" he laughed, sweeping her off her feet.

"What?" she blinked, confused for a moment until she realized he was carrying her over the threshold. She sighed a little and relaxed her head against his strong shoulder as he kicked the door closed behind them.

He was carrying her over the threshold because they were married. They'd gotten married. It still seemed like a dream. Her eyes flew open as she felt the bed come up swiftly behind her.

She heard shoes hit the ground, clothes being swept away, then she was sinking down into warm sheets, being pulled into the warmth of his body. She sighed again, thinking she was finally going to be able to fall asleep.

"Oh no, you don't," he laughed, his tongue tracing the shell of her ears and his hand smoothing over her stomach.

Suddenly wide awake, she turned her head and caught his mouth with her own. Then she froze when he touched her in just the right spot and he laughed low in his throat. She arched back against him, parting her legs and letting him back inside. Arms banded around her and her head fell back on his shoulder as everything else in the world ceased to exist but him.

Stefan knew she was asleep as her body went slack against him, her heat still rippling around him. He drifted towards sleep, still inside her, still connected to her in ways he hadn't even considered. He'd believed for years that he wanted to wait because she was too young. Because he owed it to the best friend he'd made a death bed promise to. Because they'd have the rest of their lives and there was no need to rush it. And because Jen was special and deserved the fairytale.

Now, pulling her in closer but careful not to wake her, he finally admitted to himself that all those reasons had just been excuses. He'd resisted and waited because deep down he'd known the minute he let himself have Jen, she would own him. Completely.

That every single piece of him would be all hers. He would have nothing left.

And there would be no going back.

Now, as his eyelids grew heavy and he breathed in the sweetness of sunshine and sugar and reveled in the softness of her, he knew he'd been right. They'd crossed a line tonight. He wasn't ever letting her go.

He smiled when she stirred against him, and he buried his face in her hair. He felt like he'd just run a hundred miles, and the calm that washed over him was better than any he'd ever reached before. It was her. Having her here like this brought him this peace. He'd never once imagined that she'd replace every single piece she took from him with something better, even adding back parts he hadn't known were missing.

He knew what the feeling was. He loved her. She was part of him, had always been part of him. The beauty of it stole his breath. As the dreams dragged him under, he knew he wasn't just happy, he was complete. And that was a result that had never once crossed his mind. He hadn't even thought it was possible.

CHAPTER ELEVEN

Jen could hardly believe how quickly the bakery was coming together. Jared wasted no time in signing the lease and Rogan's crew jumped on the renovations the same day. Jen watched in complete shock as Stefan and Jared failed to disagree on the security system, the renovations, or really anything. Jen had expected them to be at each other like cats and dogs, but they acted like they'd been friends for ever. It made her nervous.

"I can't believe I'm missing it," Lizzie complained.

"I hate it for you," Jen laughed, switching her cell phone to her other ear as she pretended to check out fabric samples, when she was really just watching Rogan's crew steadily working on wiring, painting, and anything else that needed to be done. "Cause Rogan could charge extra for his no-shirt dress-code for all these guys. There's just too much hotness going on here."

"Jared's band too?" Lizzie groaned. "Adam?"

"Uh-huh," Jen sighed, glancing up sideways at the tall dark guy with blue-tipped spiky hair. Adam's arms were stretched out over his head as he installed a new ceiling fan. "He's got new ink. Lilies all down his arms and back."

"I hate you," Lizzie sighed. "Take a picture."

"Hold on. Hey, Adam," she smiled up at the surprisingly shy lead guitarist of Sugar Coma. "Lizzie wants to see your new ink. Can I?" she asked, waving her phone.

Adam shrugged. "Whatever," and he went back to screwing in the light fixture. Jen snapped a picture and sent it to Lizzie.

"That's hot!" Lizzie cried a minute later on the other end.

"What's hot?" Stefan asked, and Jen jumped in surprise when he stepped up behind her, sweaty, shirtless, and totally gorgeous.

Jen's throat went dry. "Gotta go, Lizzie."

"No, I want more pictures."

"Bye, Lizzie," Stefan said loud enough for his sister to hear. "Who's hot?"

Jen smiled, licked her bottom lip slowly. "All of you, actually."

He nodded slowly, fighting a grin. "I'm glad you noticed we're all hot, maybe you can make us some iced tea."

"Iced tea?" Jen asked, as if she'd never heard of it.

"Yeah, you put water in a pot, boil it, add sugar, and instead of making it into flowers you drop in tea bags."

"I'm sorry," Jen looked at him blankly. "Were you saying something?" she asked, reaching up to run her fingers down his chest, tracing the line under his pecs and down his abdomen. "I was distracted."

He caught her hand before it could reach his waistband. "Seriously. Tea. Now."

"Oh, okay," she pouted, letting him pull her to her feet. "I'll see if I can steal some bags from Elliot."

"You do that," he growled, and kissed her before urging her towards the door. He missed the door and backed her up against the wall. This time her fingers made it to his waistband and she pulled him closer as he opened her mouth with his.

Yeah, she'd been totally wrong about Stefan not really wanting her *that* way. He'd been proving that several times a day for the last few weeks. He'd proved it in multiple ways in multiple locations and she wished he could prove it right here in the middle of her dream-come-true bakery. She simply adored being wrong.

So she tugged his jeans again, urging him even closer and got one button undone before all the whistling, cat calls, and *you two get a room* started up around them. Stefan froze, and shook his head a little as she smiled against his lips. He'd forgotten where they were.

She loved that she could do that to him.

He loved it too but the smile that moved against hers told her she would still pay for it later.

"I'm thirsty," he said.

"Hungry too," she whispered.

"Go."

She kissed him quickly, licking his bottom lip the way she knew he was getting addicted to, then headed out the door so his friends could rag on him.

Jen was still about an inch off the ground when she stepped back out onto Barracks with a hand full of tea bags and a plastic bag of sugar. She missed the black Jaguar until it pulled up to the curb, stopping her short as the window slid down. "We need to talk," Madlyn told her, pressing the door lock button. "Get in."

"Said the spider to the fly? I don't think so."

Madlyn looked at Jen over the top of her ridiculously expensive sunglasses. "Seriously, get in. We need to talk."

Jen leaned down, her arm resting against the open window. "We don't have anything to talk about."

Madlyn stared straight ahead for a minute, then she turned back to Jen, in what Jen was sure was a well-practiced intimidation tactic. "Grow up, Jen. Either get in the car, or the next person you'll be dealing with is my grandfather, and, sweetheart, you don't want to get on Winston Robicheaux's bad side. He may be retired but he's still a heartless bastard."

Jen stepped back. She'd only met Judge Robicheaux once, and that was one time too many. She wasn't the only one afraid of the old man. Angola and the state district attorney's office were equally filled with men terrified of the "hanging" judge.

"Pay attention, princess, I'm trying to help you."

Jen just shook her head and pushed away from the car. She almost felt sorry for the other woman. So much so that the princess comment didn't even bother her. "Give it up, Madlyn."

"Fine," Madlyn snapped, grabbed something out of her purse, then got out of the car, leaving it running. "You want to do this the hard way, Jen? Fine by me."

Madlyn rounded the front end and tried to hand her a photograph. Confused, Jen held her ground but she didn't take the photo.

"It's even worse than you think."

"You're pathetic," Jen said, and meant it as she headed down the sidewalk. She was so over Madlyn Robicheaux, and it felt great.

"There are things you don't know about the accident and your family."

Jen wheeled around. "Look, whatever you think you're going to accomplish, you're too late. We got married three weeks ago in Vegas. You lose. Deal with it."

Jen barely had time to savor the satisfaction of stopping Madlyn in her tracks. The Red Queen actually went a little pale.

"Vegas?" Madlyn said, recovering quickly. "Did he at least sign the pre-nup, Jen?"

"No," Jen told her. "We don't need a pre-nup, Madlyn. I don't know what your problem is. You said yourself you didn't want him. So just leave us alone."

She started to walk off when she noticed the photograph Madlyn was holding. The photograph flapped in the breeze. Jen caught a glimpse and her heart stopped. It was like a freaky, weird dolly zoom, when the camera moves back while the lens zooms in. The photograph flickered between those scarlet nails and for a moment it was the center of the universe for Jen.

"What is that?" Jen whispered, moving towards the Red Queen without thinking, holding her empty hand out for the picture while the tea bags and sugar hit the sidewalk. "Let me see that."

Madlyn let her take the photograph. Jen knew that face. She recognized that smirky half smile and wavy brown hair. Even the freckles were familiar, they were just in the wrong order. And the eyes were wrong. The boy in the picture had black eyes. Robert's eyes had been hazel. It was a photograph of Robert, but it wasn't Robert.

The buzzing she thought she'd never feel again started at the back of her skull. She smelled smoke. She knew nothing was burning and ignored it. But she could not ignore the photograph.

He was so familiar.

"I don't understand," she said to herself, feeling the edges of reality start to soften.

Not now. This wasn't happening. Everything had been going so good. But the smell of smoke was starting to choke her. She swallowed it back. "Who?" she forced the word out, reaching for anger, for anything that would keep her heart from beating any faster.

She finally looked to the one person she had never expected to turn to for help. She found the Red Queen watching her closely, and Jen knew how witnesses must feel in court when Madlyn took them apart piece by piece.

"My son," Madlyn said carefully, black eyes peeling back Jen's skin. "He looks like his father, doesn't he?"

Jen nodded, turning her attention back to the photograph and staring at it. Flashes she couldn't process fired away in her memories but nothing made any sense. She didn't even try to shake off the hand that curled around her upper arm as Madlyn walked her the few steps back to the open car door.

"I told you that we needed to talk."

"Yes, sure," Jen agreed, grateful to sit down now that the Earth was starting to spin a little too fast for her. She looked at the picture, traced the freckles, and felt her heart start to fly up her throat.

Robert's son.

Her nephew.

She had a nephew.

She had a family.

She was not alone in the world.

"What's his name?" she asked, when she could speak.

"Robert Taylor Robicheaux," Madlyn said. "We call him Robbie."

Jen nodded. She looked back down at the nine year old grinning at the camera. Even the way his head was cocked was familiar.

"Robert knew?"

"Yes, of course, we were engaged. We just hadn't told anyone yet."

Jen closed her eyes. The pain was so sharp and so hot she couldn't actually even feel it yet, but she knew when her nerve endings caught up with her brain, it would be excruciating.

She sucked in a ragged breath, and handed the photograph back to Madlyn.

If Robert had known Madlyn was pregnant, then so had Stefan.

For ten years he had let her believe she was alone in the world. Parts of her started shutting down because she just could not cope with that. She also couldn't cope with what that knowledge was setting loose inside her. She knew what it was. Even though she had never felt anything like it before. Never thought she'd ever feel anything remotely like it.

White hot rage.

Rage from an unspeakable betrayal. It was going to destroy everything.

And Jen didn't even care anymore.

"I'm so sorry, Jen," Madlyn said, and Jen felt the sincerity in the other woman's voice down to her bones. She looked at Madlyn and just knew all these years she'd been utterly and completely wrong about everything. "I never wanted to keep him from you, but I had no choice."

Jen squeezed her eyes shut, the white mist closing in as Madlyn shoved all the missing pieces into place. And no matter how much it hurt, Jen wanted the truth. All of it. "Why?"

"The trust," Madlyn said, shifting gears as she crossed over Canal and headed uptown. "Robert did not die at the same time your parents did, Jen. He lived seventeen hours."

"I know," she said, swallowing the bile rising from her stomach. She held down the button to open the window. She needed air.

"Robert inherited before he died. Legally, it can be argued that his half of the estate is not subject to the trust because he was twenty when he died. His half did not automatically revert to the trust, Jen. Robbie is his heir."

The low buzzing was back, but she fought it off as Madlyn

continued.

"You should have been with us, Jen. We're your family, not the Sellers. But you were so ill and no one wanted a huge court battle with you in the hospital and undergoing surgery after surgery. They settled."

"Settled?"

"The Sellers kept custody of you and paid the value of half of the trust to Robbie. That was put into a separate trust for Robbie. They also pay a monthly allowance for him and there is a college fund."

"Paid it how?"

"Mac Sellers paid it and my grandfather agreed not to sue the trust. Mac paid it to protect the stock. The Sellers will do anything to protect STI. Stefan especially."

"Even marry me," Jen whispered.

"Yes," Madlyn agreed. "The company is worth nearly five times what it was a decade ago. And if STI went public, the sky is the limit. But part of that belongs to my son, Jen. The settlement between Mac Sellers and my grandfather was their agreement. The Sellers couldn't legally stop you from letting Robbie have his quarter of the company. But Stefan can now that he's married to you. He didn't sign the pre-nup so all your assets are up for grabs and he has the argument that he increased the value of those assets. He'll demand the stock as part of a divorce settlement."

Jen leaned her head against the cool glass of the windshield as Madlyn's words shredded away what was left of her. Madlyn was right. Madlyn was always right. She closed her eyes.

"I'm not your enemy, Jen. I never have been. It suited Stefan for you to hate me. He spent years making sure you did. You think it was an accident you walked in on us at your graduation night? Really?"

The world ground to a slow, dying halt as Jen lost the ability to breathe and her brain simply shut down. She moved her head but she had no idea if she was agreeing or disagreeing.

"I loved your brother, Jen. We would have been sisters if Robert had lived. Let me help you."

Jen nodded this time, but everything was a huge blank.

"Do you want to meet him? I promised him we'd go to the aquarium today. Why don't you go with us? Would you like that?"

A tiny spark of hope burst deep inside of her. It was so small but it still managed to keep the devastation bearing down on her at bay just a little. "Yes," she rasped out. "More than anything."

CHAPTER TWELVE

"Wait here," Madlyn told her as she slid out of the Jaguar and walked up to the front door of the modest brick ranch. The front door opened before Madlyn could reach for the door knob.

The world warped and twisted as the little boy launched himself out the front door, hugged his mother, and headed for the car. Everything about him was painfully familiar. He was a miniature of his father. The last decade disappeared for Jen and she almost forgot that was not Robert heading for the car.

He hopped into the backseat and did up his seat belt. "Are you my aunt?' he asked, friendly and outgoing just like his father.

Jen nodded, unable to speak as she turned in the seat. It was so strange to look at such a familiar face that was still different. She could see traces of Madlyn in his eyes and his nose but the rest of him was pure Robert.

"I thought so. Uncle Stefan showed me your picture."

Jen's heart clenched. Until it shriveled and died, she hadn't even known she was still clinging to one last shred of hope that this was somehow a misunderstanding. That maybe Stefan hadn't known about Robbie.

Madlyn slid in behind the driver's side. "Zoo or aquarium," Madlyn asked, glancing at Robbie in the rear view mirror.

"Do you like sharks, Aunt Jen?"

Jen swallowed hard. The Aunt Jen razored through. "They're kind of scary," she said, the words scratching her throat. "I like penguins."

"Sharks like penguins too," Robbie laughed. "They make great snacks."

"Aquarium it is," Madlyn announced and reversed out of the driveway.

Jen had been to an aquarium before but had never paid as much attention as she did today. Robbie was brilliant. He stored facts about the fish like a little computer. Jen learned more about seahorses, stingrays, and sharks than she'd ever wanted to know. When they did finally make it to the shark tank, they sat back in the risers for a little while watching some of the fish sleep in a big pile while others swam patrol around the tank.

"He's wonderful," Jen said, her head still swimming in bittersweet pain. She could feel herself trying to drift away, but something about the grinning little boy held her back. She couldn't quite go to pieces with Robbie to consider.

Her brother's son. Her nephew. Her family.

A new strength was rebuilding the broken parts of her and she suddenly felt a strange sense of responsibility. All the pain she was feeling started to take second place to the needs of that beautiful nine year old boy. They'd tried to keep him from her. Jen understood why. Because she knew she'd walk through fire to make sure Robbie had what was his. She'd never wanted anything to do with STI or her trust fund. But Robbie might. He deserved his part of her father's legacy and nothing that Mac or Stefan Sellers had agreed to or done would stop Jen from doing what was right by her nephew. By her family.

"Thank you for this," Jen spoke the words she never thought she'd say to Madlyn Robicheaux. Maybe she had been wrong about Madlyn. Maybe she had misunderstood. Nothing really made much sense anymore except the boy watching sharks swim by. And nothing else mattered.

Madlyn took a deep breath. "Robbie is your family, which makes you our family. You need to let us help you."

Jen nodded, but didn't commit to anything.

"I'm starving," Robbie finally announced.

"Me, too," Madlyn said, as if she were surprised to be hungry. "How does a late lunch sound?"

"I'm in," Jen smiled, and meant it. Anything to spend more time with her nephew.

When they stepped out into the bright sunshine on the river front, she stopped short, her smile dying a little. Stefan stood outside the entrance, his back to the Mississippi River, watching all three of them with the oddest look on his face. He wasn't actually looking at her, he was looking at Madlyn, who was staring straight back at him. Then any final illusions that Jen had clung to that this might have been a giant misunderstanding died a very quick death when Robbie launched himself at Stefan.

"Uncle Stefan!" The cool nine year old veneer gave way to a delighted child.

Stefan didn't miss a step as he caught Robbie at full run. He gave a huge grunt then swung the boy around once, before dropping him back to his feet. They play-boxed for a minute, circling each other until Robbie got in the kill shot and Stefan pretended to fall back. The rapport between them was staggering.

"Have you enjoyed seeing your aunt?"

Robbie nodded. "She's pretty cool. She pet the stingray even though she didn't really want to."

"Is that a fact? A stingray? I can't believe you got her to do that," Stefan said, ruffling Robbie's hair. "Have you eaten yet?"

Madlyn started to protest but the look Stefan gave her over Robbie's shoulder would have made a small army flee. And while she held her ground, she immediately said it sounded great to her.

"We're going to Masperos," Robbie said. "Race you!"

And they were off, racing along the river until they could cut across to Decatur at the Brewery.

Jen watched as they disappeared around a building.

"Let's get this over with," Madlyn said.

Jen nodded, but as far as she was concerned everything was already over.

Robbie, thankfully, was oblivious to the tension between the adults at the table. He was catching Stefan up on what he was doing at school and then the conversation turned to the New Orleans 70.3. Robbie was a huge fan of the triathlons. Jen suspected it was because he worshiped Stefan. And Stefan's obvious affection for the boy was heart-wrenching.

She sipped her lemonade, ordered a fried shrimp po boy and just enjoyed watching them together. There was such genuine affection between them that she would never understand why he had kept Robbie from her. The Stefan she'd thought she knew would never do that. The Stefan she thought she'd loved could not have done it, would not have even considered it an option. But here it was, right in front of her.

Their food came, and Jen picked at her shrimp but didn't eat the French bread. Stefan and Robbie split what was left of her sandwich after demolishing roast beef po boys and red beans and rice. Stefan actually ate the French bread. Madlyn's phone rang and she excused herself from the table, but not before sending Robbie to wash his hands.

Jen watched the sidewalk through the open doors, while Stefan sat across from her in complete silence. She kept expecting him to say something. Seconds stretched into minutes as they sat there like two strangers. Then his lemonade glass hit the table just a little too hard.

"You don't have anything to say?"

Surprised he'd broken the silence first, Jen couldn't even begin to believe what he'd just said to her. Who did he think he was? He had no right to look at her like that. In that minute, she really hated him. Despite all the pain she was still fighting back, hating him was infinitely worse. Hating Stefan meant she had no idea who she even was anymore.

"How did you know where I was?" she asked, amazed at how calm her words were.

He leaned across the table. "There's an app for that."

"An app?" she echoed. "You're unbelievable."

"Seriously? I'm unbelievable? You want to explain to me why you leave for tea bags and end up at the aquarium with Madlyn and Robbie?"

"Not really, no."

"We had no idea where you were. You just disappeared."

"I trusted you," she interrupted, pushing away from the table.

"Trusted?" he echoed. "As in past tense."

She nodded, standing up. "I wanted the fairytale so bad that I let you convince me. But I always knew deep down that you didn't really love me, Stefan. I just thought you at least cared. I can't believe I was so stupid."

He was on his feet and reaching for her before she finished.

"No," she jumped backing away from him, not caring what the tourists and other diners around them thought. "Do not touch me. Just stay away from me, we're done."

"Done?"

"As in past tense," she informed him, and was out on the sidewalk before she even recognized that she was walking away from him.

"Jen." Fingers closed around her arm, but she jerked her arm back and tried to put some distance between them. She knew she couldn't outrun him but she didn't want him touching her.

"You had no right to keep him from me!"

He stopped short, and she kept walking. Then she decided she wasn't finished so she wheeled back around, surprised to see him standing where she'd left him. She couldn't believe he looked so confused.

"How could you? You knew how much I missed my family. How could you let me believe I was all alone in the world?"

She refused to let herself notice how every word she threw at him sucked a little more color out of his face. She ignored the way he iced over. She didn't care.

"And for what?" she demanded. "For money? For stock in a company that I would have given you if you had just asked for it? There was no need for you to manipulate me all these years and take away the one thing that meant something to me. But you can forget it. You'll never get it now. And if you still think you can get it as part of a divorce settlement, then you'd better think again. Because I will do anything I have to do to make sure you never touch a penny of it."

"Divorce?" the word scraped out of him.

"Yes, divorce."

"You are not leaving me." The words launched at her like frozen steel spikes, but she couldn't feel anything anymore, so it didn't mattered what he said or did.

She stared at him, then took two steps forward, meeting him head on, not caring that the ice in his expression actually burned her skin. "Stefan," she said softly, launching back steel of her own. "I'm already gone."

Maybe a sledge hammer? No, a wrecking ball. Yeah, definitely a wrecking ball would have done less damage if it'd slammed into his gut the way her words did. For a moment, he wasn't sure he was actually hearing them. His brain could just not fathom that his entire world had just exploded and fallen at his feet.

He watched her walk away, towards the black Jaguar that slid up to the curb. He couldn't even feel his feet as he started forward. "Jen," he rasped out, forcing air in his lungs so he could speak.

She didn't even hesitate. She went around to the passenger side of the Jag, and sat right down into the spider's web.

He had hardly even absorbed that this was actually happening before the triumphant look on Madlyn's face twisted what was left of his gut in half. Everything Jen had been trying to tell him about Madlyn was absolutely true. He hadn't listened to her. He hadn't believed her. Now he was going to pay for that.

He started forward, and Madlyn met him half way.

"Children are present," she reminded him.

"You unbelievable bitch," he hissed at her. "What have you done?"

She actually smiled. A wide, open mouth smile that had his hands curling into fists. "What's the matter, lover. Have I stolen your favorite toy?" she said. "Don't worry, I'll take excellent care of her. I might even let you have her back, eventually. If she wants to come back to you, but that's not likely."

His best friend had loved this woman. Stefan had dated her for two years. They had been friends for longer. She was his trusted attorney. She was family.

Now, he had no idea who the hell she was.

"What did you do?"

Madlyn's smile widened. "I just thought it was time she met her nephew. The one you refused to let me tell her about all these years."

"What?" he demanded, feeling the world lurch underneath him. Suddenly his grasp of English was called into question. Nothing anyone was saying to him today made any sense.

Madlyn laughed. "Funny thing, Jen's sketchy memory. I had no idea what a gift it really was."

"You bitch."

"You said that already."

"You know me, Madlyn," he reminded her, his voice low and controlled. "Do you really want to take me on?"

She stood her ground, something brutal flickering in her eyes. "I took you on months ago, but you just realized we were playing. I am so far ahead of you, Stefan, you'll never catch up."

"You do not want to do this."

Madlyn shrugged. "You spent so much time trying to protect her from herself, that you left your rear flank exposed."

"Robert loved you."

Every single shred of humanity evaporated from her expression, and Stefan found himself facing a cold predator that he'd never seen coming. "Don't you dare. He was everything to me. I've spent the last ten years trying to protect his son and his sister. What have you done for the last decade? You sealed her up in a perfect little bubble, then made a load of money doing it."

"You don't give a shit about Jen."

"Don't think for one second that you know me, Stefan. I protected her every time I spread my legs for you. I had the judge convinced for years you and I were together. Every weekend you spent with me and

Robbie kept him distracted. But you couldn't keep your hands off her, could you? The Kingdom wasn't enough, you had to have the princess too. Now she's on his radar. And that is all your fault."

"I'm not afraid of that old man."

"Well, then you're a fool."

He felt rather than saw the hesitation in her. "Madlyn," he said, trying to sound reasonable. "Tell me what's really going on."

She almost looked startled, but it faded so quickly he wasn't sure he'd even seen it. She just shook her head in disgust. "Just run along, Stefan. Go and make more money. The more you make the more my grandfather wants. And he's going to want a lot this time."

"This isn't over," he told her, as she walked back to her car.

She stopped at the Jag and put one foot in before turning back to him. "Don't worry. We'll be in touch."

He watched the Jag pull away from the curb. One system right after another shut down as he watched the car go around the curve, taking his wife away from him. He didn't run. He walked back to the bakery, where the crew was knocking off for the day.

"You find her?" Rogan asked, looking up from the checkbook he had spread out on one of the cafe tables in the dining area.

"Yeah."

"Where is she?"

"With Madlyn," Stefan said, sinking down in the other chair.

"Madlyn?"

"Yeah."

"What the hell?"

Stefan pushed his fingers through his hair, still too dazed by what had happened to make sense of anything. "And Robbie."

"Robbie?" Rogan sat up. "She saw Robbie today. Is she okay?"

Stefan nodded. "Other than hating my guts for hiding her nephew from her for the last nine years, she's just peachy."

"What..."

"...yeah, I know," Stefan said, suddenly very tired.

"She thinks you hid Robbie from her? Where did she get that...oh, fucking hell, I told you that you cannot trust that bitch."

"Yeah, you did." He took a deep breath, knowing that he needed to do something, but he couldn't think. His chest had been ripped open and everything was leaking out of him so fast he didn't even try to stop it.

"What're we going to do?"

Stefan shrugged. "Tequila. Lots and lots of tequila."

"Yeah, let's go with no on that. You and tequila are not good friends. Remember."

"Patron Silver and I are tight," Stefan assured him and pushed to his feet. "Where's the hippie? I need a new attorney."

Within five minutes of meeting Judge Robicheaux, Jen was not the least bit sorry the Sellers had raised her, even if their motives had not been what she thought they were. Growing up with that old man would have been a nightmare. Now she knew where Madlyn got her crazy from.

He sat in his high-backed leather chair and watched her with eyes even colder than Madlyn's. He was like some whacked-out James Bond villain. He even steepled his fingers while he talked. "The Sellers have done a pretty thorough job of conditioning you to believe they know what's best for you. They've had a lot of years to do that, several of which you were quite ill and dependent on them. Now, Madlyn tells me that Stefan has already managed to marry you. That makes things a little more difficult."

"What things?" she asked. She should never have let Madlyn bring her here. She should have paid more attention when they dropped Robbie off at Madlyn's sister's house. But the Robicheaux's antebellum mansion was only three blocks from St. Charles so she hadn't really caught on until it was too late that they were not headed to her house. Her house? Her stomach twisted. Not her house anymore. And that hurt so much more than she'd expected it to.

"My grandson's inheritance," he said gruffly, pulling her attention back. "Have you actually signed the stock over to them yet?"

Jen took a deep breath. She didn't want to hear any more of this. "I will make sure Robbie gets his portion of the trust."

"I wish it were that simple." Yeah, all the old man needed was a fuzzy white cat in his lap and the picture would be complete.

"Then just tell me what you want?"

"Direct and to the point. I like that."

He stood up and went to his desk, then brought a stack of papers with him. "First, you will retain me as your legal counsel. Then we'll begin the divorce proceedings."

Something cold seized her stomach. She'd told Stefan she wanted a divorce, but now that this man wanted her to divorce Stefan, she was no longer sure it was a good idea.

"You'll be much safer here, Jen," the judge was telling her. "Where we can look after you."

Look after her? Great, someone else who thought she needed looking after. Then it hit her. It wasn't her. It had never even been about her. It was the money, the stock and that damned company that she wanted nothing to do with. She swallowed, pushing fingers hard against her eyes. She should have stayed in Paris. She should never have come back here. Everyone here just saw dollar signs they wanted to control when they saw her.

She wanted out of here. She stood up. "I can look after myself."

"How?" the judge asked. "You're an extremely wealthy young woman, but if you walk out of here right now, where will you go? How will you get there? Do you own a car? And if you do have somewhere you can go, how will you pay for it? Do you even have the account numbers for your money? Can you access it?"

She froze, her hand gripping one of the arms of the chair, not liking the answers to any of his questions.

"You see, my dear, we are trying to help you. Now sit back down."

Her heart rate elevated then and she took a deep breath to try and stop it. She simply could not have a panic attack right now. She dropped back into the chair to concentrate on breathing through the panic. She hadn't had one in so long. She was out of practice.

And the judge just kept talking. The words sounded far away but they still sank into her like razor blades.

"Half of the Taylor Family Trust belongs to my grandson. Sellers only married you to solidify his hold over those assets. If you do not agree to sign the divorce papers, I will have your marriage annulled."

"Annulled?" she coughed. "You can't, we've already..."

His laughter was brutal and not at all amused. "On the grounds of incompetency. You sustained a very serious brain injury from the accident, Jen. You aren't competent to make your own decisions. If you don't cooperate, I will petition the judge for a conservatorship and you'll find yourself in a wonderful place in South Carolina for young women with similar problems."

The edges of her vision started to spark as the panic clawed up her throat again. That hadn't been an idle threat. The judge could make one phone call and she'd disappear. She tried to stand up again and the room titled almost forty-five degrees. She sank back in the chair and lost control of her heart rate.

Sensing blood in the water, the judge continued, "Or you can sign this paperwork, retain me as your legal counsel, and give me your proxy vote. We already have a buyer for half of the shares. Then we'll move to take STI public. That should be an easy enough choice for you to make.

Sign the paperwork and you'll be an even wealthier young woman."

"I don't want STI to go public."

His smile was not nice as he dumped the heavy pile of paperwork in her lap. He pushed a pen into her loose fingers and tapped the signature line on the papers.

"I won't sign anything that lets you take STI public," she said, around the pain in her throat.

"Sign the paperwork," he said, the false gentleness evaporating from his tone.

She looked at the page, the words danced on the page. She wasn't sure any of it mattered but she still couldn't quite make herself sign it all away. "I won't sign this." She pushed the papers off her lap and watched, fascinated as they scattered at her feet on the Aubusson rug.

"Well, then, I hope you like South Carolina," the judge said.

CHAPTER THIRTEEN

"A ny idea where Madlyn took her?" Rogan asked as he finished chilling the last of the Patron Silver in a cocktail shaker.

"No." Stefan stared at his shot glass as Rogan filled it, then moved on to Jared's glass. Jared was resting his forehead on the island mumbling about how nice and cool the marble felt.

If Stefan could have controlled his facial muscles, he would have grinned. The hippie just could not hang.

"Don't pussy out now, Marshall," Rogan laughed.

Jared reached for his shot glass, curled his fingers around it but didn't lift his head or the glass. "Need a minute."

Stefan was almost sorry he was too drunk to really rag the younger guy about not having the stones to drink with them, but he was actually hesitating about his own shot. Rogan was drinking a beer. He'd stopped the tequila a long while back, but Stefan and Jared had gotten into a pissing contest. They were both losing.

Stefan threw his back suddenly and slammed his shot glass upside down next to Jared's. "Tattooed hippie freak."

"You're just pissed cause she still loves me," Jared told him.

Stefan was on his feet, the bar stool hitting the tile floor, but someone grabbed his shirt and set him on another bar stool. Stefan stayed because the floor wasn't actually solid anymore. Grant Marshall walked around him and picked up Jared's shot glass.

"You two getting my little brother drunk?" Grant asked, lifting the Patron bottle and wincing. "Please tell me this wasn't full when you started."

"We thought it might shut him up," Rogan said.

"Did it work?" Grant laughed. "Cause if it did, I need a case of this stuff. I've never found anything that would shut him up."

"Fuck off," Jared said, but his forehead did not leave the marble island.

"You should have come to LSU, joined the frat, we would have taught you how to shoot tequila properly," Grant told his little brother, then drank his shot.

Stefan huffed and settled quite nicely into the eye of the hurricane brewing inside him.

"So," Grant said, addressing Stefan as he pulled another bar stool up. "You want to take on the hanging judge?"

Stefan nodded slowly, very slowly. The tequila had numbed him to everything except the pain of all his internal organs bleeding out and dying.

"Can you make coffee?" Grant asked Rogan.

Rogan shook his head. "It won't do any good at this point. You got about forty-five seconds before he passes out. Any more questions?"

Grant turned back to Stefan who was suddenly fascinated by the old-fashioned wall clock and how the hands were warping. "How hard do you want to play this?"

Stefan heard the question. One more shot of tequila might have made him come up with the right answer, but he hadn't had enough to be brutally honest with himself. "I'm done playing," he said, pushing himself to his feet.

Rogan was right—now he had about another forty seconds. It took him twenty to make it up to his bedroom and into the master bath, where he threw up as much of the alcohol as he could, then stood in the shower until the world stopped spinning.

Tequila? What had he been thinking?

He hadn't been thinking.

He threw up again, brushed his teeth, then got back in the shower and turned it up as hot as he could stand. He was dragging on clean jeans when his cell phone buzzed. He opened the text message and the phone almost hit the floor. Rage swept through him so fast that he actually went blind for a moment. In its wake was a calm that was so sharp, so crystal clear, that he froze instantly. No more feeling. Just clear, detached thinking.

He looked down at the picture of Jen one more time. She was curled up in an oversized leather chair, asleep. There was also a message.

So sorry, but we seemed to have broken your toy after all.

He shoved the phone in his pocket. There was just enough tequila left in his system that he thought about opening the gun safe and taking out the Glock seventeen, but he stopped at the last minute and left it alone. His brain was so razor sharp that he imagined everything from the bullet hitting the center of Madlyn's forehead right straight through to the lethal injection going into his arm and separating him from Jen forever. He dropped his hand from the safe handle.

No, he knew exactly what he was going to do. And he wasn't going to need a gun to do it. Madlyn wanted a war. She had one.

No one had the slightest clue that the Stefan Sellers that joined them in the kitchen was not the same person that had gone upstairs two hours earlier. He found Elliot and Jackson had joined Rogan, Jared, and Grant in the kitchen. They were eating the rest of the brownies Jen had made yesterday and forcing coffee down Jared.

"You want milk with that?" he asked. They all stopped at once and looked at him. Good. He had their attention.

"Sellers," Jackson Napier was the first one to speak. Jackson was one of the few people Stefan had to look up at to meet his eyes. He was also one of the few people who could keep pace with him in a long distance run. At six foot six inches he'd been a hell of a linebacker at LSU; now a hundred pounds lighter, Jackson worked for the NOPD.

"Judge send you to arrest me, Jackson?" he asked.

Jackson shrugged. "Have you done something I need to arrest you for?"

"Not yet." Stefan's smile was not nice. "Now if y'all are done snacking, I'd like to go get my wife."

"Rogan says she went willingly," Jackson said, pushing away from the counter.

Stefan turned on Rogan, who just shrugged.

"Madlyn took her to the judge's. I'm going to get her back," Stefan said.

Grant stood up. "Robicheaux will be expecting that."

"Well, then, let's not disappoint the old man."

"You need to be smart about this," Rogan said, thumping Jared on the back of his head when he snorted.

"Let me ask you something. Robicheaux gets his claws in her, how many brownies, cookies, and carrot cakes do you assholes see in your future?"

That got their attention. There was a sudden commotion, a whole bunch of *fuck that shit*, and they all moved at once. "Why don't we take a ride?" Jackson invited. "I'm off duty."

The Robicheaux's antebellum mansion was several blocks from the St. Charles house. They parked on the street out front.

"Stay here," Rogan told him. "Jared and I will go first."

Stefan didn't answer. He got out of the car and leaned against the back bumper. He wanted them to go first, so he let Rogan continue to believe he was running this show. A housekeeper answered the door, then stepped aside as Madlyn appeared in the doorway. She was lucky that he hadn't listened to the tequila and had left the gun at home. Now, he didn't even notice he was stalking across the front yard until his shoe hit the front porch.

"Stefan. You've brought your whole pack, except for Matt of course, but I'm sure you aren't interested in videoing any of this."

"Where is Jen?" Jared asked, before Stefan could speak.

"She's sleeping. She's had a pretty rough day," Madlyn said. "I doubt she wants to see you, but do come in. Grandfather has some papers for you."

He showed her his teeth. "Madlyn, I'm giving you one chance..."

"Stefan Sellers," a deep voice boomed from inside the house, pulling Stefan's attention away from his prey. "We expected you to come storming in here hours ago, son."

"Where is my wife?" he snarled, brushing past the others and going straight inside. He stopped, facing Judge Winston Robicheaux straight on, something most attorneys in Louisiana couldn't do and a whole lot of men in Angola had lived to regret.

The old judge was too arrogant to sense danger. "You were very clever marrying her so quickly this time," Robicheaux's mouth twisted into a cold smile. "It certainly complicates things, but this isn't my first rodeo, boy. When are you going to learn?"

Stefan followed him back into the office. He spotted Jen immediately curled up by the fireplace in a chair. Someone had covered her with a blanket. He took a step towards her. He would just get her and go. Maybe they would be smart and let him walk out with her. No harm, no foul.

"Not yet," the judge said, and Stefan swung back around and took the papers the judge slammed against his chest. "These are copies, of course. You might want to have a seat."

Stefan stared at them blankly. "What the hell is this?"

"I hate to spoil the surprise, but I'm filing to have your marriage annulled first thing Monday morning."

There was a stunned silence in the room, and then it became crystal clear as the papers went flying that Stefan had not brought enough friends with him. But Jackson and Rogan managed to catch him before he lunged. He let them hold him back.

"Annulment?" Stefan rasped, jerking away from Rogan.

The judge waved at him and leaned back in his chair. "That poor girl isn't competent enough to make her own decisions. You know that. Your family has always known that."

"Think about it, Stefan," Madlyn threw at him from across the room, "It means your marriage isn't legal. You really should have signed that pre-nup."

Before anyone could take their next breath, Stefan crossed the room, slid his fingers around Madlyn's neck and backed her up against the wall. The room exploded behind him but as far as he was concerned there were only two people left in the room at all. And one wasn't staying.

Madlyn grabbed at his hand, sucking in one ragged breath and finally, finally, the arrogant, smirking triumph started to melt into what she should have been feeling all along...fear. Her eyes widened as he pushed her harder against the wall.

He brought his face up close to hers. "Robert loved you," he snarled, low in her ear and felt her start to struggle harder.

"Stefan," she gasped, grabbing at his hand and prying desperately at his fingers. "Think."

"He loved you. You vindictive, malicious, bitch." The words tore out of him as he squeezed just short of actually cutting off her air. "And this is what you do to his sister? I should snap your vicious neck."

"Stefan," a voice cut through the icy haze. "Stefan," Jen was next to him. "Let her go."

Jen watched as the thing frost giants feared turned and looked at her. She took an instinctive step back from him. His eyes weren't right. He was dangerously close to the edge and once again she found herself in a situation where she had to stop him before he did something he'd never come back from. She didn't think he would actually hurt Madlyn, but she also wasn't sure she even knew who he was anymore.

"You are hurting her, Stefan. Let her go."

"Don't move," he warned her.

All the hairs on her arms, legs, and neck started to rise. She'd done this to him. He wasn't on the edge, he'd already gone over. And it was her fault. This had not been what she wanted at all. "Let her go," she whispered. She had to diffuse this situation and quickly.

Jen was faintly surprised when he released Madlyn, who immediately dragged in a deep breath and slumped back against the wall. Jen tried not to step back as he advanced on her.

"Don't you want to know how I got her to run away to Paris?" Madlyn interrupted, still leaning against the wall and breathing hard. "What could I have possibly said to her that would make your precious princess leave you?"

Stefan's mouth twisted into something bitter, but his eyes never left Jen. "Yes."

"I told her you loved her. But that you only saw a broken little girl you felt responsible for. If she loved you, she wouldn't let you trap yourself into a marriage you'd regret."

Stefan closed his eyes.

"You know the best part, Stefan? She believed every single word. It's easier for her to believe the most outrageous lies I can come up with, than it is for her to trust you."

Lies? What lies? Jen's attention focused past Stefan as the Red Queen recovered her composure with each word. Madlyn turned on Jen, going for the kill, and Jen met her dead shark eyes straight on. "You are pathetic. You don't deserve him. How could you actually believe he would keep Robert's child from you? Today is not the first time you've met Robbie."

Jen opened her mouth to speak but the floor was rushing up at her already. The buzzing was back as her mind couldn't absorb what Madlyn was saying to her. Then she looked back to Stefan who was reaching for her as she sat down hard and she understood it all so clearly. In fact she could even see it now as memories flashed through her so quickly she couldn't keep up.

Lizzie lying in the grass, a little boy held up over her, laughing as she raised him up and down and smothered him with silly kisses. Stefan grabbing the little boy and swinging him high in the air before settling him down in her lap so she could give him a bottle.

Hands were on her but she batted them away. The whole world was trying to get her attention but Jen ignored it as she faced what she had been hiding from for so long, what she'd forgotten she was hiding at all. It wasn't just her heart that was fractured into so many pieces. Her mind was too.

She really was broken. She just pretended that she wasn't. Ignored the parts that didn't work right. Ignored the things that hurt too much. Stefan really did deserve better. She should never have married him.

"Don't do this," Stefan said, sounding a million miles away even when she fought him off. "Jen," the word rasped across her skin. "I'm not leaving here without you. I have nowhere to go if you don't come with me."

She stared up at him and it was like seeing him for the first time. His hand pressed against the side of her face. "Come home."

She nodded quickly, curving her arms around his neck as he swung her up in his arms. She vaguely heard the old judge yelling, "You step one foot out of this house with her, Sellers, and I'll have you for kidnapping and assault. She needs to be in a hospital."

She turned into the warmth of the body holding her. She turned her face in the familiar safety of his neck and gave into the gray lurking at the corners of her vision. She closed her eyes.

"Don't listen to him," he said, against her hair. "They're wrong, Jen. There is nothing wrong with you."

"I'm warning you," the judge yelled, lifting up the receiver on the desk phone. "I'm calling the police now."

"I am the police," Jackson informed the old man. "Give it your best shot."

CHAPTER FOURTEEN

"This is complete bullshit," Jared said, scattering the legal papers across the dining room table.

Stefan was more interested in the older Marshall's reaction. His emotions weren't invested. Jared's were and he wasn't thinking clearly. Stefan knew this because he wasn't thinking clearly either. He didn't seem to be capable of thinking at all.

"His argument for the conservatorship is pretty strong," Grant said looking up from the papers he'd been reading for the last hour. He gathered up the papers Jared had just tossed angrily across the table and started to stack them back in order. "Tell me about her head injury." He tapped the stack of papers and set them in a neat pile.

"She had a concussion and a skull fracture. They removed part of her skull for a while to relieve the pressure from swelling. But there was never any brain damage."

Stefan could have sworn smoke was starting to wisp out of the hippie's nose. It probably should have bothered him that Jared was this deeply upset. He was obviously ready to rip someone apart. But instead of questioning the younger man's motives, Stefan found himself almost relieved to have someone as angry as he was. At least Jared could express it. Stefan had passed the point of being able to release any of the rage eating away at him from the inside out. The fallout from any reaction he allowed himself would far outweigh the advantages.

"We'll get him," Stefan said, not even recognizing his own voice as he tried to talk Jared down. "That old man has no idea what he's just bought."

Jared faced him across the table and a silent pact was sealed between them. Winston Robicheaux was already dead. He just didn't know it yet.

"Obviously there is something wrong with her," Grant Marshall said carefully, as Stefan and Jared turned murderous stares on him. Unaffected, Grant added, "I can't help her if I don't know what I'm dealing with."

"For the last time," Jared started to snarl but Stefan raised his hand and Jared reluctantly fell silent and sank back down in his seat.

"Dissociative amnesia," Stefan explained. "It's a result of emotional trauma, not a brain injury. Anything about the accident or her brother can trigger fugue states. She just checks out. She'll stop talking for a while. It can be a few minutes, a few hours, and on rare occasions a few days. Then she's fine. She doesn't remember when it happens, we all got very good at not mentioning the episodes or anything that might trigger them. It rarely even happens anymore. She's been a lot better since she got back from Paris. And yes, asshole, you get the credit for that," he told Jared before the hippie could point it out.

Jared sat back in his chair, his arms folding across his chest in self-satisfaction. "She was happy in Paris with me."

Stefan leveled his eyes on Jared. "There is a line. Don't push it right now."

"Just sayin'."

"Jared," Grant interrupted him. "You've seen these fugue states?"

Jared gave a noncommittal shrug-slash-nod and waved his hand dismissing it. "There is nothing wrong with her."

"No, there is something wrong with me," a husky voice came from the dining room doorway. All three men swung around to find Jen standing there. She was pale and still shaky. Stefan stood up, wincing as she stepped back and refused to meet his eyes. "But I made coffee," she added quickly. "Do you want some?"

"Yes," Grant sighed in exaggerated relief. "Coffee is perfect."

She nodded and disappeared back into the kitchen.

Stefan forced himself to sit back down and not go after her. Not yet.

"She seems okay," Grant said, sitting back in his chair as they waited for her to return with coffee.

"Give her another hour. You won't know anything had even happened," Jared said. "She's stronger than any of you give her credit for."

Stefan nodded his agreement, unwilling to admit he was only now really starting to get that about her.

"His argument is that someone has to handle all her financial matters. That she can't even balance a checkbook."

"That's crazy," Stefan said.

"She's twenty-two. She doesn't have a car. She went from living with your parents to living with you. The judge is saying she can't take care of herself and I don't have anything to show that she can."

"I bought her a car for her birthday," Stefan said. "She liked living at the Lake House and we're married so she lives with me now."

"The old man is clever, Stefan," Grant explained. "He's arguing that you've married her to continue controlling her inheritance, part of which belongs to his grandson."

"Part of it does belong to him," Jen said quietly, walking in with a tray of coffee mugs.

She set coffee in front of Jared and Grant, then a cup of Earl Grey tea in front of him. But she still wouldn't meet his eyes. He tried to catch her attention but she still wouldn't look at him. While the Marshalls fixed their coffee, Stefan gave in to the need to touch her and bring her close again. He wanted to wipe that haunted look off her face. She stiffened when he slid an arm around her waist. She even let him pull her close to him. But she held herself apart, didn't melt into him.

That hurt him so much, his grip on her was not as light as it should have been.

He pulled her into his lap despite her silent protest and the resistance she put up. He needed her close to him. He was freezing, and he needed her curled up against his chest, her head under his chin and her hands touching him anywhere, or pretty soon he wasn't going to be able to breathe.

He caught her face with his hand. "Stop avoiding my eyes," he said, not meaning for his voice to sound like gravel again. "Look at me." He watched, horror curling up his throat, as those beautiful brown eyes suddenly swam with moisture. "Don't," he rasped out. "Jen, don't."

He could feel her slipping away from him, but he couldn't protect her any longer. He'd messed up trying to protect her from everything and he'd ended up hurting her anyway.

He was just selfish enough to admit that if he lost her now, he really wouldn't recover. Life without Jen wasn't something he ever wanted to experience again. Nothing would make sense if he lost her now. The simple truth was he needed her. He just hadn't realized how much until he watched her eyes swim with defeated tears.

Shoving back the urge to shelter her, he reminded himself that she really was stronger than she looked and braced himself anyway before saying, "I thought we were past this whole fragile, fairy princess bullshit."

She went rigid in his arms and was on her feet before he could blink. "I am not fragile," she informed him, stepping away.

He grinned at her, relief sweeping over him like cooling rain. She was still pale and her eyes were haunted. But the tears were gone and she didn't look defeated anymore. "Oh, I don't know, you've been doing a pretty good impression of a delicate butterfly since I picked you up off the floor at the judge's house."

He vaguely caught a glimpse of Grant stopping Jared from moving.

"You did not just say that to me," Jen said, color finally starting to return to her face. Sure it was furious, angry color, but Stefan would take what he could get.

"Say what? That I'm sick of this delicate flower act? Because I've had about as much of it as I can stomach," he threw at her, and startled himself. But instead of crumbling, he watched her light up like the Fourth of July. "You didn't like that, did you?"

He stood up and she backed up, so he walked her back through the butler pantry and into her kitchen.

"Good, because I don't either. I want the girl who wears sheer stockings with little black bows on her ankles just to torture me. The one who put on that pink dress and tricked me into having sex with her before dragging me to Vegas."

"Tricked?" Jen sputtered, but he knew he had her now. Her face was raging with color and her eyes were spitting fire. "I didn't trick you. That was pretty straightforward."

"You. Tricked. Me."

"And you loved it," she shot back.

His hands were on her waist now and he dragged her up against him even as he walked her up against the wall.

"Absolutely," he agreed, covering her mouth in a rough kiss that proved he didn't think she was fragile. His whole body shuddered when he felt her teeth pull at his bottom lip, then lick the delicious little stab of pain away with her tongue.

He pushed his tongue deeper into the burning, hot sweetness of her mouth. He was starving for her and the more he tasted the hungrier he got.

But he had to be able to think. He ripped his mouth off hers, grabbed the hands that were clamped around his neck, and spun her around until she faced the wall. He shoved one foot between her feet, pressed himself hard against her, as his hands covered hers, flattening them to the wall. Her breath hitched and the surprised little cry made him forget he still had a meeting going on in the next room. He pressed his face into her neck, running his tongue along that delicious curve of her shoulder until he settled behind her ear. Screw the meeting.

"Feel that?" he asked, grinding hard against the soft, rounded curves that turned an already rock-hard erection into steel. "Does that feel like I think you're fragile?"

She shook her head as much as she could, but even pressed so tight against the wall, he could feel her body ripple with reaction. Her breathing was slow and ragged. She liked this. Staggered that she really liked it when he played rough, he gave into a fantasy he'd never admitted, even to himself.

He pushed her left hand over then pinned both of her wrists with his left hand. His right hand slid slowly down her arm, then curved around her breast. He breathed hard against her neck as his thumb slid over one tight nipple and she jerked back against him, her head hitting his shoulder despite what little room there was between them. "Does that?" He rolled the hard peak between his thumb and forefinger and she shivered against him, pressing even harder back against him

She shook her head again, turning her face into his neck, he felt her whole body go tight as he kept his hand moving down until her got under the T-shirt she wore, sighing as his hand smoothed across all that silky skin. She shivered and he tightened his hold on her, pressing harder. His fingers slid easily past the waistband of her leggings. He kicked his foot against one of hers again, spreading her legs further apart, then let himself touch what he'd been aching for all day.

She was burning up for him. Hot and wet and already really, really close. He could feel the ripples building up inside her as he pushed deep, his teeth raking across her throat as she stopped breathing. He swirled and stroked and teased until he felt her knees start to go. He dropped her hands and banded that arm around her midriff, holding her hard against him as he built a slow, steady fire inside her. One of her hands grabbed his arms, the other reached back and slid through his hair, making him sorry he'd ever cut it because he was pretty sure if she ever got a fistful of it, he'd never want her to let go. He slid out, returned with two fingers, catching the cry that escaped her with his mouth.

"You still think I see a little girl?" he rasped, his lips still touching hers as he spoke.

"No," she breathed out.

He had her right on the verge. One little twist and she'd go flying. He knew it, and the second she realized it, he said, "Now you listen to me."

She went rigid against him.

"This is what's gonna happen. I'm going back in there and finish this meeting. You are going to go upstairs to wait for me. You can take a shower but you will not touch yourself. There will be hell to pay if I think you've used that pink, sparkly vibrator. Understand?"

She nodded quickly. "Stefan." His name was a plea and he almost, almost moved his fingers and gave her what she needed. She felt so good, it took all his self-control to keep still. She tried to move her hips but he shut that down with his own.

"I will be upstairs as soon as I get rid of the lawyers, and then I'm going to show you exactly how not fragile I think you are. I'm going to fuck you so hard you won't be able to move. I'm going to make you come so many times you will never be able to walk away from me again the way you did this afternoon. By the time I'm through with you, I'll be black-tar heroin in your veins and you won't be able to go four hours without me somewhere deep inside you."

Jen went off in his arms like dynamite, catching him by surprise. He almost lost his footing and took both of them to the floor. His left hand clamped over her mouth cutting off the cry as he backed up just enough that he could bend her forward and amp up her climax with deep, long strokes of his fingers. He drew it out for as long as he could, unable to believe she'd reacted to him like that. Possibilities started forming dirty lists in Stefan's mind and he almost shoved her legging down right there and demonstrated that he meant what he'd said.

When he felt her about to collapse, he swung her up in his arms. She melted into him, still shaking, her lashes wet with tears and her breathing shattered. She was just about the most gorgeous thing he'd ever seen in his life and he really would kill the next person who tried to take her away from him. Because it finally hit home, finally became perfectly clear that he really could not live without her. She was as necessary to him as oxygen.

He carried her upstairs, leaning over her as he dropped her lightly onto the bed. She tried to roll away from him, and he grinned when he realized she was blushing like crazy. He rolled her back.

"Open your eyes," he ordered, almost losing his breath when she blinked dilated eyes a few times. His smile was slow and deliberate. "Don't think you aren't going to pay for that."

He was rewarded with a slow, deliberate smile of her own. A wicked smile. The kind he couldn't get enough of. "Promise," she breathed.

He leaned over her, kissing her deeply. "My fairy princess likes for me to talk to her like that, doesn't she?"

Her eyes darkened and she shook her head. "No. But your wife does."

Something warm and sweet rushed through him like honey. "That's right. *My wife*. Mine. Do not move from this spot."

Her hand lifted and her fingers trailed down his cheek and once again gravity became just a suggestion for Stefan as he turned his face to kiss her fingers.

"We're done," Stefan said, not even stepping completely into the formal dining room. Grant already had packed up his briefcase.

"We are so not done," Jared snarled, standing up. "I want that motherfucker's head, Sellers."

Stefan grinned, and Grant just rolled his eyes.

"Good," Stefan said. "You're hired. Consider yourself on retainer."

"What?" Jared sputtered, leaning across the table on both fists.

"You. Are. Hired." Stefan pronounced each word slowly. Then he turned to Grant. "We've got office space at the Tower you can lease. I'm assuming you'll want a satellite to work out of. I'll call our PA in the morning to get it ready for you."

"Sounds good," Grant said, standing up and grabbing his coat off the back of the chair. "C'mon, Jared, let's go. We have work to do."

"Work?" Jared exploded. "What the hell are you two talking about?"

"Too much tequila," Grant said, and Stefan nodded in agreement.

"Should have come to LSU," Stefan said, then got serious when it became clear Jared was about to go off. And the hippie looked surprisingly scary. He almost started to feel sorry for the judge. "What? You think you're going after him with pastry? Maybe force him into a diabetic coma? Was that your plan?"

Jared opened his mouth, then closed it. Then said, "I'm not a fucking lawyer."

"You are now," Stefan assured him. "You're my fucking lawyer and you better get to fucking work. Are we clear?"

Jared stared at him a second, and Stefan almost felt himself step back. He wasn't sure if the world was ready for what he was about to unleash.

"Taking him down on his turf," Stefan said, "How sweet will that be?"

Black eyes stared back at him, and then Jared grinned. "It's on."

And it definitely was. Stefan almost couldn't wait.

CHAPTER FIFTEEN

The second Stefan stepped through the door, Jen was ready for him. When he swung around, she launched herself at him full force and he had no choice but to catch her. He staggered back, and sat down hard on the bed, but she didn't let him go. She held on like a constrictor snake and for once kissed the hell out of him.

His arms went around her but she didn't let him flip her to her back. Instead she managed to catch his wrists and pin them back to the bed.

"How do you like being pinned down for a change?" she asked, pulling his earlobe into his mouth with her tongue, and grazing it with her teeth.

"Gotta say, it doesn't suck," he admitted.

She raised her head. "You like it, don't you?"

"Mmm," he nodded, blue eyes burning through her.

"I realized something," she said. "I'm an idiot."

His humor faded. "You are not an..."

She covered his mouth with her fingers. "Hush. I am an idiot. I don't know why I never realized how bad you had it for me. And you've had it really bad a really long time, haven't you?"

He watched her carefully, then nodded.

"Since I was sixteen?"

He nodded again.

"And you really kissed me prom night and told me to stay away from other boys."

He moved his face away from her hand. "I didn't want to go to jail for murder."

She laughed. "I always thought that was a dream."

"It was like a dream," he admitted. "At least it felt like one."

"No more dreams," she warned. "No more lies. No more protecting me. No more trying to keep me safe. Just the truth from now on, Stefan. I won't break. No, listen to me for a change. I did need you to protect me before and you did an awesome job. But I'm good now. I can handle it. I'm not a little girl anymore."

His grin was a shade lecherous. "I thought we'd already established that."

"I think we should reestablish it on a daily basis. Just to make sure you're clear."

"Yeah, 'cause I may not be completely clear..." he admitted, his hand going to her hips as he moved her back to position her against him. "But a daily routine for say the next forty or fifty years should help."

Jen sighed, and rocked against him. She rose up on her knees, thinking she'd take him inside her when she had a much better idea. "Stefan?"

"Hmm?" His eyes were laughing at her.

"You have a ring on your finger," she reminded him.

"What?" He tilted his head not catching her meaning until she pushed his hands away from her waist and her hair wisped down his chest. The exact second he grasped her meaning, his whole body bowed off the bed as her mouth closed over him, hotter than he could have ever imagined and Stefan discovered that he had never really lost control before in his life. Not really. Until now.

And as her heat sucked him deeper, he knew he was never going to get it back.

And when her tongue swirled and scorched and licked, he decided he really didn't care.

And any illusions he still harbored about sweet, innocent fairy princesses exploded into all out fantasies about dark, dangerous witches who spun cotton-candy into dresses and let him glimpse white hot paradise the second before he went blind from it. But before he went careening into that abyss, he grasped a handful of silk, wound it around his fingers and dragged her up. Her laughter danced all over his skin, and she rained kisses that burned all over him.

"Where the hell did you learn how to do that?" he asked between ragged breaths.

Jen shrugged, wiping her mouth provocatively. "Oh, I don't know.

I'm not sure I was even doing it right. Maybe I need more practice."

Still slow on the uptake, he didn't catch her in time when she grinned, bounced her eyebrows, then disappeared out of his line of vision.

"Jen," he hissed and then felt the back of her throat and well, he was human, after all. For a second anyway. Before she reduced him to a primitive creature who could only roar and claw the sheets off the bed.

And centuries later when his vision cleared and he fell back into his body, he opened his eyes to find her lying next to him on her side, smiling as she traced the lines of his abs with his fingers. She looked up when she felt his eyes on her.

"Do I have your full attention now?" she asked sweetly.

"Yeah," he managed, but that was the extent of his language capabilities.

Her fingers traced up slowly, until they caressed his jaw, then his bottom lip. She raised up then, pressing her hand to the side of his face. Her expression so serious, he started to get nervous.

"There's something else," she said softly. "And I need you to listen very carefully because it's important. I thought you knew it already but earlier, when I was listening to that crazy old man, I realized I've never actually told you."

"What, baby?" He tried to reassure her, covering her hand with his against his cheek. "Whatever it is, we'll deal."

She smiled at him. A completely different sort of smile. Her whole face lit up and he blinked a little as he saw her for the first time. She really wasn't a kid anymore. And she was strong, too. The resolve in her eyes undid him.

"I love you," she said, saying exactly the last thing he'd expected to hear. Her fingers pressed to his lips before he could respond. "I have always loved you. I woke up in the hospital to the sound of your voice. I came back to you. I'm yours. I've always been yours." Then because it was all too intense for both of them, she added, "So you're kind of stuck with me. Deal with it."

"I'll try," he assured her very seriously.

Laughter bubbled up out of her and her eyes shone. "And I love this house. It's perfect. And not just the kitchen. The porch ceiling, and the chandelier, and saving the fireplaces. I know the ovens were Rogan's idea, but that was completely self-serving of him because he just wanted brownies. I do get that."

He laughed, and a tiny hurt he'd never been willing to admit to suddenly floated away.

"I want to fill it full of your children. Raise our family here. Grow old here with you, and love you to my very last breath. Are we clear now?"

"Yes," he growled, rolling her suddenly. She laughed when she heard her panties rip. He shoved her legs wide and buried himself deep, finding nothing but scorching, sweet bliss again. He looked down into warm caramel eyes and let himself bask for a moment. "Now, tell me again."

"I love you," she whispered, swollen mouth smiling gently. She was so damn beautiful it chipped parts of his soul off just to look at her. "I always have."

"And I have never loved anyone else but you, Jen," he said, barely getting the words out before the rest of his brain shut down. He moved and watched her lips part and her face soften. He pulled back, then glided in, letting that plush, silken heat strip away his sanity. "You got that?" he groaned, shaking her back so her eyes snapped up to him before he went out of his mind.

"I got it," she said, and the last thing he heard was a soft laugh that turned into a moan that sent her arching and dragging him deeper, and he lost himself again. But what he found was so sweet, he didn't much care if he was ever himself again.

She'd finally done it. The parts of Jen's brain still functioning threw a party. She'd tipped him over the edge. He was gone. Stripped of every little bit of control he'd ever had. She pulled her knees back, letting him in deeper, sighing as he moved harder, wondering why it didn't hurt, and thinking maybe she shouldn't like this quite so much. She watched his face for half a second. His eyes were closed so tight. His jaw about to break until he froze over her, his mouth falling open when he blew apart. Watching that. Seeing him like that, dragged her with him a second later. And she was pretty sure, when all the pieces came back together, some of his got mixed up with some of hers. He was deep inside her, under her skin, skimming through her nervous system, and permanently lodged in her heart.

And she was keeping him there.

CHAPTER SIXTEEN

L ater Jen rested her head against his chest and threw one leg over his as she snuggled in close.

"So now, tell me about Robbie," she finally said, wincing when she felt him go very still. She pushed up on her arms so she could face him.

He took a deep breath, his whole chest rising beneath her as he dragged his free hand across his face. "As soon as Robbie was born, Mac immediately started an allowance and put money in a trust for him. When he's twenty-one, we'll give him his father's share in STI and hopefully a job, if he wants one. But right now, we can't let the judge get his hands on the company. You have to understand that. We're trying to protect it for you, Robbie, and Lizzie."

Jen nodded. "The judge wants STI to go public."

"I'm not surprised," Stefan sighed. "He's a greedy son of a bitch."

"I shouldn't have listened to Madlyn."

"Why not?" he asked, sounding strangely bitter. "I've spent years undermining your instincts about her. This is my fault, Jen, not yours. I should have seen her coming. If I had listened to you, I might have. Instead you listened to me. And look where that got us."

Jen shrugged, kind of loving where she was right then. "You should probably send her flowers."

He grinned. "I really should. Blood red ones."

"I remember playing with Robbie at the park with Lizzie."

He reached up, brushing a strand of her hair behind her ear.

"There are all these flashes. That was right before Katrina, wasn't it?"

He nodded.

"How could I forget him like that? What else am I not remembering? There really is something wrong with me. I can't trust my own mind."

"Baby," he said gently. "You had an injury to your skull, not your brain. There was no brain damage..."

"Well I am sure about one thing."

"What?"

"That you aren't telling me the whole truth again. I'm getting really good at recognizing that now, so you may as well cut it out." She wanted to smile when he opened his mouth to protest, then closed it quickly. "Just tell me."

"The doctors call it dissociative amnesia. High stress situations may affect your memory and after the last twenty-four hours, I doubt it's even still an issue or we wouldn't be having this conversation."

Jen tried to process what he told her. She'd Google dissociative amnesia later . "It's really time you stop trying to protect me from me, Stefan."

"I'll make you a deal. I'll work on not being over protective, if you'll work on trusting me."

"I do trust you," she insisted. "I do," she repeated, when he looked doubtful. One sandy eyebrow went up and she sighed in defeat. "Ok, I'll work on it."

"I mean it, Jen. We're going to have enough drama going after the judge. I need to know you and I are good."

"Going after the judge?"

"Oh, yeah. I just hired a new attorney. Robicheaux has no idea what he's started."

"Grant Marshall?"

Stefan shook his head. "Close but try again."

Jen's jaw practically hit the floor when she realized he meant Jared. "That is just so wrong."

"But it will be fun to watch." His expression turned serious. "You really didn't believe I threatened to cut off Robbie's allowance if Madlyn told you about Robbie, did you?" he said, his voice gruff, which made her smile.

"I don't remember. And you know I have problems with my memory," she said, shamelessly avoiding the question.

He kissed her nose. "I'd actually been trying to arrange a weekend for you to meet him again, but she kept finding excuses and I should have pressed harder. Now I'm going for full custody." His smile was reassuring but it was not nice.

"Good, we can't let the Robicheauxs continue to raise Robert's son,

Stefan. I don't want that old man anywhere near Robbie."

"Have you met my new attorney? He's practically rabid."

The Hawaii Five-O theme song started playing on Stefan's cell. He answered, and Jen felt suddenly cold when he straightened up and sat on the edge of the bed. "Hey, Jackson."

He nodded and gave a lot of one word responses. When he hung up, he didn't turn around right away. Jen went up on her knees behind him and wound her arms around his neck. "He's coming to arrest you?"

He shook his head, rubbing his hands across his face again. "I'm going to turn myself in."

"I've always wanted to see Mexico."

"I never run away from a fight. Besides this will be fun."

"You have a strange idea of fun."

He raised his eyebrows playfully. "Relax, I got this." He pushed off the bed. "I'm going to grab a shower."

"I am not visiting you in Angola," she warned, following him into the bathroom.

He pulled her into the shower with him.

"Not even to bring me a cake with a file in it?"

"You wouldn't eat the cake so what good would it do?"

"My cellmates will eat it."

"You've got an answer for everything, dontcha, smart guy?"

He just grinned at her as he lowered his mouth. Before he kissed her under the hot running water, he paused, "Jen, really, I got this."

"You got this?"

He nodded, rubbing his face against hers. "As long as we're solid, Jen, I can handle anything."

"You feel pretty solid to me," she laughed, her fingers curling around him and stroking him shamelessly.

He groaned against her mouth.

"I really am in complete control of this relationship, aren't I?"

"Yes," he hissed as her hold tightened on him.

"You'll do pretty much anything I say?"

"Pretty much." His forehead dropped to her shoulder as his whole body shuddered. "Tell me again," he pleaded against her skin.

"I love you," she assured him. "And whatever you've got planned had better be good."

"Oh, it'll be epic." He breathed out the words a second before he lost his mind again.

Stefan insisted she let Rogan take her to the beach. Because Grant was the one who originally suggested it would be good for her to get out of town, she agreed. By the time she and Rogan made it to her parents' old beach house, she'd already gotten a text to check out Matt Hansen's news blog and right on the front page was a picture of Stefan thrown against the hood of a patrol car being handcuffed, with Jackson looking really scary in full uniform holding up his hand to stop the camera. Matt's daily news show went live on his blog that afternoon. And what happened next was the most brilliant and insane thing Jen had ever seen. And it was, just as Stefan had promised, epic.

Matt reported on his blog that Stefan had been arrested on assault charges after his wife had been kidnapped. Matt's camera crew just happened to be set up in time for Jackson to walk Stefan up the front steps and into the police department. There was also footage shot on an iPhone of Stefan being fingerprinted and photographed. Mug shots were leaked online too. And he looked gorgeous in them, even though he was trying to look tough. The article reported in detail that Judge Robicheaux had demanded money and leveraged his custody of his grandson to try to blackmail and threaten Jen and the Sellers. The minute the judge's name hit the internet, other news blogs picked up the story, and then one of Matt's contacts at a business network ran it. They interviewed Matt, splitting the screen with video footage Matt had uploaded of their college days, and the volunteer work their fraternity had done. Then more footage of Stefan running charity triathlons and marathons. Stefan helping with the Special Olympics. Stefan working on construction crews volunteering for New Orleans Redevelopment Authority. Habitat for Humanity. Rebuilding apartments in New Orleans. Volunteering for FEMA's search and rescue. They even had a video of Stefan pulling a dog off the roof of a flooded home.

Then there was more footage of Stefan delivering meals to elderly people. Work days at hospitals and convalescent homes. Coaching kids' football games. All the things Jen knew he had done, but seeing it all in one long montage made her heart ache for ever doubting him. And she fell in love with him just a little bit more.

So did the daytime talk show cougars as they giggled and ran footage of him on a roof with a nail gun in nothing but cutoffs, work boots and a tool-belt.

"So he's basically being arrested for rescuing his wife?" one host asked Matt when they interviewed him for a morning talk show. They ran the footage again of Stefan saving that dog on a split screen with Matt's live broadcast from New Orleans. "How is that possible?"

"Well," Matt took a deep breath. "That's a complicated story, really.

Stefan's wife was involved in a serious automobile accident about ten years ago that killed her parents and her only brother." Matt went on to explain about the trust and how the Sellers had been named as Jen's guardians by Jen's own parents.

"But she's over twenty-one, isn't she?" the former beauty queen asked.

"Yes, Jen is twenty-two." Matt explained. "The Robicheauxs are alleging that due to the injuries Jen received in the car accident ten years ago, she isn't competent to make her own decisions."

"Not competent?" Her smooth voice went shrill with outrage. "You're telling me that they are trying to declare her incompetent, so they can basically stage a hostile takeover of a company?"

"That's exactly what we're saying," Jared Marshall added from next to Matt.

"We've also heard rumors that Jen is pregnant," one of the younger hosts added.

Jared grinned. "We have no comment on that."

The cougars went wild.

They were was so outraged that the Robicheauxs would try to break up these two wonderful young people starting out their life together and expecting their first child, that they immediately and predictably went on a witch hunt. It was a slow news week, which brought the major networks calling and started a parade of experts on fugue states, dissociative amnesia, trust funds, annulments, and any other detail they could use to fill air time. Not to be outdone, one network actually obtained Jen's old medical records and built a computer graphic that demonstrated how her skull had been fractured.

"This cannot be happening," Jen whispered as she watched animated pieces of her skull detach and reattach as head injury experts demonstrated that she had never suffered a brain injury.

She got a text message from Lizzie that said, "*Jen, is that your brain on TV? That is so gross.*"

That's when the stuffed animals started showing up at the St. Charles House. The porch and front yard were overrun with baby toys, cards, and candles. Someone had even made a Free Stefan Sellers poster.

By the end of the second full day of national media coverage, every court case Winston Robicheaux had ever presided over was in question. Bottom feeding attorneys were headed out to Angola in vans to talk to inmates and re-examine cases. Madlyn Robicheaux was under investigation by the Louisiana Bar and under attack by every female daytime talk show host who was outraged that she would use her own child to try to seize control of stock in a company.

And anyone who had ever written an article or book on the corruption in the Louisiana justice system suddenly got their fifteen minutes.

Jen immediately forgave the media for the animated brain graphic because soon they were featuring the front of the bakery just about every time they mentioned her name. Jared hired six people and started taking internet orders, even though they weren't actually open yet.

By the end of the fourth day, all charges against Stefan had been dropped and the venerable firm of Robicheaux, Andrews, and Robicheaux, that had served Louisiana for the better part of seventy-five years, closed down without letting any of the employees know before the doors were locked. The new offices of Marshall and Marshall opened up in Sellers Tower and immediately held a press conference promising to partner with the district attorney's office to investigate allegations of judicial misconduct.

Grant Marshall promised the citizens of Louisiana that he would not rest until they knew the full extent of Winston Robicheaux's corruption.

Stefan was unavailable for comment, according to his attorney, because he had gone to get his wife.

So Jen sat on the beach that afternoon, smiling when she noticed the runner headed towards her. She watched him for a long time, convinced the ground wasn't quite solid under his feet.

When he saw her, he altered course, and joined her in the sand a few minutes later.

"Hey, kiddo, you're up early."

She smiled as he sat down next to her, pulled off his running shoes, and sank his feet into the sand.

"I had the strangest dream," she told him, pushing the long strands of hair the wind whipped across her face behind her ear.

"Really?" He was fighting a smile.

She sank her toes in the cool sand next to his and watched the sun sparkle silver on the waves, and just like that, absolutely everything was all right.

"I dreamed Jared told the whole world I was pregnant," Jen said, trying not to smile because she really should be angry at him.

He lost his battle with the grin. "Well," he announced, jumping to his feet and dragging her up with him. "We'd better make sure. We certainly don't want to disappoint your boyfriend."

Jen yelped as he swung her up in his arms and headed back towards her parents' old beach house and did everything in his power to make sure she was pregnant before they returned to Louisiana.

A few months later, when Jen walked down the aisle in an obscenely expensive white wedding dress that skimmed tightly along her figure until it exploded in tulle, the pregnancy rumors were put to rest. No way could she be pregnant in that dress. Jared walked her down the aisle and reluctantly handed her over to Stefan, who leaned down and whispered in her ear, "Wait 'til you see my list for this dress."

She smiled up at him. The sweet smile that he had quickly learned meant trouble. "And you haven't seen my shoes yet."

Robbie was Stefan's best man, which meant there wasn't a dry eye in the house. Jen had relented and let the groomsmen wear tuxes. When it was time to cut the cake, Stefan wouldn't let anyone have a piece of his secret weapon grooms cake, which was fine—it didn't have icing, so no one else wanted any. The red velvet wedding cake Jared had made was demolished, except for the top tier. And if anyone thought the zombie bride and groom on the top of the cake was odd, they didn't mention it.

And they danced and danced and danced. Stefan wouldn't let her dance with anyone else until Mac cut in to dance with his daughter-in-law, and Rogan caught Stefan by the arm and dragged him away from her. So he danced with his mother after that. And Jen finally got to dance with the groomsmen who had been waiting impatiently all evening.

Stefan refused to let Jen change into her going away outfit so she still had her wedding dress on when he carried her over the threshold again at the house on St. Charles. Their friends ignored Stefan's warning to stay away and showed up with more champagne. They sat around the fire pit in the back and Lizzie produced giant marshmallows and sticks. Why waste a good fire?

With the city, streetcars, and Jared's acoustic guitar, they danced some more until Rogan said, "Jen, let's give him our present."

Jen agreed, sitting down in Stefan's lap which suited him just fine because it gave him a head start on undoing the gazillion tiny buttons that ran the full length of her back. "We have company, Stefan," she warned as she felt the first few buttons turn loose.

"Go home!" Stefan barked, but their friends only laughed. He was serious but too mellow to insist.

"Rogan, the envelope please," Jen said dramatically.

Rogan handed Jen the envelope and she passed it to Stefan.

Stefan gave both of them skeptical looks as he opened it. "Plane tickets?"

"Rogan," Jen laughed. "The other envelope."

Rogan grinned and took another envelope out of his jacket pocket.

"What did you do?" Stefan asked softly, but he'd already seen the eBay logo through the envelope.

She shrugged. "Open it."

He pulled out the printed auction showing one charity slot for the Iron Man World Championship. "Do you have any idea how much I love you?" he asked her.

"I really do," she assured him, and they forgot they weren't alone until Lizzie grabbed the paper away from him.

"Hawaii!" she cried. "We're going to Hawaii! Wait! We are all going to Hawaii, right?" she demanded, hands on her hips and one eyebrow arched.

Jen laughed. "Would we go without you?"

"You have school," Stefan told her.

Lizzie's smile died, and her brother laughed. "Sucker."

"My niece is due in October," Lizzie warned him. "You'll need me there. What if Jen goes into labor during the race?"

"I knew it!" Rogan exploded, and Jen and Stefan finally admitted they were pregnant. Elliot broke out more champagne and sparkling grape juice for Jen.

"Wait. How do you know it's a girl?" Stefan asked his sister.

"She just is," Lizzie said. And everyone knew better than to argue with Lizzie.

Jen laughed. "My due date isn't until nine days after the race and first babies are always late."

"Zachary was a week early," Rogan added.

"Hush," Jen warned him. "Really, what are the chances?"

Nearly eight hours into the Iron Man World Championship, with Stefan on track to shave ten minutes off his best time, Jen admitted she was in labor. When he was an hour from the finish line, race officials caught up with him on the track and gave him a message from Jen. "You wife says to remind you that the quickest way to her is straight ahead.

But if you could pick it up just a little, you're having a baby."

Stefan finished the race twenty-five minutes earlier than planned.

"Are you really in labor or were you just trying to improve my time?" he asked, sinking down in front of her, when he finally reached her at their meeting spot at the village.

"Don't kneel down. Get up. You need to walk," Jen told him, grabbing hold of his shirt and pulling it over his head, then handing him the dry long sleeve T-shirt she'd brought him. "Keep walking, I'm fine. Lizzie, get his drinks."

He pulled her up and slid his arm around her waist. "So let's walk, Mrs. Sellers."

"Shoes," she said, as another contraction started. "Take off your shoes, then drink your smoothie."

And she didn't stop bossing him around until they reached the hospital and Presley Elizabeth Sellers made her debut two hours later.

"I think this is a sign she's going to keep her daddy on his toes," Lizzie told Jen, as they watched Stefan sleeping in one of the recliners with Presley sound asleep in the curve of his arm.

Jen kissed him lightly on the forehead and his eyes fluttered opened. "We had a baby," he whispered, sleepy blue eyes dazed with joy.

"Yes," she said, gently.

He looked down and saw the perfect rosebud of a baby asleep in his arms. "She's so beautiful." He smiled up at Jen. "Tell me again," he whispered.

"Stefan," she smiled. "I love you."

"Got it," he nodded, then whispered as his eyes closed. "Love you, Jen."

He loved her. He'd always loved her. She could feel it all the way to her bones. And it was so bright and sweet it almost hurt. She kissed his forehead again, and pulled the blanket up over him. Then she pressed a kiss to the beautiful little girl in his arms. Their daughter. Their family. And that aching hollow place that she had lived with for so long was suddenly so full she almost couldn't contain it.

"Lizzie," she said suddenly.

"What?" Lizzie asked, startled because she'd almost fallen asleep.

"Look," Jen nodded at the pair as she memorized every single detail of watching Stefan sleep with their baby in his arms. "Stefan finally got his princess."

Lizzie laughed. "See, he is Prince Charming."

"Not charming," he grumbled, surfacing again. "I'm the other one."

"The other what?" Lizzie asked.

"With the sword and the horse. He kills the dragon," Stefan

insisted, still half asleep.

"Prince Philip?" Jen asked, surprised. "You're absolutely right. I should have thought of that."

He nodded. Jen leaned down to kiss him again, then pressed her mouth to his ear. "Go back to sleep. If you dream, I'll make it come true."

"Jen," he smiled, as he finally gave in to the exhaustion. "You already did."

31259154R00106

Made in the USA
Charleston, SC
11 July 2014